Tracey Nameth

AT DESTINY'S END

A Novel

TRACEY NAMETH

Copyright © 2008 Tracey Nameth
All rights reserved.

ISBN: 1-4196-9427-8
ISBN-13: 9781419694271

Visit www.booksurge.com to order additional copies.

WHAT GAVE ME THE COURAGE TO WRITE THIS BOOK?

Writing is a gift from God. I thank the Lord Jesus Christ for blessing me with such. Although all the characters, species race names and places are not real they might be considered more than fiction to me. The different characters are different aspects of my real personality. The character of Leia Tetzlaff might be considered my Superego because she's arrogant, deceiving, obsessive and a bit secretive. Where James Rawlings is the Ego because he's the balance or the reason and considers all options carefully before making a decision. Tando Ardelon might be considered my Anti-Superego because for the most part he's selfless and willing to risk all for the greater good of others. These three personalities fight inside of me each and everyday. But the Ego "James Rawlings" takes the balance of each of the other two. Therefore he's the main character in the story thus the Ego to the fullest extent. This is a work of fiction, with one exception:

My personality traits are real and present to some degree in each and every character. If you think I'm kidding, you don't know me that well.

In conclusion I wrote this novel regarding the only thing I truly can write about that nobody else knows. Myself. That might make me crazy but no more than everybody else. This novel will always keep a deep position in my soul. Thank you. P.S. don't be irked by the weird character, alien race and planet names you find throughout my novel.

TRACEY NAMETH, one of today's up and coming novelists, was educated at Mount Royal College in Calgary. He lives in Calgary, Alberta, Canada.

DEDICATED TO MY FOUR GRANDPARENTS

For Martin and Margaret Nameth who taught me
a lot with wisdom to spare.

For Frank and Velma Matai's humour. The birdie is in the middle.
They know what I mean.

PROLOGUE

Year 2116: Mars, Sol Solar System

THE AWESOME RED PLANET of Mars emerges from a total eclipse, her two moons glowing against the darkness. A tiny tan spacecraft, a Juvian Cargo Freighter firing lasers from the back of the ship, races through space. It is pursued by a giant Dominion starship. Dozens of deadly laserbolts streak from the Dominion Battleship Destroyer, causing the main solar fin of the Juvian craft to disintegrate.

Another blast shakes the Juvians as they struggle along their way. Juvian special force troopers rush past the engineering section of the ship and take up positions in the main passageway. They aim weapons toward the door. Tension mounts as loud metallic latches clank and the screams of heavy equipment are heard moving around the outside hull of the ship.

The Dominion craft has easily overtaken the Juvian Cargo Freighter. The smaller Juvian ship is being drawn into the underside dock of the giant Dominion starship.

The nervous Juvian troopers aim their weapons. Suddenly a tremendous blast opens up a hole in the main passageway and a score of fearsome armored spacesuited mercenaries make their way into the smoke-filled corridor.

In a few minutes the entire passageway is ablaze with laserfire. The deadly bolts ricochet in wild random patterns creating huge explosions. Mercenaries scatter and duct behind storage lockers. Laserbolts hit several Juvian soldiers who scream and stagger through the smoke, holding shattered arms and faces. An explosion hits right in the center of the main passageway and leaves a gaping hole in the floor.

The awesome, six-foot-tall Dominion Leader of the mercenaries makes his way into the blinding light of the main passageway. This is James Anderson, right hand man of the Warlord Jazid Gibbs. His face is obscured by his flowing black hair and bulky helmet, which stands out next to the fascist white armored suits of the Dominion mercenaries. Everyone instinctively backs away from the imposing warrior and a deathly quiet sweeps through the Juvian troops. Several of the Juvian troops break and run in a frenzied panic.

The evil James Anderson stands amid the broken and twisted bodies of his foes. He grabs a wounded Juvian officer by the neck as a Dominion officer rushes up to the Dominion

Leader. "The containers of enriched tellurium substances are not in the main cargo bay," the Dominion officer said.

Anderson squeezes the neck of the Juvian officer, who struggles in vain. "Where are those containers you stole?" Anderson lifts the Juvian off his feet by his throat. In a meaner voice James Anderson said, "What have you done with those substances?"

He obviously doesn't want to say, and looks squeamish. "We stole no tellurium containers. Aaah....This is a consular ship. We're on a diplomatic mission."

Anderson grins, then finally says crisply, "If this is a consular ship...where's the Ambassador?"

The Juvian refuses to speak but eventually cries out as the Dominion Leader begins to squeeze the officer's throat, creating a gruesome snapping and choking, until the soldier goes limp. Anderson tosses the dead soldier against the wall and turns to his troops.

"Commander, tear this ship apart until you've found those containers and bring me the Captain of this ship. Waste not one second," he said abruptly. "I want him alive!"

The mercenaries scurry into the subhallways.

THE PRESENT...

Year 2121: Yukon, Canada, Earth, Sol Solar System

"I've finally found him," the detective said.

"Where?"

"On Takara Prime. He's changed his name to James Rawlings."

"You're sure it's him?"

"I'm positive. It's him, all right. He's getting married."

Silence. "Who's the girl?"

"She's a Princess of the royal family of Takara Prime. Destined to lead that entire solar system."

The hand that held the large sapphire gem was actually trembling. "Excuse me a moment." In a gentler voice Jason Anderson said, "Amanda, you've listened long enough. Get off the com-link now." He waited until he heard the click on the extension upstairs. He paused to make certain she didn't come back on before he said, "All right. I'll make arrangements to travel out this evening to Takara Prime."

"You've got to be careful. He's killed before. It's in him."

"No one has to tell me about my son."

"One last thing," the detective said. "Somebody else is looking into this case. Maybe you're already aware of this."

"No, I'm not."

"Some guy named Stan Robinson. I'm not sure but he might be a minion to the royal family of Takara Prime. He's been nosing around, asking questions."

"Okay. I'll have it looked into. Where's this wedding being held?"

"That's a big secret, very hush-hush. I've got a lead that says it'll be at a private estate on Lake Intrepid on the northern continent."

"Can it be stopped?"

"I don't know. Maybe. If you're lucky."

"All right. Keep me informed if there's any change. I'll be in touch with you as soon as I'm squared away."

When the com-link line went dead, Anderson stood for a long time covering his eyes with his hands. How could they let him out? It was madness. Madness to let him go! For five years Anderson had waited for the call to come. Now it had actually happened.

He felt hollow. This time he knew there could be no turning back, no pity, no remorse. He wondered if he could live through it again. He cursed under his breath.

Anderson opened his eyes, and the world beyond the windows was opaque with slow-swirling fog. In the distance, like sound buried underwater, a bell tolled oh nineteen hundred. When he leaned close to the window, all he could see was his own strong, masculine face, fifty-eight years old, swimming on the dim glass.

Behind him the maid's approaching footsteps interrupted his thoughts. "Would you like to have your dinner served now, Mister Anderson, before I go?"

"I don't think I'll be having dinner this evening, Mary. I've just had some upsetting news, and I'm feeling a little queasy at the moment. Thank you all the same."

"Very well, sir. Mrs. Anderson's tray is ready."

"Would you quickly prepare my suitcase? The usual things."

"How long will you be away, sir?"

"I'm not sure. One of the larger suitcases will do."

The dinner tray was arranged for his wife's convenience. The cold orderliness of the slices of roast beef, the whipped potatoes, the perfect scarlet of the stewed tomatoes, the paper plates, the plastic utensils. It looked like a child's pretend dinner. He grasped the tray in his powerful hands, went down the hall to the turbo lift, and rode up to the fifth story of the house. With a computer scan of his hand the bedroom door unlocked, he stepped inside, and it locked automatically behind him.

The lamps on either side of the single bed looked small and separate, the glow confined to the blue silk shades. His wife was waiting for him. In her negligee, she held out her arms, the gauze bandages on her wrists almost hidden in her sleeves. He put her tray aside on the hassock, then pulled a chair closer to the side of her bed and took her hand in his. She watched him with arctic-cold eyes. After a moment she seemed to brighten. "They've found him? They've found my little boy?" she said in an anxious voice.

"Yes," he said. "I don't want to worry you."

"He's getting married," she said.

Anderson looked at her. "And that changes everything, doesn't it? Now there's someone else."

"I can't let them...I don't want them to see me like this, Jason," she said.

"I'll get back as soon as I can. I won't be gone very long."

"What are you going to do?"

"I have some business to take care of, that's all."

She sobbed a single deep breath. "You're going after him. I know. You frighten me to death."

"You know what he's like," he said, "what he's capable of." He heard his own ragged breath. "The courts let him go... Just let him go. They should've kept out of it and left us alone. He never would've got out of here. The boy's dangerous."

She reached over and touched his shoulder delicately, almost as if he and the boy were the same to her. "Don't say that. Don't you remember, Jason, how the three of us–we had good times, too."

"I try not to remember," he said.

The computer opened the door. Without hesitating, Julian entered through the door. "Evening, Miss Amanda. Evening, Mister Anderson," she said, watching the door automatically lock behind her.

"How are you, Julian?"

"Not too bad, Mister Anderson." She brought the tray over and placed it squarely across Amanda on the bed. "Old troubles and worries, I guess. But we're all gonna be doing fine now, aren't we, Miss Amanda?"

She was a tall, strong white nurse in her late forties, who saved her warmth and devotion for Anderson's wife–her precious little baby girl–Miss Amanda. While she went about coaxing the woman to have her dinner, Julian looked at him, as she did most every evening, saying silently, don't you say anything that would upset her. You know what she's liable to do. After she gave Amanda her medication and watched her wash it down with a paper cup of water, she left them to their nightly goodnights and sweet dreams.

Suddenly Anderson rose and whisked the heavy drapery apart. Through the tritanium bars guarding the windowpanes, the last of the sunlight was a glare in the fog.

"Was it the global security that called?"

"No. A man I hired."

Tears threatened to spill from her eyes. Something terrible, ominous, hovered in her voice. "That Juvian Cargo Freighter...I remember. It was so awful, so unbelievable. Most of the crew murdered."

Anderson couldn't answer. He realized he was breathing shallowly, his body tense. Madness to let him go. Madness. "I wish you'd stay home," she was saying. "Oh, I wish—"

"I love you more than anyone," he said. He kissed her on the forehead. "You have to stop worrying. I promised you I would always take care of this."

Again she found her way to tears. "Oh, I remember how it was. I remember." Slowly her head turned, and she was looking at the bars. "I'm so frightened."

He stayed beside her as Julian rushed in to sedate her and get her settled in bed. He looked at his watch. He wanted to bolt, but he felt compelled to stay. He couldn't bring himself to look at his wife again until her incoherent mumbling had stopped and she had fallen into a deep-drugged sleep. Even then, lying in that state, she was unbelievably beautiful, her rich brown hair streaked with silver.

He spent a few minutes giving instructions to Julian and returned quickly downstairs. Now the cavernous house was utterly quiet. He took up his hat and raincoat, put out the lights, and stood for a minute staring across the sofa at the living-room windows.

The fog was less solid now; only a thin skein of it hung in the air and around the bases of trees. He crossed the room. From behind books in the desk he took down the laser pistol and a box of power cells. Get this done. Once and for all. From a locked drawer he removed a badly damaged information pad and placed it in his briefcase.

Drawing on his raincoat, he went into the hall, where a light was burning and where his one suitcase was waiting by the door. He knelt and slipped the gun and power cells inside. Suddenly it came to his mind as strong as a premonition: Death waited for him on the other side of the door.

CHAPTER ONE

March 1, 2121: Lake Intrepid, Northern Continent, Takara Prime, Takara Solar System

"OOOOH, CORDETTE," said Leia Tetzlaff, one of her bridesmaids. He's the best-looking thing I've ever seen."

"You've never *really* told us where you found him." Megan Davidson teasingly joined in the banter.

"Oh, I didn't find him," Cordette answered. "He found me."

The light-hearted kidding, flattery, and feigned jealousy had not stopped since the young women in Cordette Chance's wedding party started arriving early that morning.

"She says she met him back when on vacation to the O'Ryan nebula." This was her friend since their pre-teen years, her maid of honor, Lene Fox. She was sprawled across the bed, blue eyes laughing with wickedness. "But don't believe a word of it. I never saw him while I was with you."

Besides Lene, Cordette's three bridesmaids were Megan Lee Davidson, who had been her partner in the construction of moon base *Terko;* Brenda Butler, her personal advisor; and up-and-coming space army Commander Leia Tetzlaff. The women were in various stages of putting on gowns with matching wide-brimmed hats, all in the prettiest, most delicate sky blue imaginable.

"So the truth comes out," Leia said.

"The truth is," Cordette went on, "I kept our relationship secret. Between the two of us. But after all, I prefer privacy, too. We all do."

She had been awfully lucky, she was telling them, to get Jim. James Rawlings was absolutely what she wanted. Attended by two of the Robinson's maids, a seamstress, a hairstylist and a makeup woman, Cordette stood quietly while the dream unfolded around her. They were helping her on with the long, heavy gown, flown in expressly from an Earth dressmaker.

She remembered the first kiss James had given her. She didn't tell the others how much he'd said he wanted her, needed her. How he'd said, "Let's get married as quickly as we can." Impossible to describe the evening, the moonlight. Or the lovely simplicity of the proposal from a man who must have known what loneliness was like. As much as she did.

Two heaping armfuls of tuberoses were delivered to the bedroom door. "Oh," she cried, "aren't they beautiful!" Even with the windows open the roses immediately filled the second-story bedroom with their sweet, heavy scent.

As the florist left the room, the door was momentarily left ajar, and Leia rushed to close it. "He's out there in the hall. I just caught sight of him. Oh, Cordette, can you believe you're actually doing this?"

Cordette smiled and said, "Well, I didn't set out to get married. Seven months ago nothing was further from my mind. How was I to know I was about to fall in love?"

Several women in formal dress were now gathering in the bedroom offering their assistance and advice to the bride. Looking fragile and elegant, Donna Robinson, a petite brunette, came toward Cordette, beaming, holding out her hand. "Oh, Cordette," she said, "you spoil me." "What beautiful roses. They smell of summer." She bent over the red blossoms in her corsage and inhaled deeply.

"Careful. They have thorns," Cordette said. "But they're the ones James thought you'd like best. He chose them and sends his love."

"Tell him he was right," Donna said, smiling. "I do love them."

She was dressed in a gown of lime-green silk crepe. Her hair was threaded with silver and beautifully coiffured. Everything was running smoothly, she told Cordette. No last-minute confusion, no one trying to get in who didn't belong.

They found themselves for a moment removed from the others, just the two of them, and the older woman said to Cordette, "Well, sweetheart, it's almost time. There's such a crowd. Tell me quick. I know I shouldn't ask, but where will you be staying?"

"I'd tell you if only I knew. I left that up to James. He wanted to plan things, and I was happy to let him. So he hasn't told me anything. I'm sure we'll be flying somewhere, though—in that fabulous whispercraft you and Stan gave me.

"You could've stayed right here, if only we'd thought of it. We're going away, Stan and I. He has to go to New Berlin on business for a week or so, and I decided to go with him. We'll be gone. You two could've had free run of the place."

"You've given me so much as it is. Oh, Donna, I'm going to miss you." Cordette hugged her all at once, and the depth of the moment brought tears to her eyes. Two years ago she had known Stan Robinson only as a minion to her royal family. But during the construction of *Terko*, he had become a mentor and friend. Then, when her mother passed away, Cordette had need of a private place where she could mourn and keep out of the public spotlight, and Stan and Donna had insisted that she come stay with them.

"There now," Donna was saying. "You'll be back soon." She put her arm around Cordette's shoulders, gently stroking her upper arm. "It's going to be sheer madness later on, and I'm not sure what time we're leaving. So why don't we say our good-byes now. We may not have another chance."

They looked at each other, and neither spoke.

Donna touched the bride's hand and leaned to her. "Good-bye," she whispered. "Godspeed."

"Good-bye," Cordette said. "But Donna, we'll be back in a couple of weeks. I have to be on location by month's end to christen the *Terko* moon base, remember. If things aren't too hectic later, maybe you'll grab a minute of calm with me and help me out of this dress.

"Maybe so." Donna smiled and squeezed Cordette's shoulder. "Let me know if you want anything. Now I've got to get back downstairs. I'll see you soon." As Donna kissed her on the forehead, Cordette felt more tears fill her eyes. She was entering a new phase of her life, setting out on a thrilling, uncharted path.

"Is it time?" Cordette asked Lene. "Has he gone down yet?"

Leia, at the door, shook her head and waved Cordette away. They all had to wait, confined in this bedroom, a little longer.

Lene said, "Why don't you ask him to come in and say hello?"

"Oh, no, no, no," Cordette protested. "That'd be bad luck. That's bad luck on a wedding day." She started toward the door to close it.

But suddenly there he was, walking by. Black tuxedo, white shirt, black tie, black hair, and joy in his eyes. With a fresh white smile James Rawlings looked at her over the confused flotilla of sky blue hats.

Cordette instinctively twisted away, but it was too late: Their eyes had met. She had even seen him give a slight shrug of his shoulders and a wink, affectionate and amused, his playfulness unmistakable.

"Close the door! Close the door," one of the women shouted, and the door swung shut.

All the women began laughing uproariously. The tension was broken. Tears of laughter spilled from Cordette's eyes. She wasn't really superstitious, although she had wanted to adhere to tradition. She knew she was laughing mostly from relief as she dabbed at her eyes. Finally she was able to say, "It's all right. It's all right. Years from now we'll still laugh about this."

It didn't matter now if the bride and groom saw each other. Almost recklessly Cordette looked out the big windows at the manicured lawn below, and beyond to the gatehouse, where the whispercrafts were checked as they came in. Her emotions were hardly stable. She saw two or three security men running around with handheld com-units and data pads. She realized with relief that the hordes of reporters and paparazzi were not coming after all.

Every precaution had been taken: The florists had been told that the wedding was for Stan's niece, and special messenger sent out invitations late. On the planet Miltex a shadow wedding had been created. Now the whispercrafts lined up, the valets were busily parking the half jet half helicopter vehicles in the open field, and guests were filing into the courtyard, which had been elaborately transformed with flowers.

Directly below, the festivity was unfolding. In the foreground Cordette could see the immaculate children—the ring bearer and the flower girl—awkward in formal clothes. Near the altar and the grotto of flowers a string quartet was tuning up. The wedding cake, a seven-tier extravaganza trimmed in reds and fire frogs, sat on its table, shaded under the colonnade.

Isolated, not easy to find, half covered with spider creeper plants, the house had been built on a courtyard, its two wings flanking a gracious interior garden. Since the day she had first arrived, the whole place—the views, the old-fashioned, genteel atmosphere, the soft summer light—seemed to welcome Cordette. It had turned out to be more of a home, more beautiful and friendly, than she could have ever believed. It sat on a peninsula of fifty acres of land, surrounded on three sides by Lake Intrepid—the perfect place for the private, intimate ceremony they wanted.

I'm so happy, Cordette thought. The first thing missing was her father and siblings who had unexpectedly been inspecting the mining colonies of Setlak Four more than one hundred light years away. There wasn't enough time for them to return for the almost shotgun type wedding. The second thing missing was the opportunity to tell everyone we were getting married. And that added to the unreality of the day.

With the bridesmaids assisting her train, Cordette Chance, eldest daughter of King Ewokata Chance the V of the royal family of Takara Prime made her way downstairs into the large, elaborately furnished living room, walls hung with twenty-first century paintings. Fresh-cut bouquets of lilies and roses, her favourites, adorned every table.

Cordette lingered now in front of the multiple glass doors of the bookcases that lined the three walls, glimpsing the hazy reflection of a girl in a long, flowing white dress. It was like a dream materializing.

She remembered a much smaller reflection in a mirror long ago. She'd been dressed in white organza, tied at the back with glowing white sash. Mother had been braiding her hair into pigtails. "Yes, you're the beauty," her mother had said, combing and twisting the strands of hair. "And smart, too. You'll have to be smart—very, very smart."

If only her mother could have been here. She would've approved of James. The bride was made in the image of her mother. Her hair was the same dark red-gold, thick and shinning and glorious, and she had the same green eyes.

Over her shoulder she saw the man who would give her away entering the room. Stan Robinson was a human fifty or so years old, a little under medium height, well dressed, comfortably sleek. He was wearing an ivory-colored dinner jacket, and charcoal trousers with a chalk stripe. His hair, which he wore nearly to his shoulders, had passed through several stages of blond-grayness and looked almost white.

They stared at each other for some time before either moved, and then he finally stopped staring and came toward her, took one of her hands, and said, "My goodness, you are a picture."

She was twenty-one years old, a skilled linguist, and she couldn't utter a word.

He held her at arm's length and looked at her in her white gown and veil, at the bridal bouquet, and at the little gold earrings Donna had given her for a wedding gift. "We're down to it now, aren't we?" he said, and grinned. "I still say you don't know anything about him. I wish you'd wait and let me find out more—"

Cordette lifted her fingers to her lips and whispered, "Shhh...You don't understand. I love him. If I ever stopped or anything happened to him, I don't think I'd want to go on living."

"Honey, all I'm saying is, your trouble has always been that you trust people too much."

"Be happy for me," she whispered. "Please. It means so much to me."

She caught a whiff of sweet essence of Brandy on his breath. "I love you, baby," he said. "I hope you know what you're doing."

Cordette turned, smiled, and held out her arm for him to take. "I love you, too."

A hush had come over the garden—other than the soft strains of music there was hardly any sound at all. One by one, in the breathless blue afternoon, the bridesmaids went forward like figures in a dream that take step after step without advancing.

Then the wedding march began. The music swelled, and Cordette started down the aisle. She walked slowly, shoulders squared, the motion of her legs barely breaking the front of the dress. Everyone was turning their heads and then standing in honor of the bride, Cordette Chance, who was coming down the aisle on the arm of Stan David Robinson, her mentor and friend.

The bridesmaids had taken their places flanking Father Patterson, the priest. The bridegroom was standing slightly to one side of the grotto of flowers. Cordette could see his face through her veil.

She was so happy, she could feel her cheeks burning and her eyes shining. When James Rawlings took her hand and she rose to meet him, she knew she had never been so spectacularly beautiful—not as a young girl sitting at her mother's mirror, not even in her own royal palace when she had worn fine silks and diamonds and jewels from all over the galaxy.

They turned toward the priest and stood side by side. One hand passed the bridal bouquet to the maid of honor, then lay in James' hand without pressure. She belonged to him. Although they were barely touching, she was so aware of him that she found herself thinking of the night to come—the cover of darkness, the way they would be together...Oh, she loved him. Love waited in her fingers, in her lips.

She believed in what she was doing. She believed that what was beginning here today would never be interrupted, not as long as she lived. When Cordette Chance repeated the words after Father Patterson in that clear voice, no one who heard her could question how fervently she meant it.

She was aware that James barely whispered those words, although her voice was steady and strong. She looked into his eyes, into the depths of them, where it was like looking into a black fire. She blinked for a moment, unable to bear the intensity of it, sudden tears welling up.

She recovered herself enough to repeat it after him, but James was silent. Or if he spoke at all, it was in a voice too low and husky for her to hear. He was, she thought, too moved to trust himself to speak.

The rest of it—the questions, the answers, the prayers, even the exchanging of vows and rings—seemed almost anticlimactic. Father Patterson was saying, "James, you may kiss your bride," and the guests were applauding as her husband took her into his arms. His lips were so hot they almost burned her. She understood. She understood everything about him.

The wedding reception was probably no different from the hundreds of other receptions celebrated across Takara Prime that afternoon. By oh sixteen hundred the temperature inside the courtyard had reached ninety-four in the shade. The mingled scent from the surrounding banks of flowers hung in the air with a powerful intoxication. There were buckets of Champagne and several long and windy toasts; then came the cutting of the cake, a stream of photographs both posed and candid, a few kisses that were too long or too wet, and much conviviality, laughter, and joking.

Still, Cordette was happy, she told James. She was deliriously happy. She kept trying to bring herself down to earth again, but it was no use. It took self-control, but she tried to greet all the guests, tried to smile, though just as easily she could have burst into joyous tears. The guests, as it turned out, were entirely her friends—people she had worked with or knew in some passing, unformalized way—or friends of the Robinsons'. James had refused to invite his family to the wedding. His only guest would be his best man, a bare acquaintance drafted for the occasion, who served as a witness and little else.

"I can't believe you won't invite your mother and father," she had complained.

"I'm estranged from my father, and my mother only listens to him. They have their own life. I don't want them around me. I'm on my own. Take my word for it, Cordette. It's for the best."

"Oh, come on, sweetheart. Surely you can't hate your father that much."

"Let's just say that I don't have much in common with him. He can't be around me. Just leave it alone. It's been like this for a long time. You can't possibly understand."

"But how can it matter so much for only one afternoon?"

"It matters, Cordette. It matters to me. Let's leave it at that."

More than his words, it was the anger that convinced her not to press any further. But today all that had been swept into the background.

A five-piece orchestra had replaced the quartet. Cordette and James danced the first dance, their wedding dance, and between them swirled the same sensuality as when they'd met again—after nearly seven months—only a few short weeks ago. Cordette closed her eyes and laid her head on his shoulder, and they continued to dance, without a word, in each other's arms.

Little by little, other couples joined them in a stately waltz. She felt light and graceful in his arms. The garden became a crowded blur. When the vocalist began the next selection, Cordette hardly had time to catch her breath before Stan bowed slightly and swept her off, no matter that his steps did not correspond to hers. He was getting increasingly mellow on his Brandy. "I don't want anyone to ever make you unhappy," he said.

"That's sweet," she said earnestly. "But don't worry so much, Stan."

When the dance was over, Cordette returned to James. He was with one of the older ladies, who were telling him, "The years may seem like a lot of time to you, but it doesn't look long from where I stand, looking back. Life slips so quickly through your fingers."

James smiled and said nothing. Cordette saw his eyes were moving about the garden carefully, watchfully.

The afternoon wore gracefully on toward evening.

Often the bride and groom found themselves unavoidably separated, occasionally for several minutes at a time. At twenty-nine James could be feverish with excitement or, if necessary, cool and detached. But he was never far away from her. He reveled in sweeping her away from tedious conversations, in tapping shoulders and cutting in on her handsome friends, in whisking her quickly behind the high banks of flowers and kissing her until her heart beat out of control. "I'm crazy about you," he kept telling her. "I can't stop. Let's get out of here."

"We can't," she'd say. "Not yet."

All afternoon he had never been able to satisfy his hunger for her. He nibbled her ear and said she was his entire world that he lived for her. Even when they were separated, she could still feel his embrace, hear his whisper, and almost burn with the fire of his kiss. Wildness sometimes flashed between them as pure electricity. She would be a good wife to him; she was determined to follow where he led, to make his interests hers.

It was after oh seventeen hundred when she danced once more with Stan. Some minutes later she was aware of him following one of the maids from the courtyard on some mission. Out of the corner of her eye Cordette also saw a lime-green gown cross behind a wall of guests. That was Donna, she thought. I'll have to thank her again for all this.

But before she could politely excuse herself and make her way through the crowd, Lene intercepted her and said, "I'm with Jack Quinn over there. I can't convince him you and I are old friends. Why don't you come over and say hello."

Cordette said maybe she would.

And by then it was too late to get to Donna Robinson, who was also leaving the courtyard, a few steps behind a maid. Cordette watched her go in the same direction Stan had gone. I wonder what's happening, she thought.

She returned to the veranda only to find that James was gone. Her eyes searched the crowd. Yes, there he was.

But something was the matter. Near a bank of white chrysanthemums James stood as straight and motionless as a dagger in the ground, heels together, arms crossed tight. His face was frozen. Cordette turned, following the direction of his gaze.

Through the windows across the way, she saw Donna and Stan standing in the living room talking with someone. Apparently James could see who it was, but Cordette's view was obstructed by partially drawn drapes. All she could make out were a wide-brimmed hat, the light sky blue sleeve of a gown similar to her bridesmaid's, and a woman's hands. As far as she could tell, the three of them were talking. Nothing else. And yet James stood staring at the three people in the living room with eyes hardened and full of hate.

She started toward him, and again she looked into the living room. The Robinsons were still there, still talking—heatedly, it appeared. As she watched, Stan turned and withdrew from sight. Apparently Stan was showing the woman out.

"What was that about?" she asked gently as she reached James and put her hand on his shoulder. She felt his back tighten with her touch. He didn't draw away, nor did he turn.

"Sweetheart," she said, "do you know who that was?"

After a few seconds James shook his head.

"Then what's the matter?" Cordette let out a deep breath. "Please, darling...Jim, please. Come on. Whoever it is, let's pretend she's not there. Stan will handle it. Believe me, he knows how."

When James turned and looked at her, Cordette was struck by the transformation, by his sudden air of composure. "Well," he said, "these blasted people." She saw that his hands were slightly trembling.

"It's nothing," Cordette told him. "Let's not talk about it anymore. Let's not even think about it."

His eyes gazed down at her with love. One glance and he seemed to have lost all interest in everything but her. Leaning down, he kissed her tenderly on the lips. "All right, gorgeous," he said. "Let's not talk about it."

Suddenly the orchestra started again, and Cordette stretched out her hands. "Come on, darling," she said. "Dance with me."

A moment later, as he was twirling her around, she could tell that James was stealing glances into the room. Cordette grew more and more apprehensive. She was consumed with the haunting sensation that eyes—cold, unfeeling eyes—were watching them from somewhere.

"There's no need to think of them," she insisted. "Look at me. Look at me. Keep looking at me." She rested her cheek against his and spoke to him in a whisper. "Don't you know how happy I am?" she pleaded. "Don't break this spell. We'll never have this time again."

She felt a drop of rain strike her forehead and looked up. The thunder sounded distant, but lightning flashed in the dark clouds gathering overhead. Another wet drop touched her face. Cordette laughed shakily. It was only rain, tiny warning drops.

Guests, in their finery, shrieked as they scurried into the house or under the large striped tent. Suddenly it was raining hard—gray sheets of rain, slapping against the stonewalls and windows. She and James rushed inside the long central hall of the mansion, which was brightly lit and crowded now with guests. "I love you so much," Cordette said. "You'll see. I'll make everything all right."

The light in the garden had faded to dusk, and the windows were dark with rain. Some of the guests were already leaving at the front door. Cordette and James said a few halting good-byes, but she knew they had reached the time when the bride and groom were supposed to make their getaway. As Cordette caught her breath, she leaned to her groom and said,

"Jim, everyone will start going home after this rain. Shouldn't we go up and change? It's almost oh nineteen thirty."

"Why don't you go ahead and get started," he replied. "I'll be along in a few minutes. I should say good-bye to Father Patterson."

"Oh, yes. It completely slipped my mind. Would you say good-bye for me, too?"

"Of course." He smiled. "I won't be long, but there's no use in your waiting."

And yet she hesitated. Instinct kept whispering that something was wrong, and she hated to leave him. "All right," Cordette answered at last, feeling suddenly desolate.

It was her last glimpse, indistinct and hasty, of James' figure across the crowded foyer—on his way out, following the crowd.

Gathering her long skirts, Cordette ran up the stairs, stopping long enough to tell a maid to see if she could find Mrs. Robinson and ask her to come to the bride's bedroom. "And would you please bring me the tallest glass of ice water in the house?"

"Yes, your Princess Chance," the maid said, and turned to go.

Cordette laughed. "Oh, I'm Princess Chance Rawlings now."

"Of course. I'm sorry, Princess Chance Rawlings."

"Vasha, one more thing. Since you're here, would you mind helping me undo this dress? I can't stand it another minute."

"Yes, okay."

Cordette entered the bedroom. Gifts from her wedding shower, only a few days ago, were stacked and scattered on the floor. Vases of flowers were everywhere. The maid unsnapped the back of the heavy white dress, her fingers unhooking and unbuttoning.

"Thank you, Vasha. That's all I need for now."

As soon as the maid had gone, Cordette slid the dress off her shoulders and let it fall. She crossed her arms and pulled the long slip up over her head. Once in her bathrobe, she sat at the dressing table and began to take off her makeup, which felt caked on her face. Outside, the direction of the wind had changed. She gazed at the window, where gusts of rain were lashing against it.

Hard rain drummed on the roof. On the other side of the room the windows looked across the lake, where their whispercraft was awaiting them—hidden in a neighbor's garage—the view completely obscured now because of the rain.

Gradually she was conscious of altered sound: the hiss of rain among the foliage. Windows were open somewhere, rain blowing in. She stepped out into the paneled upstairs hall, which ran dimly toward the back of the house. A door to the master bedroom stood open, and a thin band of light shone through it. Cordette listened for footsteps, for the opening and closing of doors, for voices, but there was no sound. Strange. A house full of people—and silence.

In the Robinson's bedroom only one of the small beside lamps had been left on. The light was inadequate for the big room, leaving the ceiling and the corners in shadow. The south-facing windows had been left open, and rain was pouring in on the waxed hardwood floor, sparkling in the flashes of lightning.

"Donna?" she said quietly. "Donna, are you in here?"

Cordette quickly crossed the room and shut the two windows. Her eyes filled with burning tears. Unexpectedly, after struggling all afternoon to keep her grief at bay, she piercingly wanted her mother to be there.

Suddenly it struck her as never before: She was alone—absolutely alone. Except for James. She had thought herself to be self-sufficient, but her mother had always been there, her love had always been there. Cordette had had someone—a mother, a home.

Rain was still coming down heavily, but the storm was veering away and the thunderbolts were like echoes of light in the dark clouds. Cordette was on her way back to her room when she looked up and saw James standing at the far end of the corridor.

"You look wonderful, Princess Chance Rawlings," he said as he came toward her. "I forgot how beautiful you are."

"Wait till I'm dressed. Then I'll be beautiful."

He laughed and kissed her on the tip of her nose. "I've got to get out of these clothes. Look at me. I'm soaked." His face, his voice were almost tingling with excitement, she thought.

"Is everything all right?" she asked.

"Yes. Never better. Why wouldn't it be?"

She followed him into the bedroom where he had changed earlier and where his clothes were laid out for him now. She got one of the big white bathrobes from the linen closet and took it to him.

"I don't want you catching a cold—not tonight."

She watched as he unbuttoned his shirt, removed the studs, then the cuff links, his face a mask of concentration. "I was wondering," she said. "Did you by any chance see Donna when you came up?"

He struggled and shook his head. "No. I didn't see either of them." He put on the bathrobe and knotted the sash. Turning his back to her, James stepped out of his trousers and emptied his pockets, transferring their contents to the clean, dry trousers he would wear.

"But look," Cordette said. "She left without saying good-bye."

"She probably was in a hurry to catch the transport to New Berlin."

"I guess you're right. That's what I was thinking."

As James bent over to remove his shoes, Cordette saw that his hair was a mass of pure, wet black, and she wanted to thrust her face down into it and speak with tenderness of many things. Instead she smiled and said, "I can offer you a Brandy.

Or is there something else you'd rather have?" She kissed him lightly and broke away.

But before she could leave the room, he had circled her body from behind and pressed his lips to her neck. She freed herself from him and laughed. "Just kiss me once more and then go get your shower."

Cordette left the room to retrieve the Brandy. When she returned, James took one of the glasses. "Here's to tonight," he said with a laugh, and drank it in one swallow.

Cordette took a sip, held her glass to her lips for a moment, and simply watched him.

As she started for her bedroom, she glanced around the room to make sure they weren't leaving it a wreck. James clothes lay untidily about, where he had dropped them. Cordette picked them up, surprised at how really soaked they were. His tuxedo jacket and trousers were heavy with water; even his shirt and undershirt were soaked through. Bits of debris stuck to his socks. He must have fallen down in the rain, she thought. She quickly spread his dripping clothes over the back of a chair on her way out.

She couldn't tell how many minutes passed. When he walked into her bedroom, she was standing barefoot in panties and bra. He looked at her in that way of his, drawing her toward him and making her want to cradle him. Tall, dark, a little disreputable-looking, he casually leaned back against the bedpost and crossed his legs at the ankles. He wore light gray trousers, a white shirt open at the collar, and a navy blazer. Tranquil rain was falling on the roof. "I think I'd better wait outside," he said.

"Don't be crazy," she said. "We don't have to do that kind of thing anymore." She reached out and took hold of his arm, but someone was knocking at the bedroom door. "Ah," Cordette said, throwing on a robe, "there's Donna now."

But it was Vasha edging through the door, a tray containing a glass of ice water in her hands. "I thought you were Mrs. Robinson," Cordette said, disappointed. "Do you know what's keeping her?"

"No, Princess Chance Rawlings. We're looking all over for her. Perhaps she left for New Berlin already."

"Maybe. That's fine, then. Just put the tray over there. Thank you."

James, she noticed, had gone over to the window and was studying the night. He impatiently looked at his watch.

"It's about to stop raining," he said as if to himself. "That's good."

The maid set down the tray and retreated, and James followed her out.

Cordette took a drink of water and dressed quickly. She wore a perfectly tailored suit in an indistinct black-pink crepe. It defined her figure softly, classically. She ran a comb through her hair and freshened her lipstick, then drew back to examine herself in the full-length mirror. She realized there was nothing more for her to do, and her throat constricted with emotion because now a part of her life had come to an end. She turned, moved from the side of the bed, and went out.

James was in the upstairs corridor when she found him a few minutes later. He made no effort to hide his impatience. He was walking up and down, smoking a cigarette in agitation.

"What makes you so restless this evening?" she asked.

"I guess I just want us to be on our way." He put out his cigarette, looked down at his hands, and then smoothed his clothes mechanically, fastidiously.

Cordette wasn't about to let anything upset her tonight or extinguish the tender flame kindled within her. Not tonight, she told herself.

He reached out and took her hand. "Cordette, come here. It's you and me now. I'm so proud of you." The praise, the smile, the camaraderie embraced her. "What were you going to say?" he asked.

"Nothing."

"You were. I know you were."

"But now it doesn't matter."

There was nothing wrong at all. She mustn't let her imagination get away with her, but nothing was wrong, was it?

All at once, quite nervously, she ran her fingers up under the lapels of his jacket. "Oh, hold me!" she said, pressing her face against him. "Just hold me, will you? For a minute, please." She started to laugh at herself and burst into tears instead.

He did as she asked. He put his arms around her and held her and let her cry, telling her it was all right, everything was all right, go ahead, go ahead and cry, the most natural thing in the world. Cordette couldn't help herself. The minutes were delicate, as if they shared a secret too fragile for words.

They went back downstairs to the reception to say good-bye to everyone. Yet in spite of James' impatience, it was another half hour of handshakes and kisses before they could stage their getaway. Cordette stood on the stairs and tossed her bouquet, and it made a perfect long arc into Lene's hands. "My second." Lene laughed. "It'll be my lucky number two."

At oh twenty thirty a decoy whispercraft sped toward the gatehouse, and two security whispercrafts flew into line behind it. As the small aerial motorcade shot past the gate, a barrage of flashbulbs appeared from nowhere, crackling in the night.

That should do the trick, Cordette thought. Now she and James could depart in peace. But instead of feeling relieved, she was beginning to feel more and more anxious. A maid came into the room with a tray of drinks and delicacies. "I was wondering," Cordette said, "where Mrs. Robinson has gone."

"I haven't seen Mrs. Robinson for...since it started to rain. I think someone said they left."

Uncertainty ran through Cordette. "Are you sure? I knew they were leaving on their trip, but this early? I had hoped—" She looked around at the remaining guests, and it seemed to her that they regarded her expectantly. "All right, thank you." She dismissed the maid.

Cordette took a glass of Champagne and strolled with studied indifference to the living room. A group of women sat facing each other on the twin sofas. Cordette looked for the Robinsons, searching slowly and deliberately through the length of the entire house. Donna and Stan had already left for New Berlin.

The rain had stopped. Through the window the lake glimmered between the boughs in mother-of-pearl stripes. She looked out at the sky. It had cleared completely and was rich with stars, like an immense night-blooming tree.

"Cordette?" James took her arm. "Come on. Let's go."

"I hope you'll come visit when you get back," Lene told them. "I'm just north of Takara Prime's Ellipse Ice Fields."

"We'd be delighted," James said. "You'll be first on our list."

"And Cordette, what do you say?" Lene said.

"I say...whatever James says."

The bride and groom walked out into the night, a warm, foggy summer night that smelled of summer rain. An old path wound down through towering cedar trees to the boathouse. Followed by raucous celebrants, they hurried ahead in silence, their footsteps whispering against the grass where it grew between the bricks.

In the shadow of the trees the lake was black; farther out beyond the shadows it was quicksilver. Fog coiled up from the water like wisps of smoke. They rushed past the cove where the old, rotted dock still stood, the bank now overgrown with cattails and lilies, buds thrusting above the water like serpent heads, some opened in red-throated plumage. No one noticed how the rushes were torn and strewn about; no one, including Cordette, looked closely enough to see the crushed blossoms floating silently among the reeds.

Ten feet farther along and up a ramp was the launch that would take them across the water to her whispercraft. James assisted her on board, both of them smiling and waving their good-byes as they went. Then, amid a flurry of confetti and rice, James signalled the pilot, and they pulled away into the main channel.

Behind them the company of friends turned happily back toward the mansion, remarking among themselves what a fortunate young couple they were, with their entire lives before them. Wind breathed in the rain-filled trees. Branches slowly tossed. And the night folded over the sound of their voices and footsteps and faded away.

In the cove the ebb of the water was thick with floating shoals and eddies of confetti.

The minutes went trickling by.

Till all was quiet.

There was not much blood by then. And what little stain was left in the water after nearly two hours of rain, the darkness now obscured among the water lilies. No one had seen the faces of Stan and Donna Robinson that nodded in the murky night water of the cove, held below the surface with chains around their shoulders like monstrous shawls. No one could have seen their eyes staring, hair undulating soft and lazy, like smoke, mouths parted in soundless screams.

CHAPTER TWO

March 2, 2121: The Adirondacks Expanse

THE LONE SHIP traversed the Adirondacks Expanse. The zebra-class scout ship contrary to its name looked much like the falcon that inspired her design, with a beaklike bow and sweeping wings that enabled her to streak through a planet's atmosphere. Her sleek lines were marred by various scorch marks and dents, which left her looking like an old rhino with many scars. Larger than a shuttlecraft yet smaller than a cruiser, she was better armed than most ships her size, with forward and rear torpedoes plus phaser emitters on her wings.

Her bridge was designed to be operated efficiently by four people, allowing her to carry a crew of only thirty. The engine room took up all three decks of her stern, and most of the crew served there. This was state of the art for a scout ship—about fifty years ago. Now she was practically the flagship of the Dominion fleet.

"What's the name of our ship?" asked her captain, a human man named Tando Ardelon. His brown hair was cut short and severe, which suited his angular face and muscular body that bulged across his entire frame.

Ty Kajada, the human who served as first officer, consulted the registry on his computer screen. "She is called the *Solaris*. The hyperdrive signature has already been modified."

Ardelon nodded with satisfaction. "I like that name."

On his right, an attractive woman who looked vaguely Reptilian scowled at him. "Let me guess," said Pallas Tarr. "Solaris was some ancient human who led a revolution somewhere."

Captain Ardelon smiled. "Not ancient. He lived from 2018 to 2058. He was a slave and a military tactician who led a revolt against Juviana, the greatest power in the galaxy of its day. For ten years, he held out against every Juvian legion thrown against him."

"And how did this grand revolution end?" asked Tarr.

When Ardelon didn't answer right away, Kajada remarked, "He and all of his followers were executed. Death by lethal injection is quite possibly the most graceless form of capital punishment ever invented. The injections were designed to internally burn every nerve in the body hence causing an unspeakable pain throughout the victim."

Tarr snorted a laugh. It's always good to know that my human ancestors could match my Reptilian ancestors in unspeakable acts of brutality."

"Solaris was a visionary," said Ardelon. "He paved the way for the Dominion to rule throughout most sectors in space though this entire region. But once other Dominion leaders saw he was no longer willing to keep expanding the Dominion's territory he and his followers were executed for treason."

Tarr snorted another laugh. "Now we're in the same situation he was in. Trying to reclaim the vast territories that once belonged to the Dominion not more than seven years ago. Considering what happened to Solaris, let's not put him on too high a pedestal."

"It's still a good name," said Ardelon stubbornly. Like many people, he believed that names were important—that words held power. He didn't like having to change the name and hyperdrive signature of his ship all the time, but it was important to make their enemies think that the Dominion had more ships than they actually had.

"We've reached the rendezvous point," announced the captain. "I'm bringing us out of hyperdrive." Operating the conn, he slowed the craft down to one-third impulse, and they cruised through a deserted solar system sprinkled with occasional fields of planetary debris.

"Captain Raine is hailing us on a secure frequency," reported Kajada. "Their ETA is less than one minute."

"Acknowledge," answered the captain. "But no more transmissions until they get here."

While Kajada sent the message, Pallas Tarr worked her console. "There are no Divinian ships in scanner range," she reported.

"Still I don't want to be here more than a couple of minutes." Ardelon's worried gaze traveled from the small viewscreen to the even smaller window below it. There was nothing in sight but the vast starscape and a few jagged clumps of debris. This area appeared deserted, but Ardelon had learned from hard experience that it was wise to keep moving in the Adirondacks Expanse.

"They're coming out of hyperdrive," said Tarr.

Ardelon watched on the viewscreen as a Rambler assault vessel appeared about a thousand kilometres off the starboard bow. The dagger shaped spacecraft was slightly larger than the *Solaris*, but she wasn't as maneuverable or as fast. Like Ardelon's ship, her blue-gray hull was pocked and pitted with the wounds of battle.

"Captain Raine is hailing us," said Kajada.

"On screen." Ardelon managed a smile as he greeted his counterpart on the other Dominion ship. Tessa Raine looked every centimetre a warrior, from her scarred, gaunt face to the red eye patch that covered one eye. Her blond hair was streaked with premature gray, and it was pulled back into a tight bun. Captain Raine had gotten a well-deserved reputation for ruthlessness, and Ardelon was cordial to her but couldn't quite bring himself to call her a friend.

"Hello, Tessa."

"Hello, Ardelon," she answered. The *Scorpion* is reporting for duty under your command. What's our mission?"

"Do you know the planet Quinntessa?"

"Only by reputation. Wasn't it conquered when the Dominion pulled out of that region?"

"No," answered Ardelon. "The Quinntessanites opted for the same legal status as the residents of Corvan X. Instead of being relocated, they chose to give up their Dominion citizenship and remain on the planet, under Divinian rule."

"Then to hell with them," said Raine bluntly.

Ardelon ignored her harsh words. "The Quinntessanites have always marched to their own drum. Mixed-race colonists who were trying to escape discrimination in the rest of the Dominion settled the planet. There are some Dominion sympathizers on Quinntessa, and we've been getting periodic reports from them. Two weeks ago, they sent a message that Divinian troops had arrived, then we lost all contact. There hasn't been a transmission from the planet since then. It might be a crackdown, maybe even total extermination. For all we know, the Divinians could be testing planet-killing weapons."

"They're not Dominion citizens," said Raine stubbornly.

Ardelon's jaw clenched with anger. "We can't just abandon five million people. We have to find out what's happening there, and help them if we can."

"Then it's an intelligence mission," replied Captain Raine, sounding content with that definition.

Ardelon nodded and slowly relaxed his jaw. One of the drawbacks of being in a loose-knit organization like the

Dominion was that orders were not always followed immediately. Sometimes a commander had to explain the situation in order to convince his subordinates to act. Of course, fighting a guerrilla war against one vastly superior foe would make anyone cautious, and Dominion captains were used to acting on their own discretion. Sometimes the chain of command was as flimsy as a gaseous nebula.

Captain Raine's scowl softened for an instant. "Ardelon, the people on Corvan X are from your own race. Wouldn't it make more sense to find out what happened to *them* instead of racing to help a bunch of mixed-breeds on Quinntessa?"

Ardelon couldn't tell if Raine was bigoted or just callous. He glanced at Tarr and saw her shake her head. "Good thing there are no psychological tests to join the Dominion," she whispered.

"Did you say something?" demanded Captain Raine.

Ardelon cleared his throat. "She said the Quinntessanites are not really, uh, mixed-breeds—they're hybrids, genetically bred. I've heard their whole social structure is based on genetics, the more unique your genetic heritage, the higher your social status."

"A fascinating culture," added Kajada without looking up from his console. Raine grimaced, but remained silent.

Ardelon went on, "As for the humans on Corvan X... yes, I'm worried about them. But that's a small village, and they've chosen to live in peace with the land, using minimal technology. They're not much of a threat, and of no strategic value, either—the Divinians will probably leave them alone. But Quinntessa was a thriving Dominion planet with millions of inhabitants and a dozen spaceports. When they go silent, it's suspicious."

"How do we proceed?" asked Captain Raine.

Ardelon gave her a grim smile. "Have you ever played cowboys and Cossacks?"

March 3, 2121:

Quinntessa, Falow Solar System, The Adirondacks Expanse

Observing the planet on the viewscreen, Captain Ardelon was struck by how Earth-like it was, with vast aquamarine oceans and wispy cloud cover. Quinntessa had small triple moons that orbited each other as they orbited the planet, and he could see their silhouettes against the sparkling sea. Small green continents were scattered across the great waters, but they seemed insignificant next to all that blue. A giant red sun glowing in the distance accentuated the lush hues.

On second glance, Ardelon decided that Quinntessa looked more like Miltex than Earth. Here was yet another beautiful planet stolen by the Divinians, while the Dominion looked the other way.

"One ship in orbit," reported Pallas Tarr. "A Divinian military freighter. They use those for troop transports, too, and they can be heavily armed."

Ardelon nodded and spread his fingers over the helm controls. "Let's keep it to one ship. Kajada, as soon as we come out of hyperspace, target their communications array with quantum torpedoes and fire at will. I don't want them sending for help."

"Yes, sir," answered the young human male, who was preternaturally calm, considering they were about to attack a ship that was twelve times larger than they were.

"Then hit their sensor arrays, so they have to concentrate on us."

"What about their weapons?" snapped Tarr. "I hope you aren't planning to take a lot of damage."

"No more than usual." Captain Ardelon smiled confidently and pressed the communication panel. "Vantika, report to the bridge for relief."

"Yes, sir," answered the female Rambler. She was only one deck below them, in the forward torpedo bay, and Ardelon heard her footsteps clanging on the ladder behind them. Now if Pallas has to go to engineering, they were covered.

The captain hit the communications panel, and his voice echoed throughout the ship. "All hands, Tactical Alert! Battlestations."

Like the falcon that inspired the *Zebra-class*, the *Solaris* swooped out of hyperspace, her talons bared, spitting quantum torpedoes in rapid bursts. Plumes of flame rose along the dorsal fin of the sturgeon-shaped Divinian freighter, and dishes, deflectors, and antennas snapped like burnt matchsticks. Shields quickly compensated, and the next volley was repelled, as the lumbering, copper-colored vessel turned to defend herself.

Phasers beamed from the wing tips of the *Solaris*, bathing the freighter in vibrant red light. Although damage to the hull was minimal, the enemy's sensor arrays crackled like a lightning storm. Despite her damage, the freighter unleashed a barrage of phaser fire, and the *Solaris* was rocked as she streaked past. With the larger ship on her tail, blasting away, the Dominion ship was forced into a low orbit. A desperate chase ensued, with the blue seas of Quinntessa glimmering peacefully in the background.

"Full power to aft shields!" ordered Ardelon.

"Aye, sir," answered Tarr.

They were jolted again by enemy fire, and Ardelon had to grip his chair to keep from falling out. From the corner of his eye, he saw Vantika stagger onto the bridge and take a seat at an auxiliary console. There was a worried look on her face.

"We can't take much more of this," said Tarr.

"Making evasive maneuvers," answered Ardelon.

Zigging and zagging, the Dominion ship avoided most of the Divinian volleys, but the larger ship bore down on them, cutting the distance with every second. Ardelon knew he would soon be in their sights, but his options were limited this close to the planet. He had a course to keep...and a rendezvous.

The two ships—a sardine chased by a barracuda—sped around the gently curved horizon and headed toward the blazing red sun in the distance. On the bridge,

Ardelon pounded a button to dampen the light from the viewscreen the glare was so bright. But if he couldn't see, they couldn't either. He felt the thrill of the hunt as he prepared to use one of the oldest tactics in the history of the galaxy.

A direct hit jarred them, releasing an acrid plume of smoke from somewhere on the bridge. The ship began to vibrate as they started into the atmosphere.

"Shields weakening," reported Kajada.

"Just a little longer," muttered Ardelon. He made another sharp turn, but quickly veered back toward the sun. The Divinians increased their fire, as if worried that she would escape into the planet's atmosphere. Since the *Solaris* wasn't returning fire, they had to assume she was trying to land on the planet.

"They're powering up a tractor beam," said Tarr urgently. "Their shields are...down!"

"Now!" barked the captain. Kajada's hand moved from the weapons console to the communications board, while Ardelon steered his craft vertically into the horizon, trying to present a small target. The Divinians had swallowed the bait, and now the trap snapped shut.

A Rambler assault vessel streaked out of hyperspace in the middle of the sun's glare. Ardelon knew the *Scorpion* was there, but he could barely see her on the viewscreen. The Divinian vessel didn't see her at all so intent were they upon capturing their prey.

With her shields down, the freighter's bridge took a direct hit from a brace of torpedoes, and the lightning crackled along the length of her copper hull. The freighter went dark, but she lit up again as the *Scorpion* veered around and raked her hull with phasers, tearing jagged gashes in the gleaming metal. The Divinians got off a few desperate shots, but the *Scorpion* raced past them, unharmed.

"Aft torpedoes," ordered Ardelon. "Fire!"

With deadly precision, Kajada launched a brace of torpedoes that hit the freighter amidships and nearly broke her in two. Ardelon cringed at the explosions that ripped along her gleaming hull, and he made a silent prayer on behalf of the fallen enemy. They were more arrogant than smart, but they had died bravely. Fortunately, that trick always worked on the arrogant. At a cockeyed angle, spewing smoke and flame, the massive freighter dropped into a decaying orbit.

Ardelon piloted the *Solaris* into a safe orbit that trailed behind the dying ship. "Hail them."

Kajada shook his head. "Their communications are out, and life support is failing. They have about ten minutes left before they burn up in the atmosphere."

The cheerful voice of Captain Raine broke in on the communication channel. "That was good hunting, Ardelon, and a good plan. What's next?"

"Enter standard orbit and see if you can raise anyone on the planet. We're going to take a prisoner, if we can."

He tapped the communication panel. "Bridge to transporter room. Scan the bridge of the enemy ship—see if you can find any lifesigns."

"Yes, sir." After a moment's pause, the technician answered, "Most of them are dead. Wait a second. There's one weak lifesign—"

"Lock onto it and wait for me. I'm on my way." The captain jumped to his feet. "Kajada, grab a medkit—you're with me. Pallas, you have the bridge. Keep scanning the planet, and try to raise someone. Vantika, you have the conn. Keep us in orbit."

"Aye, sir." The attractive Rambler slid into the vacated seat and gave him a playful smile. "This looks like a nice place for shore leave. What do you say, Captain?"

"I'll put you on the away team," promised Ardelon. He took another glance at the viewscreen and saw the smoking hulk of the freighter plummeting toward the beautiful blue horizon.

The captain led the way from the clam-shaped bridge to the central corridor, which ran like a backbone down the length of the *Solaris*. He jogged to the second hatch and dropped onto the ladder with practiced efficiency, while Kajada stopped at a storage panel to pick up a medkit.

Dropping off the ladder, Ardelon landed in the second largest station on the ship after engineering: the combined transporter room and cargo hold. Not that they had any cargo to speak of—every spare centimetre was filled with weapons, explosives, and quantum torpedoes, stacked like cordwood.

He drew his phaser and nodded toward the human on the transporter console. The human manipulated some old console controls, and a prone figure began to materialize on the transporter platform. Ardelon heard Kajada's footsteps as he landed on the deck, but he never took his eyes, or his phaser, off the wounded figure.

It was a female Divinian, with singed clothes, a bruised face, and bloodied, crushed legs. With their prominent bone structure and sunken eyes, most Divinian faces looked like skulls, but this one looked closer to death than usual.

"According to her insignia, she's the first officer," said Kajada.

The Divinian blinked her eyes and focused slowly on them. When she realized where she was, she wheezed with laughter. "Are you trying to save us?"

"Lie still," answered Ardelon. He motioned Kajada forward with the medkit, but the Divinian waved him off.

"Too late," she said with a cough. The Divinian lifted her brown sleeve to her mouth and bit off a small brown button. Before anyone could react, she swallowed it. "I won't be captured...by the Dominion."

"What are you doing on this planet?" demanded Ardelon. "Why don't you leave these people alone?"

A rattle issued from the Divinian's throat, and it was hard to tell whether she was laughing, crying, or dying. "You beat us...but all you won was a curse."

The Divinian's bloodied head dropped onto the platform with a thud, and her previously wheezing chest was now still. Kajada checked the medical tricorder and reported, "She has died."

Ardelon nodded. "Beam her body back to her ship. Let her burn with her comrades."

"Yes, sir," answered the human. A second later, every trace of the Divinian officer was gone.

The captain strode over to the transporter console and tapped the communications panel.

"Ardelon to bridge. Have you or the *Scorpion* raised anyone on the planet?"

"No, sir," answered Tarr. "But we detected a strong power source that suddenly went dark. It could be a Divinian installation."

"Are you picking up lifesigns on the planet?"

"Lots of them," answered Tarr.

"Pick a strong concentration of lifesigns and send the coordinates to the transporter room. Kajada and I are going down."

"Okay," answered Tarr. "Did you get a prisoner?"

"For only a few seconds—we didn't learn anything. Ardelon out." The captain reached into a tray on the transporter console and grabbed two combadges, one of which he tossed to Kajada. The *Solaris* was so small that they seldom needed combadges while on the ship; they saved them for away teams.

"I've got the coordinates," said the human technician. "It appears to be the spaceport in the city of Rya'c."

"Fine." Captain Ardelon jumped onto the transporter platform and took his place on the middle pad. Kajada stepped beside him, slinging the medkit and tricorder over his shoulder."

"Energize."

A familiar tingle gripped Ardelon's spine, as the transporter room faded from view, to be replaced by a cavernous spaceport with high, vaulted ceilings covered with impressive murals. The captain expected to see a crowd of people, but he expected them to be standing on their feet—not lying in haphazard rows stretching the length of the vast terminal. This looked like a field hospital, thrown together to house the wounded from some monstrous battle. Coughs and groans echoed in the rancid air.

His first impression was that the Divinians had wreaked terrible destruction on the people of Quinntessa, and he started toward the nearest patient.

"Captain!" warned Kajada. "Keep your distance from them."

He turned to see the human intently working his medical tricorder. This caused Ardelon to look more closely at the nearest patient, who was swaddled in a soiled blanket, lying on top of a grass mat, surrounded by filth.

The man wasn't wounded—he had oozing pustules and black bruises on his face and limbs, and his orange hair was plastered to his sweaty forehead. Although his species was unfamiliar to Ardelon, his skin had a deathly pallor, just like the Divinian's had. Ardelon took a step away from him.

Another patient finally noticed the visitors. She propped herself up with some difficulty and began to crawl toward them. Others saw the away team as well, and a chorus of desperate voices rent the air. Some of their words were incoherent, but Ardelon could make out a few phrases as the people crawled forward: "Help us! Save me! *Kill* me!"

"What's the matter with them?" he whispered to Kajada.

"A serious illness," answered the human with tight-lipped understatement."

Ardelon tapped his combadge. "Away team to transporter room. Beam us up, but on a ten-second delay. Get out of the transporter room before we materialize."

"Yes, sir," said the human, not hiding the worry in his voice. "What's wrong?"

"Something," answered Ardelon as he stepped away from the advancing tide of disease and death. "In fact it looks like everything."

CHAPTER THREE

March 14, 2121: Takara Prime, Takara Solar System

A SEA-CREATURE, attracted by the glister of the morning sun on the underbelly of their whispercraft, swam away with a frightening squawk. Even thou they were several dozen metres above the ocean they heard the creature. James refocused his attention on the craft's controls. The creature's squawk had brought him out of his momentary trance. His hands gripped and tapped the control buttons and driver stick continuously, endlessly.

A clear, green ocean stretched before James Rawlings like the facet of a gigantic emerald. Vast beds of seaweed shimmered beneath the glassy surface, looking like the fire inside the immense jewel. James spied a buoy far below them, and small, frothy waves lapped at the alien object floating in their midst. Elsewhere, a school of flying fish broke the surface and arced back into the water like a ghostly ripple. Otherwise, nothing disturbed the glistening calm of the East Deadman Ocean.

The only sound now in the cockpit of the whispercraft was a gentle rush of air through the struts, blades and ailerons. James felt as if he could fly forever on this sweet air current, but he knew he had to get lower, even if it meant losing the current. He edged the main lever down, putting the craft into a dive. The whispercraft swooped like a graceful albatross over waters that were now lime colored.

When the whispercraft dropped down to about twenty metres above the surface, its landing supports looked like webbed feet bracing for a landing on the water. But James had no intention of landing out here—he was just hoping to avoid Walgren's sensors by flying below them. At least he still had the westerly wind he needed to stay on course to the east.

As a whispercraft pilot since the age of fifteen, James couldn't believe that he had to sneak from one continent to another. In his opinion, the air currents and the lands they blessed should be as free to travel as the breeze. There had never been borders on Takara Prime before; overnight, freedom had vanished. Takara Prime was no longer part of the Dominion. The Divinian Empire had conquered it!

Over the rush of air, he called to the back of the cockpit. "Are you all right, dear?"

"Sure, James!" answered Cordette. The twenty-one year old woman fidgeted in her seat, but she was content to stare out the porthole at the glistening sea and wispy clouds. "We're flying awfully low, aren't we?" she asked.

He laughed nervously. "It only looks that way. Good currents down here." His wife knew too much about flying for him to lie to her for very long. She would be suspicious when he didn't go higher to look for faster, safer air currents. He sure hoped they could sneak into Walgren without anyone throwing a fit.

He knew he had broken the new regulations; but they had their own transportation, and they should be allowed to go anywhere. Cordette was royalty after all.

James shook his head and peered out the porthole.

"There's a squad of whispercrafts," said Cordette, pointing upward.

"What?" Scrunching lower in his seat, James peered into the glare of the reddish sun. High in the sky, at an eighty-degree angle, came what looked like a formation of snowy egrets, wending their way lazily in his direction. James checked his sensors and established that they weren't birds, unless birds had twenty-metre wingspans and were made of tritanium. He counted five approaching whispercrafts.

They must have spotted him, too, but they stayed at their high altitude, riding air currents that carried them toward him. If need be, whispercrafts could transform into a jet to increase momentum against the wind or in still air, but the constant diving and climbing made even the strongest stomachs revolt. Most whispercraft pilots refused to use jet mode for that, preferring to climb or dive very little, only to find the best currents. It wasn't only a point of pride, although it was that, too. Whispercrafts in helicopter mode simply made better rides—and the gravity suppressors exhausted less fuel—when they rode the natural air currents. Fuel consumption was a critical factor in a long haul over a vast ocean.

"Climb the wind and ride it," was a popular phrase among whispercraft pilots. That's what James would normally have done, but this trip he was trying to hide. Despite what he saw, he still hoped that the squad wasn't coming after him and his wife. With whispercrafts on his tail, he wouldn't be able to go straight to Starko, the capital of Walgren. He would have to make for some more isolated port, hoping they wouldn't follow a lone whispercraft for days on end.

Their radio crackled, making him jump. James peered at the device embedded in their console, surprised that they would communicate directly with them. It was a terrible breach of etiquette, since neither one of them have waved a wing to indicate a willingness to chat. Of course, this probably wasn't a chatting opportunity.

"Unknown whispercraft, turn back," warned a stern voice over the radio. "Traffic from Hadulla to Walgren is not permitted at the present time."

James looked with embarrassment and fear at his wife. He had told her that they might have to do some unpleasant things to be safe, and one of those things might include lying. But the gorgeous twenty-one year old gave him a brave smile, which was all he needed.

He flicked the switch and replied, "Whispercraft *Black Savour* to unknown squad, we're *not* coming from Hadulla—we're coming from Tantos. And we're *residents* of Walgren, citizens and law abiding there. This is a royal whispercraft."

"That doesn't matter—all traffic has to be rerouted," warned the stern voice coming from the peaceful squad high above them. "Royalty has been done a way with on Takara Prime. This planet is now ruled by the Divinian Empire."

Hmmm, this is serious, thought James, but he tried not to show how serious it was in his demeanor. "We're not even going to Walgren," he replied snidely. "We're going to fly right past...on our way to Sipoli."

"You're going to turn back."

"Excuse me, but you don't own these skies," he snapped at the faceless voice. "I've been flying this westerly current since last decade! We should be free to go wherever we want!"

There came a tense pause, and James let his bravado fade for only an instant. He smiled confidently at his wife, but she was starting to look anxious. "Maybe they'll see reason," he said, "and do the right thing."

The radio crackled. "You will turn back right now," warned the voice, "or we will force you into the sea."

"Or you'll *kill* me and my wife!" he muttered, although he kept the radio mute. They had given him a long pause, and now they were going to get one in return. While they waited, James used his sensors to scan the air currents above them.

Before the squad could respond, he activated the elevators on the tail section, turned antigrav to full, and soared upward. The golden nose cone sliced through the clouds, until he found a northerly flow that was fast but wouldn't take him terribly far off course. With any luck, they might conclude that he was turning around, not running.

"Whispercraft *Black Savour*, turn to heading—" James flicked the radio off before it became even more annoying.

With embarrassment, he shouted back to Cordette. "We tried to talk reasonably to them, but they weren't being reasonable. So we'll just go around."

"We're breaking the law," said Cordette knowingly. "I said we should never break laws."

"Just this once, because we haven't got much choice." He flashed her a grim smile.

The ocean had turned a teal color directly beneath them, where a cold current made the kelp scarce. As he climbed, James could see rainbows of color in the East Deadman Ocean. It swirled this way and that in various shades of green and blue for ten thousand kilometres, until it struck the third largest continent on Takara Prime—Walgren. He could now see land with his superior vision, but it was little more than a bead of rust on the shimmering horizon.

So close, yet still too far! If only we had left right away! James tried not to chide himself for getting caught up in events over which he had no control. Yes, he and Cordette didn't have to take three extra days to visit friends and Cordette's relatives in Hadulla. Somewhere in that brief period, the conquest of Takara Prime had happened and become a major part of life, even supplanting the distant robotic wars raging some three hundred light years away in the news. Free movement wasn't allowed anymore from continent to continent, or so they said. Certainly, the conquest had been nothing but distant rumors on Walgren when they departed nine days ago.

Now Divinian vigilantes ruled the skies and waters, keeping away everyone, even resident Walgrens.

"They're coming lower," warned his wife, who was straining in her seat to get a better look.

"Keep your seat belt on," he ordered her, knowing he might have to make some erratic maneuvers. In normal times, whispercrafts were never armed, but these weren't normal times. Five whispercrafts could force one whispercraft from the sky, but they would have to be fools to try that. Then again, fear and panic made people do foolish things, thought James, as he continued to flee from the squad of whispercrafts.

After thirty minutes of intense piloting, the prey and the hunters were at the same altitude, about four hundred metres above the gleaming ocean. Laterally, only one kilometre separated him from the lead whispercraft. He couldn't hear their pleas over the radio, as he had long ago turned it off, but he imagined that they were now begging him to turn back. Land was getting closer and closer—Walgren was a spill of brown and dark green across the turquoise horizon.

James banked slightly and turned toward the west. Without warning, some kind of missile shot past his window and streaked off into the ocean, leaving a red plume of smoke. Had that been a warning shot?

"Idiots!" he shouted, shaking his fist at them. With a cringe, he glanced at his wife.

"They're going to shoot us down, aren't they?" asked Cordette.

"No!" he answered through clenched teeth. "They're not going to shoot at us, because I know where the pipeline is. Hang on!"

He cut the antigrav and went into a steep dive, being careful to keep his hand near the airbrake paddles and spoilers.

There would be no more fooling around, no more running or hiding—he was headed straight for home.

Another missile streaked by the left wing of the whispercraft, coming much closer. He had a feeling that one *wasn't* a warning shot. Warfare had been unknown on Takara Prime for hundreds of years, so he had to hope that these makeshift armaments were none too deadly or accurate.

"Why don't you put out a distress signal?" asked Cordette.

Her husband nodded thoughtfully. "That's not a bad idea. We *are* in distress, and I'm not going down quietly."

He flipped on the distress signal, on all channels. The whispercrafts pursuing them were probably the Coastal Watchers, the ones charged with answering distress calls at sea. *That's some irony,* thought James, *when the rescuers become the attackers.* However, they were probably now all Divinian pilots patrolling the skies.

Leaning on the airbrakes, James pulled the craft out of its dive, and it skimmed the gentle waves of the turquoise sea. He smiled with satisfaction upon seeing the pipeline just under the surface of the shallow water; it looked like a flaw in the great jewelled facet, yet it carried much-needed fresh water. He swooped so close to the pipeline that he felt as if he could lean out the window and spit on it.

As he expected, that dissuaded his pursuers from shooting wildly at him, but his evasions had given them time to close the distance. Two of them were diving toward his position from high altitude. *Maybe they really are going to drive us into the sea!*

Cordette looked out the window with awe, having never seen her husband fly this close to the water, except when landing. And then he would be going at a much-reduced speed. There was just one problem—the air currents were slower at low altitude, and his pursuers could close the distance by staying in the upper currents. James still maintained the innocent hope that just by reaching land he could escape. Once he and Cordette were on Walgren, he rationalized no one could keep them off.

Flying only metres above the water forced him to concentrate intently, and James didn't see them coming until Cordette shouted, "James! On the right!"

He glanced over to see a large whispercraft swerve into view. Its wing nearly clipped his, and he had to tap his joystick to edge away from the sky hog. Then he saw the other one crowding him on his left—he shook his fist at him. *Are they so insane that they would wreck themselves to stop us?*

No matter how close those idiots came, James couldn't worry about them—the water was still his prime concern. At this speed, he'd be dashed into splinters if he hit it. The three whispercrafts swooped over the smooth jade water, looking like three albatrosses fighting for the same school of fish.

Finally the craft on his right disappeared from view, and he didn't have time to follow it with his sensors. With a thunderous jolt, something hit the roof of his whispercraft. James wrestled his controls to maintain altitude and not plunge into the sea; after a struggle, he managed to level his wings.

Seething with anger, he decided, *Two can play at that game! And my hull is stronger than your landing supports.* Tapping the antigrav lever, he rose rapidly and crunched into the struts, and underbelly of the craft riding him. Hanging on to the joystick with both hands, he bucked like a bronco, dumping the unwanted rider.

"James!" shouted Cordette.

James glanced out the window in time to see the attacking whispercraft spin off, its undercarriage badly damaged. Fluttering like a wounded pelican, the whispercraft hit the calm water and sent up a tremendous plume. The whispercraft wasn't completely destroyed, but it looked fairly well shattered. James felt a pang of grief, because he had never been the cause of an accident in his ten years of flying.

"Now we're in trouble," said Cordette. It was an accurate assessment.

James scowled. "Maybe they'll realize that if we can fly this well, we're not turning back."

The other whispercraft on his left now moved away to a respectable distance, and James relaxed a bit at the controls. He continued to follow the pipeline toward the shimmering silhouette of land in the distance. At this point, he would normally feel relieved and happy to be so close to home, but today the sight of Walgren only brought him dread. *What's going to happen to Cordette and me? To all of Takara Prime?*

Without warning, a missile slammed into his right wing, shearing it off. Only his quick reactions on the antigrav lever kept them from plowing immediately into the ocean. Instead the whispercraft shot upward like a leaf caught on the breeze then it lost its momentum and slowly spiralled downward, a wounded bird.

The whispercraft creaked, trying to hold together, and air howled ominously in the struts and ailerons. Cordette screamed, but the torrent of rushing air drowned her out. James tried all of his controls, but none were responsive—the whispercraft was in its death dive.

Looking out the window only made his head whirl as fast as the scenery, and James shrieked. He tried to reach back for his wife, but she was scrunched down in her seat. "Oh, my dear...I'm so sorry!"

As his whispercraft spiralled toward the pristine ocean, a tingling came over James' body. He wondered whether this was the human Calm of Death he had heard so much about. The man reached back to grab his wife's hand one last time, but her thin body shimmered like a mirage, breaking apart before his eyes. He gasped at the unexpected sight.

The whispercraft plunged erratically into the jade water, striking like a lopsided bullet and spewing a lopsided splash. Splinters from the sleek craft rained down upon the choppy waves, but James and Cordette weren't aboard.

Husband and wife stood huddled together on the transporter platform in what looked like a cargo hold full of military equipment. The entire room looked like an armory, with modular storage lockers and weapon assemblies crammed into its tight confines. Five people dressed in black military uniforms confronted them.

Cordette shivered and gripped her husband's chest. "Are they...are they Divinians?"

"I don't think so," he answered, unsure about that. James tried to stand upright and show some dignity, but he couldn't let go of his wife. He remained hunched over her thin form.

"We answered your distress call," said a familiar female, as she stepped forward and aimed a phaser at them. Leia Tetzlaff studied the two intently, not about to make any quick pronouncements.

"Leia?" asked Cordette hopefully. "You brought the royal army to save us?"

"Hardly," snorted Leia's strong feminine voice. "There is no royal army anymore. For that matter there's no royal family on Takara Prime anymore either. We're all subjects of the Divinian Empire. Including you Cordette!"

James bad-tempered instantly. "All right! What's going on?"

"James!" snapped his wife, cuffing him on the hand.

Jason Anderson chuckled. "I hope, by this time tomorrow you're pushing up daises son." Jason stepped forward and aimed a phaser at James. "Good-bye James!"

Cordette's dark green eyes widened in horror! "What are you going to do with that phaser?"

Jason grinned. "What I should have done long ago."

Leia swivelled her phaser and the phaser spit a red beam, which gnawed a burning hole in Jason Anderson's stomach. With a groan, he staggered to the door but collapsed halfway there. After he was dead Leia relaxed her phaser hand, watching James' reaction, and waited for his response.

"We haven't done anything wrong!" declared James. He hugged Cordette defensively. "Look, just beam us down somewhere on Walgren, and we'll be going. And...thanks for saving our lives."

"Saved you twice Mister James Anderson," said the officious Leia. "I could have let your father kill you but I didn't."

"Just a minute!" barked Cordette, stepping in front of her husband to protect him from Leia and her pirates. "So you killed his father instead?"

"You have to understand something." Leia stepped forward and lightly touched her own collar, showing them the Divinian rank insignias with odd markings on her forehead. "In our haste, we've gotten off to a bad start. "I'm now General Leia Tetzlaff, and this *is* a Divinian ship. But we're not here to kill anyone—we're only here to recruit new soldiers. If you help us with some assignments, we'll permit this privilege for you and your husband...and help you get commands of your own some day."

"As what?" Cordette asked. "As human slaves in a Divinian army. At least in the Dominion there was peace and freedom. How can you betray your own race? Make that choice?"

"The Dominion's rein had long since passed. I'm not betraying the human race. I'm preserving it! All humans that join with the Divinians will be forever rewarded. The choices I made far out weigh the good I had in your father's army. Take me for example I'm leader of the ninth Divinian fleet. In your father's lousy space army I was only a lonely Lieutenant

Commander but now I command entire ships. Isn't that great."

"We don't need—"

"Weren't the other aircrafts trying to kill you?"

"Uh, yeah," admitted Cordette, scratching her hardened skin colored skull. "I'd heard they weren't permitting people to travel from Hadulla to Walgren, but I didn't really believe it. Now they've destroyed my whispercraft...my transportation, my rights. I'm going to get to the bottom of this."

"The best you can hope for is to start over like me. It's not so bad. In fact I'd say your better off. Leia motioned to James. "James, you had better come with me and discuss your future. I'm offering you everything you could want. As for you Cordette you're lucky to be alive. Your family has been assassinated. I convinced my superiors to keep you alive as a favour to me. Don't let me down. We'll make a loyal Divinian follower out of you yet."

Two hours later, James was sitting in his quarters, watching a video log of Kodiak bears fishing for salmon in a wild Yukon stream. He had had bad days before but this one had to be tops. James had witnessed the murder of his father and his wife's loss of power within minutes of each other. Although he didn't care about his father, he cared about his wife and her well-being. And to top it off he was seriously considering accepting Leia's offer of joining the Divinian Empire, sworn enemies of the Dominion.

However James was no longer a Dominion officer and he never would be again given his record. There was no place for a killer in a peaceful organization. So he was free to choose his own path.

Despite their differences one thing his father and he could both agree upon: there was no place like outer space. Jason's enthusiasm had instilled in the boy a burning desire to see those strange planets and people. In fact, the young Anderson had outdone his civilian father by joining the Dominion's military. If possible, he would see even more amazing sights and do more amazing things than his dad had ever dreamed of. Although Jason Anderson hadn't realized there was a competition going on, there was.

Unfortunately, that wanderlust and ambition had been severely dampened by the long years spent on the prison world Servala V. James had been sent to military prison there when it was ruled he violated the most sacred rules as a Dominion officer. He illegally seized one hundred and three ships and murdered forty-seven people. All for his personal gain.

His father had vowed to kill him once he got out of military prison and made it his own personal vendetta to rid the galaxy of his very own son. Now James Rawlings didn't know what he wanted, except to be something different than the vindictive Jason Anderson or his past self when he was still called James Anderson.

On the viewer, he watched the great brown bears, which stood almost four metres tall, as they frolicked like cubs in the rushing stream. Catching leaping fish with a swipe of a claw wasn't easy, and the bears often failed. But they looked as if they were having fun. He realized that life wasn't worth it unless fun was involved. Unfortunately, James couldn't remember the last time he had fun.

A chime sounded at his door, and Rawlings turned off the viewer. "Come in!"

The door slid open, and a slim woman with short dark hair entered his quarters. Under different circumstances, he could have been attracted to General Leia Tetzlaff, but that had never been an option since he was married. Leia had been a bridesmaid at the wedding for heaven's sake. He jumped to his feet and stood at attention behind his desk, trying not to show the loathing he had for the leader of the ninth

Divinian fleet. She was capable, but she never seemed to have any fun.

"How do you like your rank of Lieutenant?"

"It's swell, Leia. A lot less than I expected. I was after all a Dominion Battleship Destroyer Captain."

"We all have to start somewhere. Besides you've got to earn our trust before we'll give you a higher rank. At ease, Lieutenant," she told him in a tone of voice that did nothing to put him at ease.

"Yes, sir." James put his hands behind his back and remained standing.

Tetzlaff scowled. "I've read your Dominion records, military and prison, and I'm frankly amazed. You're not a typical Dominion officer. I don't get you, Rawlings."

He opened his mouth to reply, but realized that he might make things worse. Then again, how could things be worse?

"Permission to speak freely?" he asked.

Tetzlaff's scowl deepened, because she really didn't like her officers speaking freely. "Very well."

"General, you don't understand me, and you're wrong about me."

She began to protest, but Rawlings kept talking while he had the chance. "I tried to get my Dominion superiors to act more like me and like Solaris and other Dominion leaders from seventy-years ago to embrace the power they had. They refused and were only interested in peaceful coexistence with the rest of the galaxy. A lot of good that did the Dominion. That attitude ultimately led to the destruction of the Dominion. Our ancient enemies came in droves to annihilate us. The experience I've been through is something you can't begin to understand. I had four years stolen from my life and career...and given to someone who trusted in peace. Dominion superiors treated me like a threat; others treated me like a renegade. To everyone in the Dominion, I was an oddity. Face it, my chances of rising very far in the command structure of the Dominion were dim."

"You and I have the same beliefs and value systems. We're the same in a sense. If I can help myself, maybe I should accept your offer. With your help, I'll have a chance to start over, and my career won't be capped this time."

Tetzlaff's expression softened a bit, and for the first time since she had known him, she looked at him with sympathy. "Now that's the right attitude, but I have to start you out slow and there is a job you could do. Although it's menial, it also requires command skills."

Rawlings leaned forward. "I'm listening."

"In addition to our patrol duties, we have to deliver medical teams and supplies to the observation posts along the Adirondacks Expanse. Refugees have deluged some of them. I think it will be more efficient to have a personnel shuttlecraft do these runs instead of the *Phoenix*. So we need a medical courier. You would be in command of a crew of two—yourself and the co-pilot."

Rawlings smiled gratefully. "Well, we all have to start somewhere. I'll take the job, General. Can I have the *Phoenix's* first pilot?"

"Our most experienced pilot?" said Tetzlaff, bristling at the very idea. "I think not. He's much too important and experienced to be co-piloting a personnel shuttlecraft. Your wife is a low level pilot if I'm not mistaken, I gave her the rank of ensign—you can teach her the ropes."

Rawlings nodded. "Thank you, General. I won't let you down."

"I hope not. You leave at seventeen hundred hours for Outpost Gamma III. Report to main shuttlebay." Leia

Tetzlaff started for the door, then turned back to give him a half smile. "In a way, I envy you, Lieutenant. Sometimes I'd like less responsibility."

"You managed quite a feat," James questioned her. "Just how did you get so high up on the Divinian command structure?"

"A woman never reveals her secrets. I kept your past secret from your wife and she'll never learn what we discussed here." Leia Tetzlaff stiffened her spine and put on her command face again. "One more thing: try not to get into any discussions about the Dominion with your wife. I will admit I made an example of Stan and Donna Robinson, so that the Dominion has no loyal citizens here. They almost ruined my plan for the Divinian Empire to annex Takara Prime. Keep in mind if you decide to betray the Divinian Empire, I'll make an example of you and Cordette. On this ship, we don't set policy—we follow orders. Like it or not, the Dominion are the enemy now until further notice. Understand?"

Rawlings realized Tetzlaff wasn't fooling around. "You killed them! Yes, sir," answered Rawlings. He hadn't sympathized or thought all that much about the Dominion until recently, when Leia just assumed he might be a sympathizer. This oppressive atmosphere was another good reason to get off the *Phoenix*.

"I understand. I'll stay far away from the Dominion," promised Lieutenant Rawlings.

My first command in the Divinian Empire, James thought ruefully as he inspected the squat, boxy craft known simply as *Shuttle 8*. A Type-3 personnel shuttlecraft, she accommodated a maximum of eighteen people, including crew, in very tight quarters. *Shuttle 8* had hyperdrive and a transporter, but no weaponry. According to the manifest, they would be transporting eight members of the med team, plus the two crew. What worried him were all the boxes of supplies and equipment the shuttlebay workers kept loading onto the small craft. With all that weight on board, he feared she might handle sluggishly in a planet's atmosphere.

Rounding the bow of the shuttle, the lieutenant caught sight of his reflection in the front window. He looked quite dashing in his purple and black tunic, denoting his authorization for the command of the mission. A new allegiance, a new ship, a new uniform, and a new assignment that would actually do some good in the galaxy—maybe his life was turning around.

James hadn't felt so hopeful since the day he had been released from Servala V. He tried not to think about how quickly all those hopes had been dashed.

"James?" said a familiar inquisitive voice. He turned to see his petite, soft-skinned Takarain wife. It was a weird sight seeing her in an ensign military uniform.

"You still look gorgeous in that uniform," he said with a charming smile. "I'm pleased you're alright. They didn't hurt you, did they?"

She nodded firmly. "Thank you, James. You look pretty dashing yourself. I'm all right. In fact they're treating me quite well. Probably because Leia told them to."

"Well, I've been treated exceptionally excellent also," explained James. "You never mentioned your pilot training, I should have known."

"Class two rating," she answered proudly, "although I haven't logged that many hours of solo flight. A princess uses her own pilots rather than piloting the ship herself. Of course I'm a princess no longer so I guess I have to make the best of it with my own skills."

"You will on this assignment, because I intend to get my beauty sleep."

Cordette forced a polite laugh. "Yes, James. There's so much we don't know about each other. I guess we'll find out more things about each other as we spend more time together. Are you also a doctor?"

James smiled and plucked at his purple tunic. "No, I'm just a...a medical courier. Here come the doctors."

He pointed to eight more people in purple uniforms who had just entered the vast shuttlebay. They strode briskly between the parked shuttles, and James was struck by their youth. Like his young wife in front of him, they were just starting their military careers, and they did everything with self-important urgency. He wanted to tell them to slow down, to live more in the moment. But youth must be served.

Maybe he was nothing but a glorified shuttle pilot, but it felt bigger than that. The mission felt like a step toward destiny, at least personal destiny.

After the introductions were made, James and Cordette shoehorned their passengers into the cramped compartment then they took their seats in the cockpit. A row of seats had been pulled to make room for the supplies, and the passengers were practically sitting in each other's laps. Crates and boxes took up every spare centimetre. James was glad it was only a twenty-one-hour trip to Gamma III, because they would be at each other's throats if they had to spend any more time in these tight quarters.

During his preignition checklist, James tried to think like his former friend and not miss anything. They weren't over the allowed weight for the craft, but they were darn close. He whispered to Cordette, "I think we need to compensate for all the weight we're carrying. What if we open the plasma injectors in the main cryo tank to give the impulse engines a little boost."

Cordette looked at him with alarm. "James, that is somewhat unorthodox. It would also cut down our fuel efficiency by ten or twenty percent."

"As soon as we're away from the *Phoenix's* gravity, we'll go back to normal," he assured his worried wife. "Don't worry, I'm used to doing things on the fly."

Cordette gulped. "I hope you're the one taking us out of dock."

"Yes, and you'll be glad I boosted the engines when I do."

A few minutes later, the preparations were complete, and James tapped his communication panel. "*Shuttle 8* to bridge, requesting permission to launch."

"Tetzlaff here," came the businesslike response. "You are cleared for launch, *Shuttle 8*. Lieutenant, I'd appreciate it if you returned in one piece. We've got lots of supplies that need to be delivered. Good fortune to you."

"Thank you, sir," answered James cheerfully. His fortune hadn't been all that good, and he was ready for a change in that department. For General Tetzlaff, these few words were as close as she had ever come to bubbly enthusiasm. He punched up a wide view of the area on his viewscreen and kept it on during the launch.

The *Wolverine*-class starship hung suspended in space among the dazzling stars, appearing much like a large silver monster. Double doors slid open atop the immense square section, and a tiny shuttlecraft darted out, looking like an insect escaping from an open window. The Type-3 shuttlecraft cruised to a distance of several thousand kilometres from the *Phoenix* then with a flash of light, she disappeared into hyperspace.

CHAPTER FOUR

March 16, 2121: Outpost Gamma III, The Adirondacks Expanse

JAMES RAWLINGS COULD hear a low humming noise as he cut sub-light engines and slowed the shuttlecraft to a stately drift through a sea of widely scattered asteroids. Some were only a few metres wide, while others were several kilometres wide. Slowly they approached a monstrous rock that was over eight kilometres in diameter. It was as dark as obsidian, yet its center appeared even darker. Rawlings needed a few seconds to realize that the asteroid had a mammoth hole in its middle, at least one kilometre across. In comparison with the black asteroid and the blackness of space, the chasm looked even darker—like a black hole.

Despite the deserted appearance of this region, these were the correct coordinates. "Open up a secure channel," he told Cordette.

"Yes, sir," replied the fresh faced, woman, working her board with quick fingers. "Channel open."

He tapped his panel and said, "*Shuttle 8* to outpost, this is Lieutenant Rawlings from the *Phoenix*, requesting permission to dock."

"Permission granted," answered a pleasant female voice. "*Shuttle 8*, are we glad to see you. Take dock two, the second open dock to port."

"Thank you."

"We're lowering shields and force field. Proceed when ready."

With a flash of light, the dark cavity in the asteroid turned into a blazing neon pit. Pulsing beacons guided the way to a mammoth spacedock within, and the walls of the chasm glittered with sensors, dish arrays, and weapons. Trying not to be distracted by the remarkable sight, Rawlings spread his fingers over the conn and piloted the tiny shuttlecraft into the glowing heart of the asteroid.

"Well, it's about time," muttered one of the doctors behind him.

Rawlings ignored the crack, as he had ignored so many others during the past twenty-one hours. Although the ship's sensors claimed that life support was working flawlessly, he could swear that he was beginning to *smell* his passengers.

At least Cordette had proven to be skilled, even-tempered, and unflappable.

As they cruised toward the landing dock, Rawlings glanced around the cavernous installation. He was somewhat surprised to see several unfamiliar and battered ships docked at the rear bays; they didn't look like Divinian vessels. This was supposed to be a secret outpost, but it looked more like a junkyard at the moment.

Cordette noticed it, too, and her dark green eyes darted to Rawlings before going back to her instruments. The lieutenant concentrated on the docking, although a ten-year old kid could have hit that huge target. They sat down with a gentle thud, and the umbilicals began to whir.

When Rawlings heard the clamps latch on to the shuttle's hatch, he sat back in his chair and smiled at Cordette. "We made it in one piece...without killing any of the passengers," he whispered.

Cordette nodded. She couldn't really smile at this time, but her eyes twinkled with amusement. "This job will test my social skills more than my flying."

When the hatch opened, the medical team gathered around the exit, anxious to get off. *Nothing like twenty-one hours in a shuttlecraft with strangers to give one claustrophobia,* thought Rawlings.

Without warning, the lights in the great cavern went out, eliciting gasps from the passengers. Once again, the void in the asteroid was as black as space, only without the glistening stars to give it some cheer. Seen from afar, the shuttlecraft glowed like a feeble lantern in a great hall.

A few of the passengers thanked him as they filed out, and Rawlings nodded pleasantly. He held nothing against them—in many respects, it was easier being a crewmember than a passenger on a trip like this. At least he had been occupied.

He and Cordette shut down all but essential life support on the small craft then they followed the medical team into the corridor. The last member of the team was just passing through a force-field security gate that demanded positive identification. Rawlings stepped back to let Cordette go first, but she stepped back and deferred to him.

He walked through the gate and waited for Cordette to gain admittance to the outpost. "How long do you think we'll be here?" asked Cordette.

"Maybe long enough to get a meal," answered Rawlings. "They're expecting us back as soon as possible for more of these runs. I'm afraid this assignment is going to be hectic but not all that exciting."

"We'll see," answered Cordette cheerfully.

As the party stepped off the dock, two officers met them, both wearing the green uniforms of command. One was a bald-headed Alphan and the other was a tall, antennaed Shavadai. Since both were male, neither one could be the friendly female with whom Rawlings had spoken earlier, he noted with disappointed.

The Shavadai conducted the medical team down one corridor, while the Alphan nodded politely to the new arrivals. Two white-shirted technicians strode into the landing dock behind them, and Rawlings assumed they would take charge of the cargo.

"Hello, Lieutenant Rawlings. Welcome to Outpost Gamma III," said the Alphan, with a slight smile. "I'm Ensign Mughal."

"Yes," said Rawlings brusquely. "Now if we could get a bite to eat, and maybe a walk to stretch our legs, we'll be on our way."

"As you wish, sir. However, our commanding officer, Captain Alesha Lori Zieglar, was hoping to meet with you and ask a favor."

"A favor? We're just medical couriers—what could we do for your CO?"

"I'll let her ask," said Ensign Mughal. "But I will show you something on our way. Will you please follow me?"

As they walked down a long doorless and windowless corridor, the Alphan took a right turn at a junction in the corridor, and they finally came to a row of doors. He opened one marked "Recreation," and Rawlings wondered if they would interrupt the CO during her exercise period. As soon as he got a glimpse inside the room, he knew he was wrong.

The room was full of bedraggled, sorry-looking people—men, women, and children—several of them dressed in rags. A few of them glanced at the visitors, but most stared straight ahead with vacant eyes. A handful of children were playing board games and watching video logs, but most of the people looked bored and disillusioned. Rawlings glanced at Cordette, and he could see the young woman was deeply affected by the sight. Without saying a word, the Alphan ushered them out and closed the door.

"Refugees," he explained. "And these aren't even the wounded, sick ones—the ones who survived Dominion torture and starvation. They're in sickbay, which we've had to enlarge twice. That's why we need the supplies and med team."

"I thought this was supposed to be a secret outpost," said Rawlings.

The Alphan sighed. "So did we. As you can see, the secret is out. The awkward thing is that we can't let them leave here, because it's a secret base, even though everybody apparently *knows* about it. I mean, we can't let them leave in their own ships, most of which wouldn't get very far, anyway. So we have to impound their ships and hold them, until we can find official transportation to get them back to Divinia... or wherever."

Rawlings crossed his arms. "I bet I could guess what this favor is."

"Let's go to the commissary," said the Alphan with forced cheer, "and you can have that meal you so richly deserve. The captain will join you there."

The lieutenant nodded, knowing he didn't have much choice. He wondered about the Dominion story about torture and starvation. This fake story seemed unlikely since the Dominion outlawed such things. In fact that was part of the reason James Rawlings had served time in a Dominion prison for.

As he gobbled down the finest steak he had ever gotten from a food replicator, Rawlings watched Cordette pick at the orange cabbage leaves on her plate. He felt sorry for the young woman, who evidently hadn't seen much of the cruelty and waywardness of life. One moment, a person is on top of the world, living high in a thriving colony or on a sleek vessel, and the next moment, he's wearing rags, staring at the ceiling, abandoned. James Rawlings felt sorry for the refugees, but he had seen too much in his own eventful life to be shocked by their plight.

Cordette glanced up, catching him looking at her. "What's going to happen to them?"

"They're going to start over," answered James. "They've lost everything, but they're still alive. A lot of people in the Adirondacks Expanse weren't so lucky. When it comes down to it, all we've got is our wits and tenacity."

"But the Divinian Empire should try to help them," insisted Cordette.

James shrugged. "On most issues, the Divinian Empire employs stone cold logic: the needs of the many outweigh the needs of the few. You'd better learn that, Cordette."

She peered intently at him. "You're very cynical, James."

"Just realistic. I was once idealistic like you. It's good to be like that for as long as you can, but I have a feeling that this assignment is going to break you of that. And their story of Dominion torture and starvation is absolutely bull. I know you know that."

James took another bite of steak. James looked up to see an attractive blond human woman approaching their table. Since she was wearing captain's pips, he jumped to his feet, certain he was about to meet the commanding officer of the outpost. Cordette did the same.

"Relax," said the captain wearily. "We don't stand on ceremony around here. What good would it do us? I'm Captain Alesha Lori Zieglar."

"It's a pleasure," said James, recognizing her friendly voice from his initial contact with the outpost. "I'm Lieutenant Rawlings, and this is Ensign Chance. Won't you have a seat?"

"Thank you."

"We were a bit surprised to see the scope of your refugee problem," Cordette explained.

"So were we," answered the captain. "We were hoping the *Phoenix* herself would come, and we could offload the refugees, but it didn't happen that way. So now I've got to beg—can you take a few of them back to the *Phoenix* with you?"

"Certainly," Cordette answered quickly.

James shot her a glance, and the young woman lowered her eyes, knowing she had answered out of turn. James sounded very cautious as he remarked, "It's not really in the purview of our mission to transport refugees. However, if you ordered us to do so, we'd have no choice."

Captain Zieglar slumped back in her chair and waved her hand. "Then I'm ordering you to take six of the people I've chosen. I'm sure the higher ups'll chew me out for that, but I welcome an opportunity to explain the situation to them. Having a secret outpost overrun with refugees is a bit of a security risk."

"Okay," said James. "How will you chose who goes?"

"We have two pregnant women in the group," said the captain. "I'd like to send them first. We're not exactly equipped for dealing with newborn babies here. A young couple showed up yesterday, and they claim they have intelligence to report, but they will only tell a general. There are several orphaned children—I'd like to give two of them a break."

James shook his head in amazement. "How long can you cope with this?"

"Not much longer, but we've been assured that the Empire will eventually pick them all up. Then we'll relocate this asteroid. At least now we can cope with the medical problems, thanks to you." Captain Zieglar gave him a warm smile.

"I wish we could stay longer," answered James with sincerity.

"We could use you," replied Zieglar. "We have to stay on constant vigil—not only are there the refugees, but the Dominion are experts at sneaking in and out of the Adirondacks Expanse. By the time we've discovered them, they're usually gone."

"We'll report back on the conditions here," said James.

"I wish you would."

With her napkin, Cordette daintily wiped the crumbles around her mouth. "I'm ready to go when you are."

"Right." The handsome lieutenant managed a smile and pushed himself away from the table. "Is the cargo off the shuttle?"

"Yes, it is," answered Captain Zieglar. "Do you want to interview any of the passengers you'll be taking?"

"No, I trust your judgment. It's been a short but pleasant visit, Captain."

"I'd like to encourage you to come often. Have a safe journey back, Lieutenant...Ensign." She turned and strode through the commissary nodding encouragement to the officers she passed.

James began to think that his new assignment would be a good change of pace. Out here on the edge of the Adirondacks Expanse, he had no bizarre history or hierarchy of command to deal with—he was just a medical courier bringing much-needed supplies. He would make his deliveries and go on to the next post, like the pony express. There would always be new people to meet.

He smiled at Cordette. "I think I'm going to like this job."

Ten minutes later, they were sitting in the cockpit of *Shuttle 8*, going over the pre-flight checklist. In the cavernous interior of the asteroid, it was still eerily dark, and the windows of the shuttlecraft looked opaque. Without passengers and cargo, the cabin almost looked spacious, and James wished it would stay that way for a while. However, it was not to be.

The hatch opened, and a security officer stuck his head in. "Lieutenant Rawlings, are you ready to receive your passengers?'

"Sure. I hope they're not expecting a starship."

"This is better than they're used to." The security officer stepped aside, allowing two small Abu children to enter the cabin. Whether they were actual siblings was hard to tell, but the two of them had bonded in their desperate situation; they held hands as if they were inseparable.

"Sit up front," James told them with a smile, "so you can watch Cordette pilot the ship."

"Thank you," they replied in unison, speaking so softly they could barely be heard. They both squeezed into one seat, and James didn't bother to separate them.

Two females, both, followed the Abu children obviously in the advanced stages of pregnancy. One was Nya, judging by her distinctive hairstyle—half of her head sheared and the other half with straight, black hair down to her shoulder. She looked miserable, as if resigned to some horrible fate, and she slouched to the back row of seats without a word. He guessed that the other woman was human, until she smiled at him and shook her head.

"Actually I'm a Turghan," she said.

"I've always gotten along well with Turghans," he replied.

"I can tell you have great affection for us."

Their conversation was cut short when a young Jamalan couple entered the cabin, holding hands as tightly as the Abu children had. With their bald heads and elephantine ears, they looked more alien than the others, and James recalled that Jamalans had a reputation for being brilliant but difficult. These two looked suspicious.

"We were told we'd be going to a large starship," said the male.

"You will be, as soon as we get there," answered James. "I understand you have some intelligence to report."

"But only in a face-to-face meeting with a general," insisted the female.

"I've found generals highly overrated, but we'll find one for you. Have a seat, please."

Once all the passengers were situated, James turned to address them. "I'm Lieutenant Rawlings, and this is Ensign Chance. I know all of you have had a tough time, and I would like this trip to be as pleasant as possible. But we don't have many amenities on this shuttlecraft, and the quarters will be tight. In other words, you'll basically have to sit there and not make demands on us. If you do that, I promise we'll get you to our starship as quickly as possible."

"How long will the trip take?" asked the strait-laced Nya.

James glanced at Cordette, who consulted her computer screen. "If the *Phoenix* stays on course and schedule, it should be about twenty-seven hours," she reported.

"The sooner we get going, the sooner we'll arrive." James tapped the communication panel. "*Shuttle 8* to operations, requesting permission to leave."

"You are cleared," replied a businesslike male voice. "Please maintain subspace silence in the vicinity of the station."

Beacons suddenly illuminated the depths of the great chasm, and hydraulics whirred as the docking mechanism retracted from the hatch. James sat back in his seat and smiled at Cordette. "Take her out, Cordette."

"Yes, James," replied the young woman, sounding eager to prove herself. With considerable skill, she plied her console, and the tiny craft lifted off the dock and moved gracefully through the neon pit. James crossed his arms and closed his eyes, planning on getting a little shut-eye.

Once the tiny shuttle had cleared the opening of the chasm, the brilliant lights abruptly went off, and Outpost Gamma III again looked like nothing but a craggy rock floating in the vastness of space.

James Rawlings laughed and shook his head then he put the computer pad down. For the fourth straight time, the Abu children had beaten him in a game of three-dimensional checkers. "You girls are too good for me."

They gave him identical, enigmatic smiles and looked at one another with satisfaction.

"You're a great player," said one.

"In the game," finished the other.

"Would you like to play each other?" he asked.

"Maybe sometime—"

"Later."

James nodded and looked back at the other passengers on the shuttlecraft. They were a surly lot, except for the pregnant Turghan, who occasionally flashed him a smile. The rest of the time she sat in contemplative silence with her hands folded over her extended abdomen. He didn't expect refugees who had been driven from their homes to be exactly cheerful, but they might be a bit more grateful for the ride back to Divinian space.

Then again, maybe they didn't know what they were getting themselves into. Most of them had probably been born in what was now the Adirondacks Expanse, and they had lived all their lives there. He wondered whether the two pregnant women had spouses and families to help them, or whether they were as alone as they appeared.

"You're wondering about me," said the Turghan woman with a listless smile. "I happen to be alone, although not for long." She patted her ample girth.

"I'm sorry," said James. With the others watching and listening, he wished he were also telepathic, so they could continue this conversation in private. But privacy was hard to come by on *Shuttle 8*.

"I've never seen Turghaned," said the woman. "Have you?"

"It's beautiful," he assured her. "The garden spot of the galaxy, with the friendliest people I've ever met. Even too friendly."

She nodded eagerly. "I always meant to go there one day. I didn't think it would be...under these circumstances."

Unable to say or do anything that would change the circumstances, the lieutenant turned to his co-pilot. "How are you doing, Cordette? Getting tired?"

"It's only been four hours," answered his young wife. "Perhaps in three hours more, I could use relief."

"Just let me know when you're ready. That short nap refreshed me." The young Jamalan male rose to his feet. "Is it all right if I stretch my legs?"

"Sure," answered James, "but you'll have to make do with what space we have."

"I figured that." With two steps, he stood behind James and Cordette, gazing with interest at the readouts. "Where are we, approximately?"

"We have just passed the Sha're Bivens region," she answered.

"Then we're still fairly close to the Adirondacks Expanse."

"Yes. That is where the *Phoenix* is patrolling."

"Are you a navigator?" asked James.

The Jamalan nodded. "In a way, I am. I was studying stellar cartography at the university on Ravanello VI...until it burned down."

"I'm sorry," said Cordette.

He scowled. "If you two keep saying you're sorry for every wrong committed against us, that's all you'll ever say to us. At some point, we have to stop feeling sorry for ourselves and get on with life."

"That's a good attitude," replied James, giving him a sympathetic smile. "We'll do what we can to help you."

"I know you will." The Jamalan again studied the readouts with a scholarly interest. "Our speed is hyperdrive four? That's very fast for a craft of this size."

"Common for a Type-3 shuttle," answered Cordette.

The Jamalan signed. "Where I come from, we only had sub-light shuttles. Had we ships like this, more of us might have survived."

"Tierney," said the female Jamalan, "there's no sense talking about it."

"No, I suppose not." His shoulders drooped, and he turned to James. "Is there any food on board to eat?"

Before the lieutenant could answer, there came an awful groan from the rear of the shuttlecraft. He whirled around to see the pregnant Nya gripping her swollen stomach and writhing in her seat. The Turghan woman staggered to her feet and tried to comfort her, as did the female Jamalan, while the Abu children looked on with eerie calm.

Immediately, James reached under his console, opened a panel, and grabbed a medkit. His worst fear was that he would have to deliver a premature baby, when he knew very little about delivering babies and less about Nya physiology. But a groaning, pregnant woman demanded action. He glanced at Cordette, who gave him a nod, as if to say she would handle the shuttle while he handled the medical emergency.

He vaulted to his feet and muscled his way past the Jamalan male, who seemed rooted to the spot, unable to move. When he reached the distressed woman, she was panting, and her eyes rolled back in her head. The other women stepped away to allow him room, although what he was going to do for her he didn't know.

"Are you in labor?" he asked urgently. "How far along are you?"

"Not...far...enough," she muttered through clenched teeth. "The pain...the *pain!*"

"I can do something for the pain." James opened the medkit and reached inside for a hypospray. While he loaded the instrument with a painkiller, he felt a slight shudder, as if the shuttlecraft were coming out of hyperdrive. He turned to tell Cordette that she didn't need to leave hyperdrive—it was better to keep going. That's when he saw Cordette lying unconscious on the deck, with the Jamalan seated at the conn.

"What the—"

He never finished the sentence, because the Nya grabbed him by the shoulders with incredible strength and forced him headfirst into her lap. He struggled, but the young Jamalan woman also attacked him; the two of them forced him onto his back and jumped upon him like women possessed.

James didn't like hitting women, but his instincts took over. He lashed out with his fist and smashed the Nya in the mouth, sending her oversized body crashing back into her seat. Then he gripped the Jamalan by the throat and tried to push her away, while she clawed at his face.

From the corner of his eye, he saw the Turghan fumbling in the arms locker, pulling out a phaser pistol. Whose side was *she* on? Or were they all hijackers! He didn't have time to figure it out.

James grabbed the Jamalan and yanked her around like a shield just as the Turghan fired at him. The young woman took the full blast of the phaser set to stun, and she fell upon him like dead weight. With adrenaline coursing through his veins, James tossed her off and scrambled to his feet, just as another phaser blast streaked past his head. He saw the Abu children crouched behind their chairs, watching with wide eyes.

"Don't resist!" ordered the Turghan, aiming her weapon to get another shot. "You won't be harmed!"

The only weapon at hand was the medkit, and James threw it at her with all his might. His aim was good, and the metal box bounced off her head with a thud, causing her to collapse to the deck. James dove for the discarded phaser and came up with it just as the Nya jumped on his back. She was as determined and as strong as a sumo wrestler, and she shoved his face into the deck. Twisting around, he smashed her in the mouth with an elbow, and she slid off his back with a groan.

James crawled out from under the dead weight and staggered to his feet. He checked to make sure that the phaser was set to low stun before he fired at both her and the Turghan.

With all three women immobilized, he turned his attention to the Jamalan male, who was furiously working the shuttle controls. "Move away from there!" he ordered hoarsely. "Or I'll shoot!"

When the man didn't move immediately, the lieutenant drilled him in the back with the phaser, and he sprawled over the conn. From the stationary stars visible through the window, James realized that they must have come to a full stop.

The only ones left to subdue were the Abu children, and they seemed content to stare at him with a mixture of curiosity and fear. *What kind of world is this?* Panting heavily, James stumbled into the cockpit to see how much damage the hijackers had done. He knew the Dominion were desperate, but to hijack an unarmed shuttlecraft was ridiculous!

He bent over Cordette to check for a pulse and make sure she was still alive. She was, although a contusion on her skull was staining her skin with red blood. Lying on the deck beside her was a length of metal pipe, obviously the weapon the Jamalan had used to disable her. At least he had put down the hijacking and gained control of the ship—for the next several minutes. He had to act fast before the attackers came to.

Keeping an eye on the Abu children, he set down the phaser pistol and grabbed the medkit to attend to his wounded wife. Just as he loaded a hypospray with a coagulant, James felt a peculiar tingle along his spine. In the next instant, he realized it wasn't peculiar at all—it was a sensation he had felt many times. A transporter beam had locked onto him!

James reached for the phaser pistol, but his hand had already started to dematerialize—he couldn't close his fingers around it. Helpless, he stared at the Abu children, and they stared back like strawberry dolls, until everything in the shuttlecraft faded from view.

CHAPTER FIVE

HE MATERIALIZED NOT on a transporter pad as he expected, but directly inside an old-fashioned brig, with bars across the door. He charged forward and smashed into the bars, rattling them but not doing any real damage. The outer door whooshed open, and a wild-eyed Reptilian woman entered, wielding a Bolaa phaser rifle.

At least she *looked* Reptilian, although closer inspection led him to wonder, because her forehead ridges were not very pronounced. But the contemptuous scowl on her face sure made her look Reptilian. "Back away!" she said with a snarl.

"Or what?" he demanded. "You'll hijack my shuttlecraft? You've already done that. But maybe you want to torture me—see if I know anything."

"The captain will be here in a moment," she replied. "Just shut up until then."

"What vessel is this? Are you Dominion...or something else?"

"This is the *Solaris*," said an authoritative male voice.

James turned to see a commanding figure in a tan jacket enter the brig. He stared, because it appeared as if the brown-haired man looked familiar to him.

"I'm Captain Tando Ardelon," said the man, meeting James' hostile gaze. "And yes, we are Dominion. Despite that, we mean you no harm."

"People keep telling me that," muttered James, "but somehow I don't believe it. You cracked open my co-pilot's skull, and you attacked us without provocation."

"Your co-pilot is receiving medical attention right now." Ardelon gave James a grudging smile. "And it sounds like you defended yourself fairly well. I'm glad we backed up our infiltration team, but we can't afford to leave anything to chance."

James shook his head in disbelief. "All this to hijack an unarmed shuttlecraft? If that's the scope of your ambition, it's a wonder the Divinian Empire pays any attention to you at all."

"Shut up!" snapped the Reptilian woman, threatening him with the phaser rifle.

"Stow it, Pallas," ordered the Dominion captain. "He's got a right to be angry. Don't worry, Lieutenant, it's not you or your shuttlecraft we want. It's your cargo."

"What cargo?"

"Aren't you carrying medical supplies?"

"We were, but we're empty on our return trip."

Ardelon scowled in anger and stepped over to a communication panel beside the door. He slammed it with a clenched fist. "Ardelon to bridge. Do we have a report yet on what they found on the shuttle?"

"Yes, Captain," answered a calm male voice. "We found only personnel—our own and the shuttlecraft's co-pilot."

"You're sure of that?"

"Yes, sir. No supplies were found on the shuttlecraft, other than standard issue medkits. The wounded parties have been transferred to the *Scorpion* for medical attention."

From the captain's clenched jaw, James assumed this was very bad news. "All that trouble for nothing," he grumbled. "Ardelon out."

"Not for nothing," said the woman called Pallas. She glared at James. "We still have *him* and the shuttlecraft. And he's a doctor."

James shook his head. "No, I'm not—I'm just a medical courier who was in the wrong place at the wrong time. But I don't get this—if your people needed medical attention, why don't you just join the refugees? You could turn yourselves in."

With a heave of his broad shoulders, Ardelon stepped closer to James. "It's not us. We've got several million people in extreme danger who can't be moved. Pallas, open the cell door."

"Are you sure?" asked the Reptilian in shock.

"Let him out. If we're going to help them, the lieutenant had got to help us of his free will."

Looking as if she disagreed wholeheartedly with this decision, the woman stepped back and pulled a lever on the other side of the room. She kept her phaser rifle trained on James as the bars retracted into the bulkhead.

"I'm not joining the Dominion," declared the prisoner as he stepped forward.

"I'm not asking you to," said Ardelon. "I'm asking you to help us save millions of lives. I presume that's why you joined the medical branch—to save lives."

James remained tight-lipped, unwilling to admit that altruism had only been one of several reasons, and maybe not the most important. He had already decided to say and do as little as possible, while waiting for a chance to escape.

The Reptilian woman scowled. "Do you have a name?"

His lips thinned, because James knew he was on shaky ground. Anything he did to help these people could land him in a Divinian prison for the rest of his life, but antagonizing them could get him killed. *Better to keep my mouth shut.*

Pallas walked over to the communications panel and hit it with her fist. "Tarr to bridge. Kajada, have you tapped into the shuttle's computer yet?"

"Yes, I have," answered the same efficient voice that had answered them before.

"What's the name of our guest in the brig?"

"The Divinian computer identifies him as James Rawlings. But our Dominion database identifies him as a Dominion Battleship Destroyer Captain named James Anderson."

Ardelon blinked with surprise and stared more closely at his prisoner. "Are you Anderson or Rawlings?"

James' jaw clamped shut, and he took a deep breath. Unfortunately, if he admitted to being *Anderson*, his chances of escape from this crew would be nil.

"Come on, answer," said Pallas Tarr, levelling her phaser rifle at him. "Every prisoner of war is allowed to give his name, rank, and serial number."

"My name is James Rawlings and under orders from my Divinian superiors I have been impersonating James Anderson for quite some time. My DNA and facial appearance was even altered to match that of the real James Anderson's."

"You expect us to believe that?" scoffed Tarr.

"I don't really give a damn what you believe!" snapped James. "What are you people but a bunch of two-bit space pirates? I find *you* hard to believe."

Tarr started to swing the butt of her phaser rifle at his head, but Ardelon gripped the rifle and stopped her. "Calm down! We haven't got time for this. Whether he's James Anderson or Lucky the Leprechaun, it doesn't matter—he's the only link we've got to the medical supplies we need."

Breathing heavily, the woman tried to shake off her anger, but a fire still burned in her dark eyes. Despite his status as her enemy, James couldn't help but feel a kinship with this volatile woman. Like him, she harboured a bitterness and anger that couldn't be easily assuaged.

"What race are you?" he asked.

"I'm half-Reptilian and half-human," she answered with some resentment. "I guess we're both pretty whacked out. You with your altered DNA and me with my mother mating with a human."

Ardelon waved his hand impatiently. "There's time to get to know each other later. Right now, Lieutenant Rawlings, I have to show you something."

"What if I don't want to see it?"

"I think you'll want to see it, because after you do, I'll let you go."

"Just like that?"

"Just like that. You can't do us any good stuck in this cell, but you can save a lot of lives if you're free. Let's go." The captain led the way out the door, and James followed, conscious of Pallas Tarr at his back, aiming her phaser rifle at him.

After walking a few metres down a narrow corridor, Ardelon came to a ladder embedded in the bulkhead, and he climbed upward into a small hatch. With a glance over his shoulder at Tarr, James followed the captain, and they emerged in a longer and wider corridor. James got the impression that the *Solaris* was a rather small vessel, no more than a scout ship or an assault craft.

Ardelon strode down the corridor like a man with pressing matters on his conscious and time running out. What made a proud, competent man like this turn into a rebel in a ragtag fleet? These were the first Dominion soldiers he had met since before he went to a Dominion prison, and Captain Ardelon, at least, didn't fit his preconceptions.

Pallas Tarr, on the other hand, was more the kind of person he thought would be attracted to the Dominion. She seemed a bit unstable, low in self-esteem, and angry at life. In short, she was damaged goods. Her Reptilian side probably relished the prospect of dying a glorious death battling the imperious and callous Divinian Empire.

They entered a compact, clam-shaped bridge, and a human swivelled in his chair to glance at James before turning back to his instruments. Maybe everyone on the *Solaris* was mad, even the dignified Ardelon.

Through the narrow cockpit window, he saw a Rambler assault vessel off the bow, as well as his own star-crossed shuttlecraft. What could the Dominion hope to accomplish with these three little ships out her in the middle of nowhere, a stone's throw from the Adirondacks Expanse? Like the attack on his shuttlecraft, this whole thing was surreal.

"Before you show me anything," said James, "I want to make sure that my co-pilot, Ensign Chance, is all right."

"Kajada, hail the *Scorpion*," ordered Ardelon, "and have them put Ensign Chance on screen."

"Yes, sir."

"While he does that," said the captain, "let me ask you if you've ever heard of a planet named Quinntessa."

James nodded. "I know it was on a list of planets in the Adirondacks Expanse that were turned over to the Divinian Empire."

"Yes, but it wasn't evacuated like most of the Dominion colonies. The Quinntessanites chose to stay and live under Divinian rule, but something terrible has happened there."

"I have located Ensign Chance," interjected Kajada.

"On screen."

James turned with interest to the small viewscreen spanning the front of the bridge. The blank image switched to a view of a bustling sickbay, and Ensign Chance was lying on an examination table with a fresh bandage around her head. Upon seeing James, the former princess of Takara Prime sat up weakly.

"At ease, Cordette," he told her. "Have you been treated well?"

"As well as can be expected, I suppose. What happened to the shuttlecraft?"

"The passengers attacked us, stopped the shuttle, and then we were intercepted by these two Dominion vessels. Cooperate, but remember that you're a prisoner of war."

"Yes, James. Are we going to be held long? Or exchanged?"

"I don't know." James glanced at Ardelon, who stepped in front of the screen.

"You and Lieutenant Rawlings will be released soon, along with your shuttlecraft," promised the captain. "Please try to rest. I'm sorry that our methods were violent, but the Divinian Empire barely negotiates with *us*." He motioned to Kajada, who ended the transmission.

"Satisfied, Lieutenant?" asked Pallas Tarr.

James shrugged. He wasn't going to argue with someone who was aiming a phaser rifle at him.

"Kajada," said the captain, "put on the video log and explain matters to the lieutenant."

Kajada tapped his console. On the viewscreen appeared a beautiful, aquamarine planet, sparkling in the vivid light from a distant red sun. The surface of the planet had to be ninety percent ocean, with small green continents scattered across its vast waters. James had seen many Class-M planets, but none more lovely than this one.

"Quinntessa," said Kajada matter-of-factly. "It was a thriving world, inhabited by about five million people, mostly of mixed-species ancestry. The only thing that has protected them so far is the relative isolation of population centers on the various islands and continents."

The image shifted to a modern city street, which appeared to be deserted, despite sunny blues skies and balmy weather. Some kind of dead animal lay in the gutter, and there appeared to be a humanoid corpse sprawled in an open doorway. Trash and leaves skittered across the empty thoroughfare, borne by a gentle breeze. It was an eerie scene, reminiscent of a planet ravaged by warfare, only without the full-scale destruction.

"This is the city of Tobay," explained Kajada, "as we observed it five days ago. The streets are deserted, because a devastating plague has struck this continent. The disease is similar to anthrax, only several times more deadly and contagious. It is caused by an unusual combination of three prions, which are transmitted by air, water, saliva and other bodily fluids."

Now the view changed to the interior of some cavernous hall, where sick people lay in haphazard rows stretching the length of the room. It wasn't a hospital, so James had to assume the hospitals were all full. Coughs and groans filled the disturbing scene. Three visitors in white environmental suits moved among the sick like ghosts, or angels. When the video log showed close-up views of dying people with distended stomachs, blackened faces, and open sores, James had to look away.

"Point taken," he muttered. "But our Divinian Empire must have the technology to deal with this. As you said, it's now a Divinian planet."

"Maybe they do but your so called Empire doesn't protect its people. The Divinians have abandoned them," answered Kajada, "except to station ships in orbit to stop any attempt by the inhabitants to leave the planet. Divinian troops on the ground have destroyed ships and spaceports and shut off all communication with the outside. A quarantine is in effect, and the entire populace has been left to die."

Tarr peered into James' eyes. "Ask yourself, why *this* planet? Why *now*? Quinntessa is as advanced as any planet in the Dominion, but it's been cut off, abandoned. Nobody cares what happens there. You couldn't pick a more helpless place. But we still have time to help them, because of the distances across those huge oceans."

James sighed and held out his hands. "I'm one medical courier with a shuttlecraft. What do you expect me to do?"

The Dominion are explorers and warriors, not healers," said Ardelon. "We're rounding up all the doctors and nurses we've got, but we only have a handful of them. Plus we don't have enough drugs or research equipment to do the job. You have access to everything we need."

James felt trapped on the cramped bridge, torn between doing his duty and doing what was right. His preconceptions about the new Dominion had crumbled even further, and he felt as if he understood them. They were not wild-eyed pirates and opportunists; they were people trying to help other people.

"Is there a drug that's proven effective against this disease?" he asked.

"To a degree," answered Kajada. "According to records, Rotherum KAE can prolong life, but it is not a cure. When the prions combine into a multiprion in the host's body, death can result in as quickly as forty-eight hours. The multiprion can be removed via a transporter biofilter, but that is extremely time consuming. The best way to stop the spread of the disease is to find the transmission vectors and shut them off. That is precisely what the Divinians are doing with their quarantine."

"And that's the situation in a nutshell," grumbled Tarr. "So will you help us?"

James paused before answering, although he knew he would say yes. His first duty was to reclaim his shuttlecraft and his co-pilot and get away from these people. After that, when he had time to think about it logically, he would decide how far to go in helping them.

"All right," he murmured. "Do you have those records you've been talking about?"

Kajada nodded and pulled an isolinear chip from his console. "This also contains the video log you saw."

James took the chip, but as he withdrew his hand, Pallas Tarr caught his wrist in a tight grip. "Can we trust you, Anderson?"

He didn't pull his hand away, because her touch was warm and charged with life. As he gently pried her fingers from his wrist, he gave her a charming smile. "Call me James please."

"Okay, James." She smiled back, but it wasn't a friendly look.

"We'll meet you right here, at these coordinates," said Ardelon. "How soon do you think you can get back?"

He shrugged. "I would guess three or four days. I'll have to fake a requisition or divert supplies going somewhere else."

"If we see anything but a shuttlecraft coming toward us, we'll head into the Adirondacks Expanse," warned Ardelon. "And the deaths of millions of people will be on your conscience."

"I've already got a lot on my conscience," said James. "Can I go now?"

Ardelon nodded. "Vantika, will you escort him to the transporter room?"

"Yes, sir." The Rambler motioned to James, then led the way into the corridor.

When they were gone, Ardelon remarked to Tarr, "Do you know how much help he can be to us?"

"You mean, with medical supplies?" she asked.

"Not just that. I don't buy that he's just a Divinian operative who's impersonating James Anderson. He is the *real* James Anderson. But somehow along the way he's one of the many humans who have joined the ranks in the Divinian Empire. I think he still has sympathies for the Dominion. The possibilities that he can eventually help us spy on the Divinian Empire are endless. We have to try to recruit him."

"I thought we just did."

"I hope so," said Ardelon, his eyes narrowing.

In the briefing room of the *Phoenix*, Brigadier General Robert F. Makepeace and General Leia Tetzlaff sat in stunned silence after viewing the video log and hearing James' story. In addition to the three of them, two other people were present: Cordette Chance and Lieutenant Don Jones, an expert on the

Dominion. Brigadier General Makepeace had a human name but was in fact a Makaj who had lived close to six hundred years, and even he appeared at a loss for words.

Finally Leia Tetzlaff scowled and turned to Cordette. "Do you corroborate Lieutenant Rawlings' story?"

The young human woman gingerly touched the small scar on her head. "I can't corroborate all the details, but I know we were attacked by the passengers. Looking back now, I can see that the distress of the pregnant woman was a diversion. When Lieutenant Rawlings went to attend her, one of the other passengers must have hit me on the head. I only know that I woke up in sickbay on a Dominion ship with this head wound. But I believe Lieutenant Rawlings must have handled himself quite well, because the passengers who revolted were also receiving medical attention." Cordette glanced at James, and gave him an appreciative nod.

"I actually regained control of the shuttle," he explained. "But before we could leave, the Dominion ships arrived and transported me directly to their brig."

"And then they showed you this video log and told you about the plague on Quinntessa?" asked Tetzlaff, sounding suspicious.

"After they found out we weren't carrying any medical supplies," James added. "That's all they were looking for."

"Did you hear the names of any of these Dominion officers?" asked the brigadier general.

"No," lied James immediately. He didn't know why he lied about that, except that he felt oddly guilty about betraying the Dominion's confidence. Perhaps Ardelon, Pallas Tarr, and the others were known Dominion, but if they weren't, he wouldn't be the one to identify them.

"What can you tell us about their ship?" asked Brigadier General Makepeace.

James shook his head. "It was small, older, nothing special. They weren't about to show me around. I've told you the truth, sir. I can't imagine that sending a med team and supplies to Quinntessa will give the Dominion any strategic advantage, and it could save millions of lives."

"So you want to collaborate with the enemy?" Tetzlaff asked snidely.

"I want to save lives," answered James, appealing to the brigadier general. "If we don't cooperate, they'll just keep attacking our ships until they get what they want. And if any sick Quinntessanites escape from the planet and reach Divinian space...I don't need to tell you what might happen."

The Makaj pursed his lips and rubbed the dark spots on his left temple. "There may be a secret Divinian organization conducting unauthorized operations on Quinntessa. If so I want to know about it. Lately as our Divinian Empire keeps expanding certain elements have been plotting against each other for their own benefit. This could result in a breakdown of the status quo or the current state of how things are run. And that would be very bad for my interests. I'm inclined to agree with you, Lieutenant, but I can't *order* anyone to go on a mission like this. You would have to depend upon the Dominion for protection, not us. We'll brief the medical teams, and if anyone wants to volunteer, you can take them. That is, if *you* wish to volunteer."

"I do."

"Count me in, too," said Cordette, nodding her head resolutely.

"Sir, I strongly advise against this course of action," declared General Tetzlaff.

"Duly noted." Brigadier General Makepeace rose to his feet. "These are strange times, and they require strange deeds. Lieutenant Rawlings, take a shuttlecraft and strip all the Divinian signage; requisition the supplies you need. I myself will brief the medical staff and ask for volunteers."

"Yes, sir," replied James. "You should also tell Divinian Command to get those refuges off Outpost Gamma III, and give them all a good interrogation."

"Good idea but Divinian Command doesn't have to know about it until after I interrogate them. I'll have a ship dispatched to get them immediately. Also if you confront any Divinians, or other species working for Divinians, say you're on a private, humanitarian mission, or say you're a Quinntessanite. Don't pose as members of the Dominion or the Divinian Empire unless you have to. Wear civilian clothes, and take as many precautions as you need. Dismissed."

After the brigadier general had left the briefing room, Tetzlaff stopped James and whispered, "I don't know what you're up to, but remember what I told you earlier you and Cordette will be executed if you betray us."

James stared her down. "I figure there's a good chance I'll be killed on this mission. I'd love to give you a fat big kiss before I go."

Tetzlaff stared at him in shock, utterly speechless, but there was a yielding in her eyes that made him smile with victory. "I thought so." He strode away, still grinning.

Later in Tetzlaff's large private quarters aboard the *Phoenix* she heard footsteps behind her, and she turned to see her servant, Leedora, shuffling toward her. The young human woman Leedora looked more twisted and wasted than usual, and there was a worried look on her youthful face.

Since Tetzlaff had given orders not to be disturbed this evening, she rose to meet the young woman with a mixture of irritation and concern. "What is it, Leedora?"

"Sorry to interrupt, General," said the young servant, lowering her head respectfully. "Sub-Emperor Tuplo from the Central Command is on the emergency channel."

"Tuplo, eh?" Tetzlaff tried not to show her apprehension over this bit of news. Tuplo was a new ally of hers since Tetzlaff had joined the Divinian Empire, but he was also now her superior in the pecking order of the Central Command. She would never say it aloud, but Tuplo had become something of an annoyance since his recent promotion. And the fact that he was of the true Divinian race and not a human like Tetzlaff who had just joined the Divinian Empire made him sort of condescending towards her at the best of times.

"I'll take the call."

"Yes, sir."

"And not a word of this to anyone!" ordered Tetzlaff as she strode toward her private study.

"Yes, sir," muttered the young woman with resignation.

Upon reaching her study, the general went in and locked the door behind her. Although this room had been secretly built by Tetzlaff to conduct her covert operations, there were other servants in her quarters, and Tetzlaff had not gotten where she was by being careless. Plastering a confident look onto her angular face, Tetzlaff approached the communications console.

On the screen, Sub-Emperor Tuplo scowled with impatience. "I don't like waiting."

"Hello to you, too," Tetzlaff said with forced joviality. "Thank you for bothering me on my night off. I was having entirely too much relaxation."

"This is an emergency."

"What?" scoffed Tetzlaff. "Has the Dominion swarmed across the Adirondacks Expanse?"

The Adirondacks Expanse was *her* responsibility, and she resented anyone telling her how to manage it.

"Nothing quite so dramatic...yet. The Melosha Council summoned me this morning—they're very worried about that plague planet. What is it called?"

"Quinntessa."

"Yes. They found out about our losing our troop transport, and they know the Dominion have taken charge."

Tetzlaff laughed out loud. "The Dominion only have a handful of ships in the area at best. And they're no match for us. They couldn't take charge of a junk shipyard."

"The Melosha Council is worried about the civilian population if that plague gets loose."

"It's not going to," declared Tetzlaff irritably. "We have a spy on the lead Dominion ship, and she informs us that they aren't planning to evacuate any of the Quinntessanites. Even the Dominion aren't that stupid. Besides, where would they take them? But they are trying to cure the disease, and it's worth giving them a chance to do that. After all, we still have a garrison of soldiers on Quinntessa, and we'd like to keep them alive."

Sub-Emperor Tuplo warned darkly, "There's a faction on the council who would like to dispense with halfway measures and just destroy the planet."

"I'm sure there is. There's always a faction who want to destroy things, but in this case it's entirely unnecessary. It could also plunge us back into war with the more hardcore Dominion splinter groups."

Tuplo shook his head worriedly. "You had better be right about this, my friend, or no power in the galaxy will be able to protect you."

"Of course I'm right," insisted Tetzlaff with more confidence than she felt. "As we've seen before, panic is worse than plague. The Melosha Council had no business meddling with military polices in the Adirondacks Expanse. Tell them to go back to reforming the slave trade."

Tuplo chuckled, obviously relieved by Tetzlaff's bravado. "I won't tell them that, but I will tell them that the situation is under control."

"You do that. I'll get back to you in three days, and keep you updated on any developments. Tetzlaff out." As soon as the image of Sub-Emperor Tuplo faded from the screen, so did the smile on Tetzlaff's face.

Her thin brow knit with concern, the Divinian general went to her door to make sure that no one was in the vicinity. She closed it and double-locked it. Then she went to her communications console and set it for a low frequency that was seldom used, except for antiquated satellite transmissions. There was a series of old alien satellites in the Adirondacks Expanse that were thought to be inactive. In truth, it was a subspace relay system employing technology that was far more advanced than anything the Divinian Empire possessed.

Tetzlaff's fingers trembled as they paused over the console. Even though her transmission would be encrypted and indecipherable to anyone but the intended recipient, she chose her words very carefully:

"Problem on test site. Outsiders present. Will try to delay overreaction from masters. Suggest you proceed to quick conclusion." She signed it with her codename, "Wattley."

When she sent it, a lump lodged deep in her throat. Tetzlaff knew that her message would not be well received, and her secret benefactor would be very angry. Very angry, indeed would they be.

CHAPTER SIX

March 21, 2121: Quinntessa, Falow Solar System, The Adirondacks Expanse

WHEN ARDELON REACHED the bridge, Kajada glanced at him, and Vantika gave him a quick smile. On the screen was a view of the graceful blue curve of Quinntessa's horizon, as seen from orbit. The planet looked serene yet vibrantly alive, kept that way by an enlightened populace. Yet hidden within those wispy clouds, balmy seas, and dimpled land-masses was a deadly enemy committed to wiping out all humanoid life.

"Lieutenant Rawlings has set up Clinic One on Hajee," reported Kajada. "Visual contact will be possible in sixty-five seconds."

"Bring it up when you can," ordered Ardelon. Like everyone else, he wanted to see some tangible results for all their hotheaded effort. Would they do some good today? Or were they risking their lives in order to swat at flies on a corpse?

While they waited, Vantika leaned back in her seat and looked at him. "You know what I said about wanting to go on shore leave? Never mind. I know where my duty is—right here."

"That's big of you," said the captain with a grim smile. When times got tense, he welcomed the Rambler's dark sense of humor. In truth, he would need Vantika on the bridge, with Pallas down on the planet's surface.

"In range," reported Kajada. With a flash, the viewscreen revealed a static-filled image with several blurry figures moving about. In a few seconds, the image cleared to make it plain that they were inside a portable geodesic dome. People stood patiently, waiting for inoculations from the efficient medical team. A couple of the medical workers were Dominion, but the majority were personnel from one of Makepeace's Divinian divisions.

The equipment and facilities were first-rate, thanks to James. The lieutenant had gotten everything they needed, but in small quantities, due to the confines of the shuttlecraft. Ardelon still found it hard to believe that James had stolen all this stuff, but he wasn't going to question a gift. The man had accomplished his mission, and that commanded

Ardelon's respect. The captain couldn't really be sure of the loyalty of those around him, so he had to trust in their character.

James sat down in front of the viewer, a satisfied grin on his bearded face. "As you can see, Captain, we're open for business, and it's booming! The word has gotten out in only a few hours. We're offering inoculations of Rotherum KAE and a wide-spectrum antiviral compound—the same thing all of us got. It should prolong onset—and relieve symptoms—until we can do more research. If we catch anyone within forty-eight hours of contracting the disease, we're using the transporter biofilter in the shuttlecraft to remove the multiprions."

He was jostled slightly by two confused patients, and James lowered his voice to add, "Being on the outskirts of the city was a good idea. We're only getting those people who are still relatively healthy. As soon as I can get away, I want to take the shuttle and find any local doctors who can tell us how this developed."

"Be careful," warned Ardelon. "Wear the suits in the city—it was hit hard."

"We will. What about Clinic Two?"

"We're getting ready to beam down to Kozak," said the captain, "but it doesn't sound like the plague has hit there very hard. They're more interested in keeping people *out*."

"Are you sure that's where you want to set up?"

"Yes, because we need a control site with relatively few cases—that's the best way to isolate and track them. At least that's what Dr. Cross says, and Kajada agrees."

"Well, we're busy here," said James, being jostled again. "I'll report in later. Away team, out."

James Rawlings rose to his feet, feeling very claustrophobic in the crowded dome. Although few of the patients appeared outwardly sick, he was acquainted enough with it that they might be. Plus the Quinntessanites were alien in appearance and dress—each one a combination of various species, each person dressed in a colourful, billowing costume with ribbons and braids. It was as if they were headed for a masquerade party or to perform at the circus. Although James had served with numerous humanoid species, he found it bewildering when he couldn't identify people by species. Perhaps that was the point, he thought ruefully.

When he looked more closely, he could see that many of the Quinntessanites' flamboyant attire were soiled and tattered. In their haunted eyes, he saw that their comfortable lives had been wretched apart. They were either ill, grieving, or in shock; they hadn't yet reached panic, but their self-respect was starting to slip. He smiled at them as he passed, but the Quinntessanites were lost in their contemplations of demise.

James strode out of the portable dome into the crimson sunshine and flower-scented zephyr of late afternoon on Quinntessa. He took a yawning lungful of the sun-drenched air, then held his breath when he realized that it probably contained the deadly prions. He reminded himself that he was now in the medical division—his main concern was other people's health, not his own. If he were serving on the bridge in a battle, he wouldn't be worried about his life, only doing his duty. It had to the same here, on this weird front.

Fighting this enemy was harder, he decided, than fighting a well armed, advanced starship. At some point, a starship would reveal itself and stand to fight—but their tiny enemy would always stay cloaked, if they let it. Now that the clinic was set up and people were being helped, James knew he had to find a way to go on the offensive.

He strode toward the unmarked shuttlecraft, formerly called *Shuttle 8*, where people were also gathered. Only they were waiting for acquaintances and family to exit the small craft, not enter. He saw Cordette escort a very weak patient to the hatch and hand her over to her waiting friends. There was much bowing of heads and many expressions of gratitude, and the thin Cordette looked gratified herself.

"Bed rest," she cautioned the patient. "Check back with the doctors in forty-eight hours."

James hated to interrupt this heart-warming scene, but he felt the need to keep moving. "Cordette," he whispered to her, "wrap this up, because we have to go."

"Go where?" she asked in horror. "But I have more people to bring through the biofilter."

"They'll have to wait."

"Some of them can't wait," she insisted. "Tomorrow will be too late."

James guided Cordette back into the shuttlecraft, away from the curious eyes and ears of the patients. "We're logistical support," he reminded her, "not doctors. Don't make me order you."

"Technically, you can't order me," replied the young woman. "Since we're here on an unofficial, private mission, Divinian chain of command doesn't apply."

James sighed. "Okay, bring through one more. Then we've got to gather information."

"How about *two* more?" she begged.

He nodded with acquiescence and sunk into his seat in the cockpit. With joy on her smooth silky face, Cordette returned to the transporter console at the rear of the craft. James could see her dilemma—helping individuals gave one the feeling of immediate triumph, while research and long-term planning might not help at all. But if they hoped to save Quinntessa, they had to rid the whole planet of the bug, not just a few individuals.

A muscular Quinntessanite with brown hair and sharp tusks materialized on the transporter pad. He staggered off, and Cordette rushed to help him into a seat. For the first time, James felt as if he recognized a patient's species, or at least part of it. The man had the bulk and unpleasant features of an Anteaus.

"Can you help us?" asked James. "Where in the city are the doctors? I mean, where are people going for medical care?"

The part-Anteaus looked up at him, and the brute actually seemed to smile. "Glad to help. The spaceport and the arena are supposed to be emergency hospitals. But I wouldn't go there—no one ever leaves."

"Where are they doing research?" asked James.

The patient shrugged his broad, furry shoulders, "I suppose, OSI."

"OSI?"

"The Organization for Species Improvement." He shook his woolly head. "I forget, you're strangers here. Some species do not breed naturally with others, and medical intervention is needed to produce a child. In vitro fertilization, cloning, genetic transplants—whatever is needed—they've done it. There are OSI clinics all over the planet."

James turned to his readouts. "Could you show me on a map of Hajee?"

The hulking citizen rose to his feet and moved slowly toward the hatch. "I don't need to—you will see the giant red complex in the center of the city. It's the tallest and biggest. But I've got to warn you—"

"What?"

The Quinntessanite stopped, looking undecided about spreading unpleasant news. "I heard they closed their doors—not letting anyone in or out. Check for yourself."

"We will, thanks." James made a note in his log and muttered to himself, "Organization for Species Improvement."

He heard a thud, and he turned to see another patient stagger off the transporter pad. Cordette caught her—a sleek woman with yellowish-brown skin and feathery grey fur on her forehead and neck. While Cordette attended to her, James turned reluctantly to his pre-flight checklist.

As soon as Cordette escorted her last patient off the shuttlecraft, James told her to clear the area. He felt guilty about leaving the medical staff alone, but they knew this was no paid vacation. They could request help from either the shuttle or the *Solaris*, he told himself.

Cordette jumped in the hatch and closed it after her; the young woman looked energized by the day's work. "Thanks for letting me do two more, James. I told them we'd be back soon—there are so many who need help."

"We can help more of them by finding the origins of the infection," he reminded her. "Did you hear anything about how it started?"

"No," she admitted. "I talked to a few people, but they don't know what happened to them. They're still in shock.

"Okay. Get ready for takeoff."

As soon as the area was clear of pedestrians, James fired thrusters, and the shuttlecraft rose swiftly from the bluff. It swerved over the ocean and the crashing waves far below and quickly reached an altitude of three thousand metres, where James left it. From the outskirts to the center of the city was a short jump in a shuttlecraft, and he wanted to get a good look at everything along the way.

The rolling countryside was startling in its lush growth and natural beauty. The Quinntessanites obviously enjoyed an unhurried but civilized life, with time to walk rather than ride. The only thing out of place was a thin line of sick people wending their way along a footpath to the new clinic. *How had they found out about the medical team so quickly?* wondered James. *Maybe hope is also contagious.*

The shuttlecraft flew over a sparkling bay, filled with what looked like seaplanes and small sailing ships, bobbing peacefully in the surf. All that was missing were people. James tried to imagine this city a month ago, before tragedy crept up on it. Hajee must have been a bustling paradise, with a populace so confident in their future that they could exchange the Dominion for Divinian rulers. Now their ambitions and dreams were grounded, just like the seaplanes bobbing below him.

The shuttle flew over s orange-colored beach and a picturesque boardwalk lined with charming three-story buildings. There were actually a few people milling about on the boardwalk, haunting deserted cafes, watching the afternoon sun glitter on the bay. A few pedestrians waved at the shuttlecraft as it passed over, apparently happy to make contact with the visitors. Despite the fact that the handful of people on the boardwalk could plainly see each other, they didn't interact. They obviously preferred their solitude.

The city was large but not oversized, with broad, tree-lined boulevards, ample green belts, and tasteful buildings that didn't dwarf the civic planning. But without any people, it looked like a model of a city, like something on an architect's desk. James glanced at Cordette and could see the sight of empty streets below them saddened the young woman.

"What do they do with the bodies?" she asked tenderly.

"They may vaporize them with phasers," suggested James. "Burn them...I don't know." He was about to suggest she help him look for a big red building, when the landmark appeared on the horizon, shaped like a symmetrical tree.

When he flew closer, James could see that the ruby-red building was actually a massive pyramid built in the Mayan style. It was the central keep of an oval fortress with high, curving walls and billowing battlements. The entrances were minimal—one south, one north, at the tips of the oval. Inside the walls were nine smaller square buildings with the pyramid holding down the center. The sharp angles of the pyramid, and the oval, rounded walls made an odd placement.

While he circled the complex, looking for somewhere to land, James watched for movement within the walls. He spotted none—it seemed to be as deserted as everyplace else. The few optimists on the boardwalk were keeping a forlorn vigil for the rest of the city.

There was no landing pad or strip inside the walls, and the spacings between the buildings were just small enough to keep him from landing on the grounds. Outside the southern wall was a landing pad with the wreckage of some kind of vehicle on it. A path led to an archway in the wall and one of the two obvious gates.

As James circled, he pressed the communications panel and broadcast on all local frequencies, "Shuttle to Organization for Species Improvement. We're a private medical team, here to help you fight this disease. Please respond."

They listened, but there was no response, as James circled lower. The shuttlecraft neared the tip of the pyramid when Cordette suddenly shouted, "Raise shields!"

James did so a moment before a beamed weapon shot from the tip of the pyramid and strafed the shuttlecraft. He slammed on the thrusters and zoomed away before the pyramid got off another shot.

"Wow!" He whistled. "You're a lifesaver."

"No damage," said Cordette, still watching her instruments. "We were scanned, then I caught an energy surge. I thought it might be advisable to raise shields—"

"To save our lives. Good quick thinking. Someone in there wants to keep us out."

The young woman shook her head. "It could be automated. Our drop in altitude may have tripped the scanners, and the scanners tripped the weapon. I'm not reading any lifesigns, but there's a lot of shielding."

"Then let's land outside." James banked toward the landing pad outside the southern gate. As he zoomed over, he noticed that the wreckage on the pad appeared to be fairly recent but already scavenged, some of it placed in neat piles. The debris was scattered badly enough to make landing hard, so James looked elsewhere.

He picked a nearby park and landed in a gently rolling meadow of wildflowers and playground equipment. He gazed out the window at the empty swings and slides; although no one was present, he swore he could hear the cries, shrieks, and laughter of the absent children.

"Suit up," he told Cordette.

"We've already been exposed," she pointed out.

"Yes, I know, but I want anyone who sees us to know we're outsiders." James worked his controls. "I'll put on security and enable remote transporter control."

Assisting each other, they put on their environmental suits and armed themselves with phasers. Before the attack, James might not have considered a phaser necessary; now he adjusted his weapon from low to medium stun. Despite the apparent desertion of the central city, *something* had given them an unfriendly welcome. He wasn't convinced there was nobody home inside the mysterious OSI fortress.

As soon as he stepped out of the hatch into the field of wildflowers, James was sorry that he couldn't enjoy the late afternoon breeze. He could feel the sun warming the silken fabric of the suit that covered every centimetre of his body, and he wished he could take it off. With a sigh, James motioned to Cordette, and she followed him toward the wreckage on the landing pad.

He didn't step directly on the platform. He preferred to walk around the debris. Maybe he was being overly cautious, but James knew that a wrecked spaceship could leave numerous toxins and dangerous substances. He could see exposed fuel tanks and no indication whether they were full or empty. Despite his protective suit, he felt oddly vulnerable in this ghost town, and he agreed with Ardelon—*take no risks that don't have to be taken.*

As James passed the wreckage, he mused whether the pyramid had shot down the ship, or whether they had simply made a poor landing. The debris had been picked through too much to tell him anything.

He saw Cordette checking the wreckage with her tricorder, and she shook her head. "No lifesigns," her voice boomed in his hood.

"Let's try knocking." James motioned to the gate in the circular wall then took the lead. They moved cautiously down a well-manicured footpath and approached a rectangular archway at the elongated tip of the oval-shaped fortress. The door itself was metal, windowless, and solid, although the wall appeared to be made of a ruby like stone. James could see no mechanism that would open the door, except for a small slit for card entry at the side of the door.

In frustration, he knocked, although he doubted whether his gloved knuckles would make any noise whatsoever on the smooth metal. There were no signs or markings, no indication that this complex had once been a vibrant center of commerce and health care. Judging by the variety of hybrids on Quinntessa, the Organization for Species Improvement must have been busy day and night.

Cordette's eyes stayed riveted upon her tricorder, so she didn't see James remove his hood. "Hello!" he shouted as loudly as he could. "Is anyone in there?"

The harsh wind whistled ominously through the turrets of the fortress, making it sound like banshees wailing for the dead. But no living voice answered them.

Cordette shook her head. "James, it's highly unlikely that—" She stopped suddenly and stared at her tricorder. "Eleven lifesigns approaching rapidly on foot."

"From the complex?" asked James, looking at the door.

"No, James. From the northwest...outside the wall."

Reacting quickly, James put his headgear back on and stepped away from the gate. He wanted to get a better view of the wall to northeast, but he didn't like the fact that they were exposed, out in the open. "Start heading back to the shuttlecraft," he ordered Cordette.

"Yes, James."

They scurried down the path, keeping in a crouch, but they didn't move quickly enough. As they reached the landing pad, a squad of infantry jogged around the corner of the wall and dropped into firing position on knees and bellies. A few of them arranged mortars and other equipment.

"Get down!" shouted James. He and Cordette dove into the dirt just as the squad opened fire. Their deadly beams raked the brush and twisted metal on the landing pad, causing leaves, twigs, and molten metal to pelt James and Cordette. As he cowered in the dirt, James realized that phasers set to stun were not going to do the job.

He squeezed the combadge in his glove. "Rawlings to shuttlecraft. Two to beam back. Activate now."

When nothing happened, he stared at Cordette, and she shook her head. She mouthed something, but he couldn't hear her. Since wireless communications had broken down, and James didn't like the poor visibility, he ripped his hood off. Then he set his phaser to full.

"Surrender yourselves!" shouted a voice.

James looked at Cordette, who pulled her hood off and pointed to the attackers. "A dampening field."

He motioned to her to keep moving, all the way back to the shuttlecraft. Scurrying on her hands and knees like a lizard, the young woman darted from one clump of brush and debris to another.

"Surrender? By whose authority?" he shouted back.

"By authority of the Horrell Coalition!"

Horrell Coalition! James lifted his head from the dirt to peer at the black-clad soldiers. They were a well-trained unit. They broke from kneeling positions and scattered to cover, moving ever closer to him. James glanced around but couldn't really get a good look at them then he caught sight of some of the soldiers. They were true Divinians not just another species in the Divinian Empire but true Divinians. Apparently whatever element in the Divinian Empire had established them on Quinntessa had felt it necessary to give them a fake cover as this so called Horrell Coalition.

"We're just a medical relief team!" he called out.

James heard a loud whooshing sound, followed by a tremendous concussion that shook the ground like an earthquake. He covered his head as dirt and flaming debris rained down on him, scorching his environmental suit.

"Surrender!" shouted the hidden Divinian. "Or die!"

Surrounded by a patrol of well-armed Divinians who were this Horrell Coalition, cut off from the shuttlecraft, unsure what had happened to Cordette, James needed a big diversion. He aimed his phaser at one of the exposed fuel tanks and fired a searing blast. The tank ruptured in a fireball that ballooned high into the dusky sky. James was driven to the ground, as more flaming debris rained down.

A dampening field! He recalled the equipment the Divinians had set up the moment they charged into view, just before they opened fire. While the wreckage on the landing pad continued to burn like a bonfire, James scurried forward and found a vantage point atop a decorative mound. Searching for the place where the Divinians had rounded the wall, he quickly spotted two metal boxes on tripods.

Without time to think, James aimed his phaser and opened fire. Despite the beams whistling past his head, he didn't finish firing until he had completely destroyed the two portable dampening boxes. Then he rolled down the hill and cowered in the dirt from a barrage of phasers and concussion mortars, which turned the ground into quivering jelly. He began to sink into quicksand.

Desperately he tapped his combadge. "Rawlings to shuttle, beam me up now!"

As a phaser beam melted a chunk of his environmental boot, James tried to float atop the liquified soil, but he only succeeded in burying himself deeper. The withering fire never stopped, and he was sure death was near...until he felt a tingle along his spine. The lieutenant curled into a ball until he was certain that he had transported from the fire zone.

Dripping mud, James rolled off the transporter pad into the cabin of the shuttlecraft then he dashed to the transporter controls. Ripping off a glove, he set to work retrieving Cordette. An explosion sundered the ground just outside the craft, and James staggered. His fingers pounded the console as they worked.

With a surprised but grateful look in her eyes, the young woman tumbled off the transporter pad four seconds later. James didn't wait to greet her—he hurried to the cockpit. Even before he got into his seat, he had punched up the shields and ignited the thrusters. He sunk deep into his chair at the same moment that the shuttle left the ground.

Their shields took a direct hit, and the shuttle rocked—but James maintained control as he zoomed into the darkening sky. The ruby pyramid was lit up like an amusement park by the explosions and light beams hurled at them. With James on the conn, the shuttlecraft weaved back and forth through the barrage, undamaged.

Cordette staggered into the seat next to him. Her environmental suit was scorched and ripped like his, but unlike him she had a dribble of blood on her hip. He realized she had been injured.

"Are you hit?" he asked with concern.

She shrugged, but her arms quivered for a second. "It's just a scratch—from a rock, not a phaser."

"Let's get back to camp and have it looked at." James gave her an empathetic smile.

"We didn't find out much," said Cordette with a grimace.

"And we probably won't until we figure out a way to get into that OSI complex." After making sure they had swung well wide of the pyramid, James set course for the clinic. He mused aloud, "Do the Horrell Coalition have control of that place? Or were they just in the neighbourhood?"

The young woman shook her head. "We don't know. With their dampening equipment, they could stay hidden from our sensors. Or they could transport in."

"Later tonight we'll pay them another visit," said James with fortitude.

CHAPTER SEVEN

A HUGE RED PYRAMID with boxy angles and long staircases commanded the center of the city below them. It glistened in the midday sun like a jewel. Pallas Tarr had difficulty taking her eyes off the awe-inspiring landmark. But she had to watch her instruments as Ardelon brought the *Solaris* down for a rare landing. They had decided to make an impressive landing rather than just transporting down.

Ardelon had agreed to this only because the *Scorpion* had returned with more medical supplies, scrounged from a dozen Dominion hideouts. The *Scorpion* was taking their place in orbit, ready to respond to an emergency or fend off a Divinian attack.

Tarr cycled through her checklists as they prepared to land in a fallow field about three kilometres outside of town. She looked out the window to see the charming streets of Xifo swarming with people during the midday break.

"Pallas, let them know who we are," ordered Ardelon. "But let's keep our shields up."

The Dominion engineer nodded and opened the local frequencies. "To the people of Kozak," she announced, "this is the Dominion vessel *Solaris*. We are here to offer medical assistance. Repeat we are here to help you during your medical emergency. We will land in a field three kilometres southeast of—"

"Don't land!" a voice broke in. "Traffic between Hajee and Kozak is not permitted."

"We haven't been on Hajee," she snapped back. "We can inoculate your citizens and help you beat this plague."

"We have no plague on Kozak!" insisted the voice from the ground. "And we don't wish to anger the Divinians. Quinntessa is no longer a Dominion planet. It's not your problem. Dominion vessel, we urge you to turn back!"

Ardelon slid a finger under his throat in the universal sign to cut them off. Tarr did so gladly. "Nice, reserved rude pig like people," she muttered.

Vantika looked serious. "They probably *are* nice people, normally. But they're afraid. They must have seen reports from Hajee."

"They can't hide forever," said Tarr. "The disease is airborne, so they'll be exposed to it, anyway."

"Nobody thinks like that," said Vantika with a listless smile. "This is the kind of thing that happens to somebody else...someplace else."

"So far," added Tarr.

Ardelon heaved his broad shoulders and edged the craft into a gradual landing approach.

"They haven't fired at us, so I think I'll land. Remember, Pallas, you do the talking. You and Kajada will be the ones who stay and make the arrangements. We need to exchange information, and research any cases they've had. We have to find out the situation on the other continents as well." Ardelon turned to Tarr. "Are we ready?"

She studied her readouts but found nothing abnormal. "All systems are in the green."

"Stand by for landing." The attack craft, which seemed small in space but gigantic as it drew close to the ground, dropped into its final approach. Ardelon fired thrusters and set her down in the barren field.

Tarr braced for impact, but the landing was surprisingly gentle. The *Solaris* tilted on her landing legs as she settled into the furrows, but the aged ship held together.

Ardelon smiled at her. "You can let your breath out now."

"Nice landing. That's not what I'm worried about." She looked pointedly at him. "What if they won't listen to me?"

"Just give them a little of that famous Pallas Tarr charm," replied Ardelon. "If that doesn't work *command* them. They'll listen to you." The captain tapped his communications panel. "Kajada, meet Tarr at the transporter. We'll wait her until you signal that it's safe to leave."

"Yes, sir," replied the human male.

"Good luck," the captain said to Tarr.

"If I had any luck, would I be in the Dominion?" With a scowl, Pallas rose to her feet and strode off the bridge.

Thirty seconds later, she entered the cargo bay, which had been turned into a flying laboratory. A handful of researchers looked on as she crossed to the transporter platform, where Kajada waited. She nodded to him, who handed her a combadge and a holstered phaser pistol. As she added these accessories to her plain brown uniform, Tarr glanced again at the researchers and doctors. They looked scared. They had trained all their lives for this battle, but they had never been on the front before. The fight would be until the bitter end, because this enemy took no prisoners.

Pallas tossed her short black hair, prepared to stride out there without an environmental suit. She told herself that she had been inoculated with the best drugs the Dominion had to offer, and the biofilter would remove the multiprions whenever she transported back. But no one could be calm about-facing death so directly.

"Are you ready?" asked Kajada.

Tarr nodded and stepped upon the transporter platform, her hand resting on the butt of her phaser pistol. Opening and closing the hatch on this old ship was a pain, so they had decided to transport outside the ship. "Activate," she told the operator.

A moment later, she and Kajada materialized on the other side of the hull, a few metres beyond the *Solaris*. There was nothing around them but rich, loamy soil piled in rows, awaiting seed. About ten metres away, a spring gurgled in the center of an old artesian well, and an orchard of venerable fruit trees rose beyond the well. In the distance, Tarr saw a cloud of dust on the dirt road, and she pointed it out to Kajada.

He checked his tricorder and nodded wisely. "There are four hovercraft headed toward us. Twenty people, total."

"Are they armed?"

"There are no unusual energy readings. They must have small arms."

She tapped her combadge. "Tarr to transporter room. Stand by for emergency beaming."

"Yes, sir," answered the human on duty.

Tarr stood her ground as the small craft sped toward them. When they came within range of her sharp eyesight, she could see the fear and anger on their distinct faces. These Quinntessanites looked wild, almost fierce, in their colourful, billowing clothes, unfurled ribbons, and windblown hair. They were all hybrids she had never seen before, because they had never existed before; and they existed nowhere else outside of Quinntessa.

The four hovercraft stopped at a respectful distance, and five riders in each jumped out and started forward. The brashly garbed welcoming committee didn't appear to be armed, but they did look angry and upset—and uncomfortable with both emotions. As they got closer to the stoic human and the scowling half-Reptilian, their fierce expressions softened, and some of them gaped openly at Tarr. Most of them fell back to talk in hushed whispers, and only a handful of them kept coming.

The one in the lead was a big, red-haired humanoid with a cherry-red complexion and fine black hair growing down his neck into his flashy tunic, which had puffed sleeves and black braid. His age or ancestry would be difficult to guess, but from the way the others fell back and let him approach alone, she assumed he was the one to deal with.

"Hello!" she said, trying to muster some of her allegedly famous charm. "I'm Pallas Tarr, chief engineer of this vessel."

He stopped and bowed respectfully. "I am Opher, the governor of Xifo, a Royal Son of the First Light Constellation. I beg your pardon, but we are not accepting visitors at the moment. Now leave."

"We're like the plague," countered Tarr, crossing her arms. "You'll get us whether you want us or not. You can't just cut yourselves off from the rest of Quinntessa and hope it doesn't happen to you. Help yourself by helping us study this disease and find the transmission vectors."

"How do we know *you* aren't carrying the disease?" asked Opher suspiciously.

"We just arrived. We've got tests, inoculations, and records about this disease. Our ship has a laboratory and a clinic." Pallas shook her head, growing impatient with this begging. "Listen, we just want to combine forces—if we find that we have to quarantine Hajee or someplace else, we will. Just work with us."

Opher smiled and held out his hands. "Let us show you around and prove to you that we don't have this terrible problem on Kozak."

"Not a single case?" she asked, disbelieving.

He shrugged. "Not that I've seen. Granted, I'm not a doctor. Are you?"

"I've said I'm a ship's engineer. But we have doctors on board—let them examine a few of you. We'll include an inoculation and a trip through our transporter's biofilter, which will take out the fully developed multiprions."

Opher bowed to her, but there was an amused sneer beneath his smile. "As you wish. Lya! Addison!"

Tarr watched curiously as two Quinntessanites ran forward to do his bidding. "I have a favor to ask. Would you two go aboard this ship and allow this Dominion medical team to examine you?"

One of them, a tall woman with long, apelike arms, grimaced with alarm at the idea. "Can we trust them?"

"We have their guests here with us," explained Opher, motioning to Pallas and Kajada. "There should be no danger."

While this conversation was going on, Tarr caught sight of another colourful dressed Quinntessanite training a tricorder on her. When he saw her looking at him, he folded the device shut and melted into the crowd that was gathering.

She tapped her combadge. "Tarr to bridge. We're going to take a tour of the city, and we have two locals to beam aboard for tests. They're about two metres in front of me."

"We're locked on," replied Ardelon's voice. "As soon as they're aboard, we'll head back into orbit. You're doing great—maybe we'll make you an ambassador."

"I'm holding out for major," muttered Tarr. "Team out."

She and Kajada stepped away from the *Solaris* and motioned the others back as well. Still looking frightened, the two sacrificial Quinntessanites clutched hands as they waited to be transported aboard the strange ship. Judging by the welcome given to the Dominion, Tarr guessed that the Quinntessanites had already gotten a good dose of Divinian threats and propaganda. Or maybe they were just cautious people by nature, despite their ostentatious appearance.

When the two finally dematerialized and the *Solaris* lifted off into the lustrous blue sky, the Kozakians seemed to relax for the first time. Tarr saw Opher talking to the man with the tricorder, and she hoped they had gotten a clean bill of health. For people who didn't believe the plague could touch them, they sure took a lot of precautions.

She glanced at Kajada, who raised a noncommittal eyebrow. Tarr wanted to head back to the ship and keep moving, letting these ungrateful people fend for themselves. But they had to confront this disease right here, right now, or they might have to chase it over every centimetre of the Adirondacks Expanse for years to come.

Governor Opher walked toward her and held out his arm like a gentleman. His red hair and cherry skin glistened with a healthy sheen, and he looked as strong as a Reptilian. With a sigh, she took his brawny arm, but only so as not to offend him. Several other Quinntessanites smiled and nodded with satisfaction, as if some event had transpired of which she was not aware.

"Have you ever been to Quinntessa before?" he asked as he led her toward a hovercraft. Kajada followed closely behind them.

"No," answered Tarr. "Why would I?"

"The way you look. Excuse me, but you are half-Reptilian, aren't you?"

She nodded. "And half-human."

Opher's dark blue eyes twinkled with respect. "Half-human and half-Reptilian. I've seen computer simulations, but never the real thing! And you were conceived naturally?"

Tarr bristled. "Well, I wasn't there, but that's what they tell me."

"Incredible! Obviously, they sent you to Quinntessa because of your unique lineage?"

"No, I'm here by chance. The Dominion doesn't have the luxury of picking and choosing who they send places."

She stopped at the door to the hovercraft, expecting Opher to open it, which he quickly did. If they wanted to treat her like royalty, she would oblige. Tarr slipped into the open vehicle ahead of him, and Kajada followed, keeping a close eye on their hosts. They sat in the back row of seats, allowing a driver and two more passengers to climb into the front. The other locals crammed into the remaining hovercraft as best they could. All four vehicles lifted off the ground at the same time, as if linked then the caravan glided smoothly down the rough dirt road.

For the first time, Opher turned to Kajada. "And you, sir, are a full-blooded human?"

"Yes I am."

"I myself am Nafrayu/Turghan on my mother's side, Alphan/Shak'l on my father's side. Here we pride uniqueness—the more unique, the better."

He turned to stare at Tarr with unabashed adoration. "You, Pallas Tarr, are very special indeed."

"Aren't there any full-blooded species who live here?" she asked impatiently.

"Unibloods, as we call them. Of course, there are." The tall man looked wistful for a moment as the hovercraft cruised slowly between rows and rows of flowering vines. The smell of ripe fruit was fragrant on the steamy breeze. "Quinntessa wasn't always like it is now—isolated—with all this strife and uncertainty. We used to have many visitors, great commerce, and spaceports in every city. A lot of unibloods came here to help us with our breeding programs, and just decided to stay."

"So you are saying that the majority of Quinntessanites are genetically mixed," concluded Kajada, "while unibloods are a minority, mostly newly arrived immigrants."

"That's right," agreed Opher. "If you stay here long enough, your children will undoubtedly be unique."

"Why is that?" asked Kajada.

Opher smiled. "You've got to understand where our ancestors came from. They were persecuted all over the galaxy for being of mixed blood. Mixers, they were called in some places. Hundreds of years ago, our ancestors banded together to form a colony that would always be a refuge for persecuted mixbloods, but they did much more than that—they established the Sect of Exclusivity. It became our creed to combine species in as many permutations as possible. And some that weren't possible."

"You employ artificial means of procreation," said Kajada.

Opher stuck his chin out defensively. "Only when necessary. Most Quinntessanites don't have families and children in the accepted sense. We have constellations, which are communal dwellings...a type of clubhouse. For the most part, adults tend to raise their children alone, and the absent parent or parents are regarded as donors.

"We select the genetic traits of our children very carefully, weighing what kind of life we want for them, how much medical intrusion we're willing to allow. And, of course, how attracted we are to the donor." With a glance at Pallas, his defensiveness faded. "To be granted such blessings naturally, as you have been, is a great gift."

No matter how attractive the messenger, the sentiments were still disturbing. Maybe it was the Reptilian in her, but Tarr found the idea of total dependence on genetic engineering to be unnatural. She switched her stare to the buildings that had come into view: tidy three story houses with intricate metal fences and spacious balconies. Quinntessanites rushed onto those balconies to watch the caravan of hovercraft as it entered the city. No one waved or shouted, but they didn't throw bricks either. Tarr felt like the centrepiece of an impromptu parade before a respectful but fearful audience—the leader of a conquering army.

They passed an open-air market, and the hovercraft had to slow down to accommodate all the pedestrians. It seemed almost like a holiday, with so many happily decorated Quinntessanites strolling under the cheerful pennants and striped canopies. The goods in the marketplace were bountiful, ranging from fresh fruits and roasted vegetables to utensils, musical instruments, and more flashy clothing. At first, Tarr tried to pick out the different species in the faces and bodies she saw, but the Quinntessanites were such a hodgepodge of different traits that it became impossible. It was easier to consider them all one race that came in infinite varieties.

As they pulled away from the market, she saw a full-blooded Bolaa, who came charging after them in pursuit. But their hovercraft moved more swiftly than a Bolaa on foot, and they skittered around a corner and were gone.

"Where are we going?" asked Tarr.

"The Organization for Species Improvement," answered Opher, straightening the magenta cuffs on his billowy shirt. "Then to the First Light Constellation, my home. But I want you to note that the people of Xifo do not seem sick, or in a panic. Yes, we have protected our borders from the terrible tragedy on Hajee, but what would you expect from us? You are looking for transmission vectors, and we have sealed off the obvious one."

Tarr gazed at the wealthy city all around her, with its stylish shops, grand commerce buildings, blooming parks, and contented populace. She did find it hard to believe that they were on the verge of annihilation. "You must have some sick people," she pointed out.

"Yes," the governor assured her. "We are going to OSI now to interview the scientists and the few patients we have. The finest minds on the planet are found at OSI."

He reached forward with a cherry hand that was ringed on the wrist with fine black hair, and he brushed her wrist. "I would consider it a great honor if you would have supper with us at the First Light Constellation."

"Yes, Kajada and I will eat with you."

Opher bowed his head apologetically. "We'll make other arrangements for Mr. Kajada to dine with fellow unibloods at the Zoran Constellation."

Tarr frowned at him. "Are you telling me that Kajada can't eat at this fancy club of yours?"

"He can't even go in the building," said Opher.

While Tarr sputtered, unable to find the exact words to rip this trifling young man up one side and down the other, Kajada held up his hand and declared, "I would prefer to eat with the Zoran Constellation. We are on a fact-finding mission, and it would be wise to interview the uniblood community. Perhaps they are not as immune to the disease as the hybrids."

Opher smiled gratefully. "I think Kajada understands. The Zoran Constellation is every bit as grand as the First Light Constellation. Ah, here we are."

Tarr looked up to see them approaching a gigantic red wall. Behind the red wall loomed the pyramid she had seen earlier, looking like a mountain with intricate steps carved into its gleaming sides. The four hovercraft made a small circle and came to a stop, sinking softly to the ground.

Opher bounded from the hovercraft and ran to the other three vehicles. As they conversed, Tarr and Kajada sat patiently, their eyes moving between their hosts and the astonishing structure looming before them.

"They're hypocrites," Tarr whispered to Kajada.

He shrugged. "Maybe. But every culture has a social order, even if it is not as pronounced as this one. It is not unusual for a persecuted group to duplicate that persecution in another form. Otherwise, the Quinntessanites seem to be prosperous and well adjusted."

"At least this place hasn't been devastated by the plague," said Tarr with relief. "We're not too late."

Opher returned to their hovercraft, while the other three vehicles lifted off the ground and glided away. "I told them you weren't a security risk," he explained. "That's correct, isn't it?"

"If we were looking out for ourselves," answered Tarr, "we wouldn't be here at all."

The governor nodded in agreement. "Yes, I suppose, we haven't been fair to you...or to our neighbors. But we've fought so hard to keep our home, and our way of life. Our ancestors built this colony from nothing—in the farthest corner of Dominion space. The early years were very hard, and our founders suffered greatly—I'd like to show you our histories sometime. We put up with the Dominion, we put up with the Divinian Empire, and now these radical factions from the Divinian Empire—but one thing is certain, we're going to keep our home-world."

"But you would sacrifice your citizens on the other continents?" observed Kajada.

"They have the same technical capabilities we have." countered Opher. "If they can't cure it, neither can we! And you forget—the Divinian splinter group that's been quarantining our planet destroyed all of our long-range vessels. The only way to get across the ocean now is by sea-glider, and that's not the way to move supplies and sick people. We have no way to get off the planet, no way to get help—"

"Until we came," said Pallas.

"All right," he conceded, "you came. And how long will you stay here? My guess is that you'll leave the moment more Divinian ships show up, which could be any minute."

Then we'd better hurry," said Tarr, striding past Opher toward an archway in the red wall. Kajada walked after her, leaving the Quinntessanites to gawk at the audacity of their guests.

Leaving his three comrades with the remaining hovercraft, Opher followed them to the gate. In the archway was a heavy metal door, which didn't suit the exquisite red stone of the wall. Beside the door, Tarr noticed what looked like a card slot, but their host paid no attention to it.

"Just stand here," he explained. "We'll be recognized."

Sure enough, the door opened, and Opher led the way inside. The walkway sloped downward, with handrails on either side. Tarr realized they were headed underground, into a network of tunnels. The lighting came from luminescent strips embedded in the walls, ceiling, and floor of the ruby corridor. Their footsteps echoed plain against the dull stone as they descended.

In due time, they came to a shiny metal turbolift, which opened invitingly at their approach. They stepped inside the well-appointed chamber and, following Opher's lead, stood quietly. After a jarring ride that made Tarr dizzy, the doors opened, and they found themselves in a extravagant office, furnished with mementos, plaques, and awards. There were so many chairs arrayed against the walls that Tarr decided this was a waiting room, with no one waiting.

A chime sounded, and a small bookcase in the corner spun around. A little man wearing a white laboratory coat stepped off the platform and gave them a crinkled smile. From the riot of spots and bumps on his face, it was impossible to tell what species his ancestors might have been, but it was certain that he was old. Grey hair sprouted in unruly clumps from his head, eyebrows, and chin, only adding to his elf like appearance.

"Hello! Hello!" he said, striding forward. "I am Dr. Johnson. Welcome to OSI." Although he tried to include all of them in his conversation, his purple eyes drifted toward Pallas Tarr. "Yes, yes...remarkable."

"Dr. Johnson," said Opher warmly. "Glad you could see us personally." This is Pallas Tarr and Kajada from the Dominion vessel."

"Has their ship left the ground?" asked Johnson.

"Yes, it's back in orbit."

"Good, good," said the little man with extreme relief. He turned apologetically to Pallas. "We still worry about the Divinians more than anything else, and we don't want to give them any excuse to punish us. Although it may not seem like it, I'm glad you're here."

"You people are in denial about this plague," said Tarr. "You can't hide from it and hope it goes away."

"I told them we didn't have any cases," insisted Opher.

Johnson scratched his wiry goatee. "I'm not sure of that anymore. It's possible that we could have had some plague cases and not recognized them. People could have died in the countryside without our knowing it. We need to cooperate with these people to find out."

Tarr took an isolinear chip from her pants pocket. "I've got all the Dominion data on the previous outbreaks."

He took the chip and shrugged. "I've seen the data, including some Divinian files you could never obtain. I didn't tell Opher, but we have samples of the prions, smuggled out of Hajee before the quarantine. We were studying the disease, but it moved too quickly for us to save Hajee."

"Then you know this is serious," said Tarr.

The doctor nodded somberly as he paced the quiet library. His shuffling footsteps were the only sound, except for the far-off drip of a faucet.

"It's more serious than you think," he began. "Much more serious. This strain is just as dangerous as previous strains—but even more contagious. My theory is that it's a chimera, a genetically engineered combination of two different organisms. In this case, it would be the original virus combined with a less deadly disease that is easy to contract. So we have a disease that was already deadly, only now it's more contagious than ever."

"Who engineered it?" asked Opher, shock spreading across his handsome face.

Dr. Johnson shook his shaggy grey mane. "That's unknown. We don't even know what the second organism is, and I've got people in this building who disagree with me—they think it evolved naturally. We've just started looking at this thing, and it could take months, or years, to crack it. And we may not have that much time—either from the disease or the Divinians."

The little elf looked into Pallas' eyes. "And no one is going to allow us to leave the planet, are they?"

She cleared her throat and returned his frank stare. "No, we have to fight this battle right here, right now. Win or lose."

"Aren't there drugs that can delay the onset?" asked Opher hopefully.

"Yes, but there's no cure," stressed Dr. Johnson, his pace turning into a nervous jog. "Only by tracking it back to its origins can we hope to snuff it out. Now that we've got a couple of Dominion ships and the means to move quickly around the planet, let's use them."

"I'll get you together with our doctors." Pallas tapped her combadge, but nothing happened.

Johnson smiled slyly. "That won't work in here, my dear. No, no. I would suggest that we have as little contact with your ship as possible, in case the Divinians show up again. In fact, there's a garrison stationed east of here in Michasa, and they keep a close eye on us."

"So we'll exchange records and personnel as needed, while you two stay with us to coordinate the research. Your ships will do the fieldwork—as they're already doing on Hajee. But direct contact with your ship should be kept to a minimum. Also, it might help if you two didn't go around openly proclaiming your identity as Dominion. Just say you're Quinntessanites."

"With *these* clothes?" asked Pallas, pointing to her drab uniform.

"Yes, yes, we'll do something about that." Johnson gave Kajada a crinkly smile. "You, dear man, could make a fortune while you're here—in donor fees. Wouldn't require much work on your part—we can extract your DNA. It's quite harmless I assure you."

While it was not possible to embarrass Kajada, he did manage to look offended. "That is the most unappealing job offer I have ever received."

The little man shrugged. "Not to fear, it is entirely your decision. Turghans are so similar to humans that we've learned to use them almost exclusively. But never mind about that. Are we agreed on how to proceed?"

Pallas could feel the leadership of this mission slipping away from her, flowing toward the charismatic little doctor. Then again, they needed help desperately. And he was right, if the Divinian faction that was behind this showed up in force, all bets were off. It was a good idea to make the Quinntessanites self-sufficient, as eliminating this disease was going to be a long, hard job, even if they were successful in containing the outbreak.

She looked at Kajada, and the human man raised an eyebrow, awaiting her decision.

"Sounds like a plan," she said. "We'll stay with you and coordinate."

Dr. Johnson clapped his gnarled hands. "Superb! Superb! I feel very confident that we can fight this chimera. Our people have a lot of natural resistance built into their genetic makeup."

"Do you have biological warfare?" asked Tarr.

"No!" squeaked the little man, looking horrified at the idea. "We've never had war of any kind, biological or otherwise. The Divinians could have wiped us out anytime they felt like it, with conventional weapons. There's no reason the should introduce a disease—or that anyone else should."

Tarr nodded, more troubled than relieved by that thought. As she had asked James days ago: *Why here? Why now?*

CHAPTER EIGHT

A LOUD, WRACKING COUGH sundered the silence of the examination tent, and a thin, naked man shook uncontrollably on the metal table. He looked old and used-up, although that may have been a result of the disease. For all James knew, he could have been a young man in the prime of life. This disease attacked every organ at once, bringing on instant aging.

Two medical workers in white gowns and hoods leaned over the old man, conversing silently inside their headgear. James stood nearby, waiting to see if the patient had to be transported to the shuttlecraft. Finally one of the doctors turned to him and shook his encased head.

"He's too far gone," said a disembodied voice in James' hood.

The lieutenant didn't need any further explanation. He had seen plenty of patients like this one in the last few hours. Although the multiprions that caused the disease could be removed from their bodies by the transporter biofilter, their weakened bodies could not be repaired. Two many other opportunistic diseases had taken over; too many organs were failing; too many healthier people needed attention.

Unable to watch any longer, James waved to the doctors. "I have to check something." They waved back and grabbed hypos that would alleviate the man's suffering but not prolong his life.

Feeling constricted inside his hood, James stepped out of the examination room into a primordial night. The sky above was sugared with stars, and the dead city cast a boxy silhouette in the distance. The clinic's lights were the only lights between their encampment and the stars.

A clutch of Quinntessanites waited nearby, staring at him. After a moment, he recognized them as people who had carried the old man in. Their gaily striped and billowy clothes were soiled and tattered, making them look like an impoverished theatre company. From their concerned yet hopeful faces, he knew they wanted some reassurance, but he couldn't give them any. It wasn't even his place to talk to them, but James knew that if he didn't, no one else would. He removed his headgear and walked toward the people.

"Will the governor be all right?" asked a female who might have been attractive before worry and tragedy carved herself into her mahogany face.

James looked frankly into eyes that were perfectly round. "I'm sorry, but the doctors say he won't recover."

A man with puckered purple skin pushed his way through the group to confront the lieutenant. "But the transporter—we saw others being cured!"

"Others who were infected but not that sick," explained James. "We have to catch it within forty-eight hours. I'm sorry."

He started to walk away, but the man, who was good-sized, grabbed James' shoulder and whirled him around. "That's our *governor* you're talking about—the chief of the Sun Constellation! You have to save him!"

James tried to remain calm as he pried the Quinntessanite's fingers off his shoulder. He also tried to ignore the way the man had spit into his face. "We're medical workers, not miracle workers. We're trying to save as many as we can, while we make the others comfortable."

"You'll save him!" shouted the man. "Or I'll tell the Divinians you're here!"

James glanced worriedly into the night sky. "I'm pretty sure they already know we're here. I met a few of them in town, around the OSI building. What are they doing there?"

"You're evading my question!" sputtered the man.

"No, I'm trying to help people in this place...and getting shot at, threatened, and exposed to plague for my trouble!"

When the man wouldn't calm down, two of his friends grabbed him in an emotional hug. "Don't make it worse, Vukelic," begged a woman. "We knew he was very sick. Let him go."

"They are only trying to help," insisted another friend. "Let's get in line for inoculations."

With lingering anger and denial, the purple man glared at James. The lieutenant knew he should show more sympathy, but death was all around, breathing down their necks, and he wanted to survive. "What are the Divinians doing around the OSI complex?" he asked again.

The man looked past him, grief finally taking the place of anger, but a pointy-eared lad stepped forward. "They're shooting down any ships that can leave the planet. Those have been their orders for a while."

"And what about OSI? A weapon in that pyramid tried to shoot *us* down."

"That's their regular security," said the boy, sounding proud. "It's to protect trade secrets from their smaller competitors."

"Some secrets," muttered James. "Thank you. Once again, I'm sorry."

He hurried off before he could get involved in more grief, sickness, and death. With the *Solaris* and *Scorpion* in orbit, James wasn't that concerned about an attack from space, but he didn't like squads of Divinians popping up here and there. If that crack patrol ever decided to attack the clinic, they could wipe them out in less than two minutes. It was doubtful the ships in orbit could respond quickly enough to help.

He crossed the flower garden to the shuttlecraft, which was parked on a grassy hillside overlooking the ocean. The hatch was open, and a feeble yellow light spilled into the darkness. In the gloom, the shuttle looked like a panel wagon belonging to a couple of traveling dirt-poor cowboys. It was too dark to see the ocean, but the waves crashed soothingly to the shore; the monotonous sound gave a false impression that all was well.

He stepped into the shuttlecraft, about to blurt orders, when he saw Cordette sprawled like a limp starfish in the pilot's seat, fast asleep. She looked so peaceful, he didn't want to wake her up, but they were endangering the clinic by being here.

"Cordette!" he snapped, dropping into the seat beside her. "Prepare for takeoff."

Cordette bolted upright, blinking her eyelids. "I'm sorry, James, I don't know what happened—"

"I know what happened—you got tired. But don't worry about that. We've got to get out of here. Can you take over the checklist?"

"Yes, James." Cordette's hands dropped onto the board, and she was instantly at work.

James tapped the communications panel. "Shuttle to *Solaris*."

"We hear you," replied Ardelon.

"We're assuming orbit, because I'm worried that the shuttlecraft is endangering the clinic. The Divinians on the ground are out to get every ship that can leave the planet."

"Understood," said the captain. "But the situation may change quickly, because we're out of contact with Tarr and Kajada on the other continent. We've got no reason to believe they're in danger, but they're not responding to hails."

James frowned. "Is there anything I can do to help?"

"No," muttered Ardelon. "They went into a building where there may be shielding. And sometimes those surplus combadges can fail without warning. Let's give them a little longer."

"Okay. After we get in orbit, I'd like permission to beam down to the planet to scout Divinians and a medical facility."

"Is this necessary?"

"I think it is. We've got to get records and find out how this thing started. The problem is, Hajee is a ghost town—everything is boarded up. The only ones out and about are Divinians. How have they avoided the plague? I'd like to know."

"Okay, but keep in touch."

"You've got to take over the transport duties for the clinic," said James.

"We just entered synchronous orbit, and the transporter is going full time, no waiting."

"Okay, shuttle out."

James punched up the launch sequence, as Cordette stared at him with concern. "We're going back to that place?"

"Yes, but we're not going to march right up and knock. Let's launch, and we'll discuss it on our way."

James and Cordette beamed into what they thought was an empty administration building near the OSI complex. When they shined their lanterns around the dark workroom, James was glad he had insisted they wear environmental suits. They were surrounded by hundreds of shrill rodents, interrupted in the middle of dining on three dismembered corpses.

When the rodents advanced, teeth bared, James raked the front row with phaser fire; they fell back, squealing. The line of charred rodents pointed the way to a second door, and James jogged in that direction, keeping the light in front of him and Cordette.

The door was automatic and should have opened at their approach, but the power was off. He trained his lantern back on the rats, several of whom were bravely sniffing their footprints, trying to decide if these intruders were a danger or more food. "If they get close, shoot at them," he ordered Cordette.

"Yes, James," replied the young woman with a tremble in her voice.

James stepped back and surveyed the area around the door, finding an access panel that might control the mechanism. Since Quinntessanite technology was based on Dominion technology, James had no trouble opening the panel and determining which circuits he needed to disable to allow it to open manually. He didn't have much hope of restoring electrical power to the building, but he wanted to be able to open a door without blasting through it.

A flash of light caught his attention, and he whirled around to see Cordette firing at a wave of scurrying rats. "Keep them away!" he ordered her.

James wormed his gloved fingers into the crack between the two halves of the door. Using every muscle in his upper body, he pried the door open, as Cordette backed into him. She fired continuously at the rodents, but a sea of fur surged across the floor, caught in the wavering light of their lanterns.

"Get out!" James straightened his arm, forming an archway and holding the door open for the woman. When she didn't move fast enough, he grabbed her and shoved her through the door. With a final glance at the frenzied rats, James turned the light away and plunged the room back into darkness. With his hold on the door weakening, he squeezed through and let it snap shut behind him.

They found themselves in a deserted corridor, which was fine with James, since he wanted to search for the best observation post. He picked a direction and started walking. Cordette shuffled behind him, keeping an eye on their rear. With no lights except for their portable lanterns, it almost seemed as if they were exploring a mine.

Midway down the hall, they came upon a door that bore the universal pictograph for stairs. James gave it a push and found that it wasn't locked or automatic. He held the door open and motioned Cordette ahead of him, while he took a last look down the length of the bleak hallway.

Once in the stairwell, James decided that they might as well stake out the highest ground. He pointed up the stairs then took the lead. Upon reaching the top landing, he was confronted by another automatic door. While Cordette held the light for him, he opened the access panel and disabled the circuitry, allowing him and Cordette to push the door open.

When they stepped onto the flat roof, they were unprepared for the sight that greeted them. Quinntessa's triple moons had just risen, casting an eerie green light upon the dark cityscape. With their intricate wrought-iron balconies, sharp angles, and terraces, the buildings looked like giant mausoleums.

James turned off his lantern and motioned Cordette to do the same. Then they crouched down and took a good look at their surroundings. Arrayed along the roof were a few communication dishes and antennas, plus some environmental equipment, but little else of interest. Moonlight bathed the pyramid, making it look yellow instead of red.

The two of them dashed to the edge of the roof and peered over a wrought-iron railing at the street below. From a height of about seven stories, they had an excellent view over the wall into the OSI complex, where they could now see smaller buildings in addition to the pyramid. They also had a commanding view of the street in two directions. The only disadvantage of having a post on the roof was that they would be visible by air surveillance. But thus far, they hadn't seen any Divinian aircraft, and James didn't think they would have to worry until morning.

He got into a comfortable yet effective reclining position then removed his hood. After a moment, Cordette did the same. "What are we looking for?" she asked.

"To see if anybody is in that place. If there's someone home, we have to attract their attention without alerting the Divinians. Let's just be ready to gather information...and move fast if we get the chance."

As the two of them watched the massive pyramid and deserted street, time hung suspended over them like the glittering moons. It seemed as if they were the only people in the universe, keeping a vigil for a long-dead traveler who would never return home. Even though the buildings were standing, and the infrastructure of the society remained in place, this city was dead. James wondered if the survivors in Hajee could be relocated somewhere else on the planet, allowing them to start over.

Cordette tapped James on the leg, jarring him out of his daydream, and she pointed to the east end of the street. He peered in that direction but could see very little in the shadows.

So he took a small scope from his pack and adjusted it to his eye.

Immediately he spotted a squad of Divinians strolling down the street, probably the same ones who had attacked them on their last visit. From their movements, it was clear they thought they owned the neighborhood and had nothing to fear. James still wondered if they were connected with the OSI complex—or had just discovered a good place to trap unsuspecting shuttlecraft.

Maybe I can find out.

As the patrol drew closer, unaware of the watchers on the roof, James turned to Cordette and whispered, "Remember that payload we talked about beaming into the complex?"

The woman nodded. They had discussed transporting themselves directly behind the walls then had decided to send an inanimate load first. After collecting a few objects to send down, they had finally decided to scrap that plan until they were more desperate.

James went on, "I want you to return to the shuttle and beam the package into the complex. Put it on the other side of the wall, where that shrub is. See it? The Divinians should pass by there in about a minute, but wait for my signal."

"Yes, James." Cordette looked for the shrub and checked the coordinates on her tricorder. Then she pressed her combadge. "Chance to shuttle. One to transport—now."

With a twinge of dread, James watched his wife vanish into the night like a swirl of dust caught in the moonlight. He had really come to rely on Cordette, and he didn't like being without her, even for a few seconds.

Creeping along the lip of the roof, James peered through the wrought-iron lattice. He could see the unsuspecting patrol, strolling the street with a swagger typical of conquering soldiers. This time, they were wearing some sort of gas masks, although no protective clothing—just their regular black uniforms. He appreciated the way they skirted close to the red wall in order to avoid a clump of debris in the street.

When they were only a few steps from the shrub on the wall, James tapped his combadge. "Activate now."

Gazing down at the complex from above, he saw a blue ripple race along the interior of the wall, as if a force field had rejected an attack. The blue anomaly moved outward in concentric circles, like a ripple in a pool, flowing over the walls and encompassing the unsuspecting soldiers. They screamed in agony, and half-a-dozen of them collapsed to the pavement. The others staggered, although some recovered quickly and aimed their weapons at the wall, which had seemingly attacked them for no reason.

The Divinians cut loose with a withering blaze of fire, which only carved a minor dent in the impervious red stone. Nevertheless, the defences of the complex reacted as if a full-scale attack was in progress. A red beam shot from the tip of the pyramid and melted a screaming Divinian. Now the rest of them stopped firing and beat a hasty retreat, dragging four of their comrades with them.

James heard a snort and he turned to see Cordette watching the curious spectacle. Subconsciously, she rubbed her injured hip.

"Did the package get through intact?" he asked.

"I don't know. The transmitter stopped working, and heavy-duty shields blocked our sensors. We had an isolinear chip in there with all of our data, so maybe they'll take notice."

James nodded with satisfaction and turned his attention to the stunned Divinians. One of them crawled away, but three of them lay completely still, as still as death. They had been the closest ones to the wall, and James had a feeling they were not going to get up.

He whispered to Cordette, "Whoever is in that complex, they're not allied with the Divinians."

Cordette started to reply, but a howling noise interrupted her. Screaming out of the night came a missile that slammed into the red wall, exploding with a thunderous concussion that shook the whole street. Cordette and James were hurled away from the edge of the roof into a thicket of antennas. Red hail rained down upon them, and it took James a moment to realize that the ruby gemlike pellets were bits of the wall.

He crawled to the edge of the roof and peered into the acrid smoke and swirling embers. He was amazed to see a gaping hole in the wall, with sparks glittering around its edges.

Movement caught James' eye, and he looked up. From the top of the pyramid, the deadly red beam raked a building farther up the street. James was curious about the target, but he couldn't stick around long enough to study it. The heat from the pyramid's weapon was scorching, turning the air into an inferno. He rolled away from the edge of the roof, yanking his headgear back on.

Scrambling to his knees, he spotted Cordette crouched by the door to the stairwell. He dashed toward her, and the two of them tackled the door; with their adrenaline pumping, they pushed it open in seconds. Just as a monstrous explosion shook their building, they ducted into the cover of the stairwell.

After scurrying down a flight of stairs, Cordette and James finally took a moment to catch their breath and slump against the narrow walls of the enclosure. "Well while they fight it out we're caught in the crossfire," observed Cordette, panting.

"This would be a good time to get into that complex," breathed James. He flinched from another blast that sounded altogether too close, as bits of plaster and dust fluttered down on them.

"First thing's first," rasped Cordette, "I say we get out of here."

"Good idea." He tapped his combadge. Rawlings to shuttle—two to beam up! Right now!"

They dematerialized just as an explosion ripped off part of the roof, causing beams and debris to cascade down the empty stairwell.

Back on the shuttlecraft, safely in orbit, James didn't take time to congratulate himself. He charged to a console and scanned the breach in the wall, while Cordette slumped into the closest seat.

"There's a hole that goes all the way through," said James, "and there's no force field. We could beam right inside—onto a walkway."

"The shooting?" asked Cordette.

"Has stopped for the moment—both sides are quiet. If you don't want to go I'll go by myself." He checked the other readouts.

"I can't let you go alone," said Cordette, rising wearily to her feet. She pulled the hood back over her head and checked her suit. "We need to know what's in there."

After making sure that the shuttle's orbit was stable and her status was good, James punched in commands and motioned his wife back onto the transporter pad. "Phasers at maximum."

"On maximum," she agreed, drawing and checking her weapon. With the lieutenant deftly handling the controls, Cordette faded into a glittering shimmer. He jumped onto the platform after her, levelled his phaser, and vanished.

The two visitors materialized inside a gloomy walkway that sloped downward. It would have been well lit in daytime, thanks to a ragged hole in the wall about seven metres behind them. James pushed Cordette along, because there was a lot of moonlight spilling through that crevice.

As they descended into the walkway, James felt a handrail at his side, and he grabbed it. There were enough red pebbles and debris to make walking treacherous. He turned on his lantern and played the yellow beam upon the glistening walls of the corridor. The entire thing was made of the same red material as the exterior. James knew he could learn more from a tricorder reading, but he didn't want to take his eyes off his surroundings.

"Look here," said Cordette. She pointed her lantern beam straight down the corridor until it glinted off shiny metal. "Looks like a door."

He nodded, motioning her to go on. If they both had to return fire, it would be better to have the shorter person in the lead. Suddenly the strips of light glimmered in the floor and ceiling of the corridor, causing the visitors to drop into a crouch.

"It's just the lights," James said with relief, rising to his feet.

He felt a slight tremble, and looked back in the direction they had come from. At the far of the corridor, the red jade appeared to be moving—sliding—and he wondered if it was a trick of the light. Looking closer, he realized that the walls of the corridor were slowly oozing toward the breach, as if they were trying to heal it. He couldn't take time to watch this phenomenon, because Cordette was already moving toward the gleaming door.

James shuffled after her, his booted feet making hissing sounds on the smooth red stone. When they reached the door, it slid open at their approach, revealing a small, tapering enclosure within.

Cordette fumbled for her tricorder, but James touched her arm. "It's a turbolift."

She looked up and nodded nervously. This time, James led the way inside, and Cordette followed, keeping a watch on their rear. There were no buttons to push, no controls to operate. The doors whooshed shut, and the lift moved so quickly that James felt a heave in his stomach and slight disorientation.

The doors opened a moment later, revealing what appeared to be a cluttered waiting room. Diplomas, plaques, citations, and letters hung on every spare centimetre of the walls, while jumbled bookshelves filled the rest. The furniture looked old and comfortable, as if this were a good place to read a paper, have a discussion, or take a nap. By the turbolift was an umbrella stand with three striped umbrellas stuck in it.

James stepped gingerly into the room, surveying the walls for other entrances and finding none. Cordette slowly followed him into the room, her phaser levelled for action. They hardly noticed when the turbolift doors slid shut behind them.

Suddenly one of the short bookcases began to revolve, revealing a small man in a white laboratory coat. His face was a remarkable road map of the most startling traits of half-a-dozen different species, and his broad smile was equally universal. He wore no protective clothing, and his grey hair bristled energetically as he strode across the room toward them.

"Welcome! Welcome!" he called, clapping his hands together. "Your perseverance has paid off. I thought we wouldn't be having any more customers for a while, but here you are!"

"We're not customers," said James through his speaker. "There's a plague going on out there."

"Let me show you our plans," said the little man. He crossed to a bookshelf and took out a large photo album.

"According to our scans, the male will be uniblood human, and the female will be uniblood Takarian. Your child will be quite unique, and we can increase your chances of conception considerably. We'll also have to watch for the genetic clash between human DNA and Takarian DNA. Sometimes that combination can cause a miscarriage."

James pulled off his hood, thinking the old man couldn't hear him properly. "We're here because of the plague—not to have a child."

The old doctor frowned with disappointment. "You've changed your minds then. That's too bad. You two would produce an excellent offspring. It's a big step, I know, but OSI will always be here for you when you're ready."

"Hey fellow. Do you have a few screws loose up there? Tell us what you know if anything about the outbreak up there?" snapped James, losing his patience.

"Don't waste your time," interjected Cordette. He glanced over to see Cordette intently studying her tricorder. "He's a hologram."

James peered closely at the little doctor, who gave him a crinkly smile in return. "I've never seen a hologram this good before," said the lieutenant. It appears this one has been programmed to deal with prospective parents. Are there any *real* people in this building?"

She shook her head. "I can't tell. The shielding is very thick—I can't see anything beyond these walls. I doubt if our combadges would work."

James tapped his badge immediately. "Rawlings to shuttle." There was no response. Rawlings to *Solaris*." The only sound was the bubbling of a small aquarium on a corner table.

The elf like doctor chuckled warmly. "If the expense is a problem, let me tell you about our instalment plans. Or perhaps you qualify for financial assistance. Let me check."

"We want to see where the procedures take place," demanded James. "We want the grand tour."

"Right this way!" chirped the kindly doctor. He started for the turbolift, then stopped and shook a finger at himself. "Sorry, sorry, I keep forgetting. You'll have to remove your weapons. Regulations, you know."

With a scowl, James holstered his weapon, and so did Cordette.

"No, I mean, leave them here." He held out a spotted, grey-furred hand. "I'll put them in my drawer—they'll be safe."

James' hand hesitated on the butt of his weapon. It seemed unwise to hand it over at this point. "Maybe we'll just be leaving," he said, edging toward the lift. "Just tell us how to get out safely."

The friendly elf clapped his hands with joy. "The decision is in! You have been accepted as patients on full scholarship basis. Your pregnancy is completely free!"

"We'll be going now," insisted James.

"But it's time for your anesthesia."

Something sharp pierced James in the center of his back. He struggled to reach it, but he couldn't in the bulky suit. An instant feeling of well being spread over him, and he stopped struggling, using all of his facilities just to stand on his feet. Swaying back and forth like a drunkard, he tried to remember why he had come in here.

James caught sight of some movement in the room, and he turned very slowly—in time to see Cordette pitch forward onto the carpet. For the first time he realized that something was wrong.

A throaty chuckle emanated from behind the revolving bookshelf, and he tried to focus his eyes in that direction. A figure in a blue environmental suit stepped into the waiting room, trained a phaser rifle on him, and pulled the trigger.

All feeling in James' body disappeared, and his head rolled into a black pit.

CHAPTER NINE

PALLAS TARR LOOKED DOWN at the patient, who showed the strong sabre tooth tiger traits reminiscent of a Gairwyn, although in a more muscular body. Through the gauze of a protective canopy, the patient nodded weakly at her, Kajada, Dr. Johnson, and governor Opher. Tarr looked around the intensive care unit, impressed with the efficiency and quality of OSI's infirmary. Their tour had been extensive, and they hadn't even seen the obstetrics ward, the biggest wing of the complex.

"This patient is our best in-house possibility for a case of the plaque," whispered Johnson softly. "We've had other possible cases, but all of them have recovered. I gather that's not the typical profile. What do you think, Mr. Kajada."

Kajada studied a large electronic pad containing the man's medical records. "At a glance, it would appear this man has a respiratory infection, not the plague. I would like to have our doctors look at this data, as well as the patient. Can we contact our ship and beam him up?"

The little man sighed, as if this would be possible but inadvisable. "I suppose we'll have to risk it. Why don't you take time right now to go back to the surface, where you can use your communicators."

"How far underground are we?" asked Tarr, beginning to dislike this arrangement.

He shrugged cheerfully. "Two hundred metres or so, that's all."

"I don't think being cut off from our ship is going to work," she declared. "If this is your only facility, we'll have to move most of the work to the *Solaris*."

"Pardon me, said Opher. "What about the two healthy people you took earlier?"

"That's another good reason to get in contact with our ship." Tarr began to pace the ICU, growing impatient with the time this was taking. The tour had been a good idea, but it still felt as if they were in a diplomatic stage, when they needed to be on the offensive.

"Governor Opher can take you to the surface," said the old doctor reassuringly. "I'll get this patient up there, and we can make all the arrangements we need. I know you understand the need for us to distance ourselves from you, but I also realize the necessity for *some* contact. I do."

"See you later, Doctor," said Tarr. "Thank you for all your help."

The tiny fellow gave her a crinkly smile and waved both hands. Opher patiently herded them away from the intensive care unit.

The governor looked relieved to get this unpleasantness behind them, and he asked conversationally, "Don't you think it's possible that the disease has bypassed Kozak? We're a long distance from anywhere."

"What's possible," admitted Tarr, "but if you had seen conditions on Hajee—"

"Quinntessa has awfully big oceans," Opher reminded her. "They give our planet much of its character, and they protect us. You'll grow to love them."

"We don't plan on staying here for a long time," she grumbled. They paused to let the door open, and the air rushed outward into the corridor; the facility used uneven air pressure to keep contaminants out of patient areas.

"Who knows how long it will take to squash out this terrible disease," said Opher. "But I know you can't be a Dominion officer for the rest of your life, Pallas. You'll have to look for peace eventually, and no place would suit you better than Quinntessa. Here you would be worshipped, part of the social elite. You could be whatever you wanted to be."

She scowled. "I'm a ship's engineer, and you don't have any ships."

"Not now, but we're a resilient people. We'll build up our merchant fleet again. You can help us." Opher glanced at Kajada as they stepped into the red-ruby corridor. "In fact, I would say that *all* of the Dominion could blend into our society with ease. You have skills we need to rebuild, and we would welcome you with open arms. Where else can you go? None of you can ever return to Earth, and most of your homes in the Adirondacks Expanse are gone. The Divinian Empire will hunt you down."

"Your reasoning has merit," agreed Kajada as their footsteps echoed dully in the undistinguished corridor. "The Dominion doesn't have a plan to return to civilian life. They lack long-range planning skills."

"Who needs a plan when winging it for all these years will do," Tarr grumbled.

Opher pounded his fist into his palm. "I'm going to bring it up at the next Canyon Constellation—sanctuary for any Dominion crew who wishes to settle here! After you help us save our home, it can become *your* home."

The governor smiled warmly at Tarr, but she was still thinking about what Kajada had said. "Do you really think we should start planning to get out?"

The human male looked pointedly at her. "Service in the Dominion can only end one of three ways: retirement, imprisonment, or death. I would prefer to see my comrades in retirement than in either of the other circumstances."

"That's very thoughtful of you," replied Tarr dryly.

As in most times, she couldn't disregard Kajada's logic—they *should* have an exit strategy from this crazy life. *But peace? Retirement? A return to civilian habits?* After the last several months, these notions sounded like pipe dreams. Tarr wondered what had brought on Kajada's sudden concern for the future. The nearness of so much death, she decided, could give anyone an encompassing sense of humanity.

The trio finally reached the turbolift at the end of the corridor, and the doors whooshed open at their approach. Opher motioned to his visitors to enter first then he followed them into the gleaming metal chamber. The doors breezed shut.

Again, an odd feeling of dizziness and disorientation came over Pallas, but it was gone a moment later. They stepped into a corridor that sloped upward and was lit with luminescent strips embedded in the red stone. She led the way, eager to get out of the underground complex. There was no reason for the OSI facility to seem so claustrophobic, especially for a person who lived and worked on a small scout ship, but Tarr nearly ran for the exit.

The outer door opened as she jogged toward it, and she dashed into the warm, afternoon sunshine. Their hovercraft was parked right where they had left it, and the crowd of onlookers had shrunk but had not entirely disappeared. She tapped her combadge and growled, "Tarr to *Solaris*."

"Pallas!" answered the relieved voice of Captain Ardelon. "Are you all right? You've been out of contact for almost two hours."

"I'm sorry about that, but their medical facility is underground, and we had to take a tour." She proceeded to fill him in on everything that had happened to them, including the fact that the bug might be a chimera.

"I'll get our researchers on that," promised Ardelon. "The two people from Kozak that we examined are healthy, although one of them has one of the prions in his system."

"We've got a sick person we'd like to beam up," said Tarr, "along with some records. Also, we'd like to get a couple of doctors down here to go over their files. They claim that Kozak hasn't had any cases of the disease."

"Let's hope they're right. Maybe this won't be as bad as it looks—a larger continent to the south appears to be clean, so far."

"One other thing, Ardelon." Tarr chose her words carefully. "When this is all over, we may want to lay low for a while. The governor of Kozak wants to offer sanctuary to members of the Dominion who would like to stay here and blend in with the populace."

There was no immediate response from Ardelon. "Captain?" she asked.

"I heard you. There are days when that offer would sound pretty good. Ask me again when it's all over. Right now, we've got work to do."

After making arrangements that would keep the transporters and medical teams busy for hours, Ardelon leaned back in his seat on the bridge of the *Solaris*. He gazed at the watery blue sphere shimmering in the sun and wondered what it would be like to live down there. It had to be better than dodging Divinian warships, and hiding out in the Adirondacks.

With a sigh, he glanced at Vantika on the ops console. "Any word from Rawlings?"

"No," answered the Rambler.

"Try then again," he ordered. "I'd be a lot happier if we could just maintain contact with all of our away teams."

Vantika worked her console for a moment then shook her head. "Rawlings isn't responding, and their shuttlecraft is still unmanned."

Ardelon scowled and balled his hand into a fist. "Let's send a pilot to that shuttlecraft, just in case the entire Divinian fleet shows up."

"Connor is coming on duty in four minutes. We could send him."

"See to it personally that he gets there," he ordered. "Tell him to stand by the comm. channels and stay on alert."

"Yes, sir." Vantika jumped to her feet and strode off the bridge, leaving Ardelon alone to contemplate the enormity of their mission.

Their first day had gone almost too well, considering the obstacles. Ardelon wasn't a pessimistic man, but he had a strong belief in fate. Something terrible and unforeseen was about to happen—he could feel it. But he wouldn't worry about it. Destiny had drawn them all to this forgotten corner of the galaxy, and maybe this would be the place where their idealistic pursuit came to an end, one way or another.

The situation in the conference room onboard the *Phoenix* grew tense. Sub-Emperor Tuplo sunk into his chair, a scowl darkening his bony, black façade. Like everyone else in the conference room, he cowered from the angry outburst of Sub-Emperor Zaha, who pounded the table with a beefy fist as he ranted. The object of his wrath was General Tetzlaff, who stood watching her new friend, hoping Tuplo would defend her, or at least save her dignity.

No, it's not to be, thought Tetzlaff. She was to suffer this humiliation alone, with Tuplo letting her twist in the wind.

"I cannot believe you let this condition fester as you have!" thundered Zaha, chief of the Melosha Council. "That planet endangers our very existence, and then to let the Dominion run wild on it...is inexcusable!"

There were grumbles around the room as the other members of the council agreed with their leader. So Tetzlaff let her eyes wander out the large window to the glorious view of the Tamsin Shipyards, high in orbit over the amber clouds of the planet Galyn Major. She envied the builders floating in the skeletal frame of a future starship at the next dock. Those menial workers could see the result of their work at the end of the day, while she had to think strategically—decades and centuries down the road. And in this matter, she had kept her own council, so even her friends couldn't speak for her.

"Brigadier General Makepeace outranks me and has his own agenda. If I had been in charge of the whole situation it would have been under control. And am I allowed to defend myself?" she finally asked. "Or is it a given that you're going to destroy Quinntessa and be done with it?"

That gasbag Zaha apparently needed to take a breath, because he just waved at Tetzlaff to speak. The military general appealed to Tuplo and her other allies. "First of all, you act like Quinntessa is in Divinian space. Technically it is, but it's also in the Adirondacks Expanse. We are prohibited by treaty with the Dominion from sending warships in there."

To mocking laughter, Tetzlaff nodded her head. "Yes, I know we often break that rule. However, the more splinter Dominion groups *does* monitor us—as we monitor them—so we're very careful. Sending enough ships to fight off the regular Dominion and kill everything on a planet is bound to bring them running in full force. You've got to ask yourselves—should we start another full-fledged war with the Dominion over this threat? Before we're ready to annihilate them for once and for all. I think not."

The laughter faded, and they were finally listening to her. "As for the Dominion, we have a spy on their lead ship. We have a garrison of three hundred mobile infantry on the planet—we know exactly what the Dominion is doing. Like any do-gooders, they're committed to fighting the disease and ending the outbreak. That's a job that needs to be done, and we don't really have the stomach for it. According to our reports, they're maintaining the quarantine, keeping the Quinntessanites on the planet. Who knows? They might succeed. We can always crush them later."

"That's taking a terrible risk," warned Zaha, glowering darkly at Tetzlaff. "The Dominion regulars are unprincipled scoundrels who can't even be loyal to their former masters. If they get sick, they're just as likely to pull up stakes as remain there, spreading the disease elsewhere. After we all get the plague, we won't be able to punish you sufficiently."

There were grumbles of agreement after that remark, and Sub-Emperor Tuplo rose to his feet, waving down the others. "I believe my friend Tetzlaff is thinking rationally, but we can't be rational where this plague is concerned. We have to be *irrational*. We should muster enough ships in that region to make sure that the quarantine of Quinntessa holds."

The majority barked their agreement to this remark, and Tetzlaff could see the compromise forming. Tuplo hadn't gotten where he was by being a fool.

The Sub-Emperor lifted his chin confidently. "We must be ready to destroy the Dominion at a moment's notice, if they fail, but not so rashly that we alert more splinter Dominion groups. If we slowly assemble ships in the region, we'll eventually have enough to scorch the planet into dust and escape before splinter Dominion groups can react. Something that's done is history, not a threat."

There was polite applause at this remark, and Tuplo looked pointedly at Tetzlaff. "What do you say, friend?"

The slim general knew that she was the military governor and could do as she wished in the Adirondacks Expanse, until they replaced her. Tuplo was right. When people panicked by a plague—especially *this* plague—they did act irrationally. She could not be sure of holding her post if she failed to seize this compromise, and the compromise would at least buy her time. *I can justify it to myself, but can I justify it to my silent partner?*

Tetzlaff decided to deal with that later. Right now, the entire Adirondacks Expanse was close to slipping from her grip. "I believe that plan is doable," she said with a tight-lipped bow. "I'll begin to assemble ships already in the Adirondacks Expanse, and we'll send another warship through every day, disguised as a merchant ship. We'll use proximity to the ancient seven collapsed stars to mask our fleet."

Zaha scowled, not liking the fact that he hadn't gotten credit for the compromise. "I want a list of all the ships in this operation."

Tetzlaff nodded. "That list will be so highly classified that I will entrust it to the keeping of the Simmeria Command."

That should keep your grubby hands off it, she thought to herself.

"Tetzlaff is right," declared Tuplo, clasping his old comrade on the shoulder. "Every detail about this operation is highly classified. Breathe of it to no one, not even your closest mistress."

They all laughed, breaking the tension in the conference room. While the others congratulated themselves on their good sense, the sub-emperor whispered to the general, "I saved your ass this time."

"All the same," grumbled Tetzlaff, "I don't like people telling me how to do my job. I won't forget your interference."

She turned and stalked out of the conference room, thinking very little about Tuplo and all the self-important sub-emperors and generals. Tetzlaff was only worried about what she would tell her secret benefactor.

Nothing, she decided. If they could keep this operation hidden from the Dominion, and most of the Divinian Empire, perhaps they could keep it hidden from *him*. With any luck, the experiment would soon be over, and Quinntessa would be nothing but a distant, unpleasant memory.

James Rawlings came awake from what seemed a confused dream, which seemed to consist of a single image: that of the figure in a blue environmental suit, which had trained a phaser rifle on him and fired. James rolled over the wide, comfortable bed and pulled an armload of silky covers to his chest. Although it felt natural to remain asleep in this plush splendor, he suddenly realized that he wasn't supposed to be in a bed. He sat up and blinked at the blankets, his silky pajamas, and a large, tastefully appointed bedroom done mostly in white antiques. Sunshine streamed in through the French doors, as did the gentle sound of the surf pounding against the shore.

James scrambled out of bed, stepping onto cool, purple, rustic tiles. Atop a white armoire, he found a pile of clean clothes; a pair of calf-length brown boots stood on the floor. The clothes appeared to be of traditional Quinntessa design—blousy shirts with colourful stripes and braids, brocaded pants with flashy buttons and cuffs. Since he seemed to be alone in the bedroom, he stripped off his elegant pajamas and put on the bizarre clothing, which turned out to be warm, well made, and comfortable.

"Hello!" he shouted angrily. "What am I doing here?"

There was no response, except for a flurry of footsteps that sounded far off but quickly became louder. A moment later, the white door flew open, and Cordette stood there, looking very festive in her Quinntessanite ribbons and braids.

He gawked at her. "What's happened to us?"

"I don't know, James. I woke up in that bed, the same as you. You were still unconscious, so I just got dressed to have a look around."

James strode to the door and stared over her head at a sunny hallway that seemed to open into a large living room. "Where are we?"

"We seem to be in a beach house. I think that's what you would call this place." The small woman stepped aside to allow him to enter the hallway.

James rushed from room to room, almost thinking he was in a vacation resort on Atlantica. Every room was light and cheery, with comfortable if not sumptuous furnishings.

There were two bedrooms, a bathroom, a recreation room with exercise equipment and videoscreens, a compact but functional kitchen, and a living room; his grandfather would have called it a sitting room.

Charging back into the master bedroom, James brushed past Cordette and crossed to the French doors. He threw them open, stepped outside, and felt the sun-kissed, misty sea breeze strike his face. The sun was so bright that James had to shield his eyes, but he could tell that he was standing on a peach colored observation deck that commanded a view of a narrow orange beach and a few lichen-covered boulders. Beyond the boulders stretched a shiny sea that looked like saskatoon berry syrup with cream floating on top of it.

Cordette stepped onto the deck beside him. "What does it mean?"

"Let's think. The last thing I remember is that we were in that waiting room, talking to the little man—the hologram. Then something shot me in the back—"

Cordette nodded her head vigorously. Yes, it felt like a dart. We were probably drugged."

James scowled angrily. Before I passed out, I think I remember seeing somebody else...they were laughing."

"Who was it?"

He shook his head. "Someone in a blue environmental suit. But who knows, it could've been a hallucination...or another hologram. For all we know, *this* could be a hologram... one big holodeck."Cordette squinted into the bright sunlight. "Possibly, but there must be two thousand places on Quinntessa that actually look like this."

"That's true." James spotted some stairs going from the deck to the tiny beach, and he bounded down and leaped into the sand. Running, he circled the beach and jogged to the side of the house. To his surprise, the view was virtually identical in every direction—an endless horizon of sparkling ocean.

Off the front door of the house was a small landing pad and a rickety pier that went about eleven metres into a picturesque lagoon. Except for four palm trees, there was nothing else.

They were alone on a tiny tropical island.

James heard a shuffling sound, and he turned to see Cordette walking up behind him. Her step wasn't as energetic as usual, and he saw deep furrows on her smooth, brow.

"What's the matter?" he asked. "Your injury bothering you?"

She touched her hip. "No, not too much. I just feel a little weak...probably a side effect of the drug."

James nodded, gazing from the white beach house to the shimmering blue horizon. "I'd enjoy the view if we weren't stranded. I don't suppose it would do us any good, but we should search the house for a radio, flares, or anything we could use to signal for help."

"We should," agreed Cordette. "We'll also need food and water."

They returned to the house and soon found that food and water would be no problem. Fresh water ran freely from the facets, and the kitchen shelves were stocked with freeze-dried food in metallic bags. It was the kind of food that might be found in survival rations, but there was enough of it to keep them alive for several weeks.

The water pouring from the taps fascinated James, and he traced a pipe under the kitchen sink into the foundation of the house. Going outside, he found a water shut-off valve at the side of the house, and he probed the sandy ground with a stick to find the underground pipe. More investigation revealed that a large pipe lay submerged in the ocean only a couple of metres under the water. Both he and

Cordette decided that this pipe brought fresh water to the isolated isle.

It seemed like an awful lot of detail for a holodeck simulation, and they reached the grudging consensus that their island paradise was real.

James dragged two chairs onto the deck off the master bedroom, and they sat there and watched the morning sun rise higher in the sky. This helped them make a guess as to cardinal points, and James drew a compass in the sand with an arrow pointing north.

"Why are we here?" he finally asked. "I can guess how, but not why."

"We must have been spared for some reason," answered Cordette. "It would have been easy enough to kill us. If so, we're probably under observation."

James looked around at the multihued expanse of sea and sky. "Under observation? But how?"

"By long-range telescopes or scanners," she said, looking up. "Or maybe there's equipment in the dwelling."

James jumped to his feet and charged through the French door into the bedroom. Over the French provincial vanity table was a mirror, and there was another one in the bathroom. In fact, there was a large mirror in every room.

In the second bedroom, he grabbed the floor-length mirror and tried to yank it off the wall. An electric shook jolted through his body, and James flopped to the floor, twitching like a fish in the bottom of a boat. Cordette rushed into the room and wrapped her arms around him, and he could feel her trembling warmth. Despite the shock and disorientation, he soon stopped shaking, and his head began to clear.

A cheerful chuckle emanated from the doorway, and James twisted around to see the elf like doctor in his white lab coat. He clucked his tongue at them disapprovingly. "Please don't remove any of the furnishings. No, no. We only *rent* this house."

With a snarl, James charged toward the doctor then he stopped himself. "You're not real, are you?"

"Nonsense, I'm Dr. Johnson. Don't get insolent with me. Yes, yes, you are the subjects of an experiment, but it has to be done, don't you see? If we can get enough data on the disease this way, then we can spare all the Quinntessanites who aren't already infected. We can step back and let you save the planet. You'll be saving millions of lives by your cooperation."

"How do you know we'll contract the disease?" asked James.

The little man pointed a spotted finger at Cordette. "Because she already has it."

James felt as if he had been stabbed in the chest, and he turned to look at his wife. Her startled face went through three expressions: shock, anger, and a dawning realization. He remembered her injury, her recent lethargy, and the way she had been sleeping at odd hours.

"But she's been inoculated," protested James. "The same as I've been."

The grey-haired doctor scratched his goatish beard. "We were wondering about that. But her physiology has obviously been altered by what we call genetic drift and in fact we believe she's a clone of the original Takarain woman she's pretending to be. What about it, dear? Did that affect you somehow?"

Cordette lowered her head, and the young woman seemed to shrink into her eccentric clothes.

James didn't quite understand what this doctor was saying. But if his wife were a clone or not he would still defend her against this unruly hologram. "You don't have to answer him," said James.

Her voice quivered as she answered, "I'm sorry I never told you James. But I died when I was eleven or at least she died. Her family couldn't bare to live without her and so they made me which is a clone of her. But Takarain cloning is somewhat flawed and they told me that the process of it have given me a depressed immune system—it's a known side effect. What choice did I have but to live? This has always been the way with Takarain cloning techniques."

James tried to conceal his astonishment when Cordette flat out told him her secret. James had not been expecting a revelation of this sort at all, much less one, which suddenly shook the very foundation of his marriage. For James it was a lot to take in. Like a weird hazy nightmare, which would haunt him forever. His wife was a clone of the real Princess Cordette Chance of the royal family of Takara Prime. Correct that, the former royal family of Takara Prime. It shot through his soul like a star going supernova.

"Then you got injured," said the little man. "That was an intervention of fate; it introduced the disease directly into your circulatory system."

James snapped out of his dazed state. "But I'm not infected?" muttered James, hating himself for asking.

"No, Lieutenant. So far, the various Dominion precautions are working in your system, but I can't imagine it will take long, considering your constant, unprotected contact with the Takarain clone. How long it will take—that is a question of great interest to us. The two of you are almost perfect subjects for this test."

James could contain himself no longer, and he charged the pretentious little ogre. His entire body passed through the image standing in the doorway, and he crashed into the wall in the corridor.

The doctor reappeared to add, "Please behave normally toward the woman, just as you would toward any loved one." With a blip, he was gone.

James picked himself up from the floor and gazed determinedly at Cordette. "Listen, we will find a way out of here. All you need to do is go through the transporter biofilter."

"Within forty-eight hours," she said solemnly. "It's probably already been twenty-four hours. I'm more concerned about preventing *you* from contracting the disease."

Not knowing what else to do, James took a step toward her, and she motioned him back. "No, James! You have to protect yourself, even though it's probably too late. I'll be getting sicker and sicker, and you'll have to stay away from me."

"No, I have to get us out of here," promised James. "In time to save you."

Through the open window in the second bedroom, he caught sight of the blue silhouette of the ocean; it seemed as vast as space, stretching into the wavering horizon. Also through the window came the timeless crunch of the surf against their spit of land, wearing it down a few centimetres a year. Time hung heavily on this island, and freedom seemed eons away, in another galaxy.

It dawned on James that *time* was their new enemy.

CHAPTER TEN

IT WAS A QUIET moment for everyone present. Dr. Johnson and Dr. Cross were grinning, and Kajada, while not grinning, looked satisfied. The patient lying before them in the clean room enclosure was not sick but possessed two of the prions that caused the plague. If the third were present, they would combine to form the multiprion that brought on the full-scale infection. Pallas Tarr understood that much.

She had been on the bridge of the *Solaris*, scanning for James and Cordette, while running computer models for the researchers, when she was summoned to the cargo hold. The Dominion's equipment had meshed nicely with OSI's equipment to produce a state-of-the-art laboratory in a clean room enclosure, and now they had their first success. She could see the excitement among the others, but she wasn't quite sure of the reason.

She stared through the clear screen at the Quinntesaanite lying unconscious on the metal table. "Why is it such a good thing that this woman is almost sick?" she asked Kajada.

"Because she possesses a prion not previously seen in any of the other Kozakians we have examined," answered Kajada. "And her exact movements can be traced. She arrived on Kozak less than four weeks ago, before the quarantine, from a small continent known as Tanas. This continent lies west of Hajee, so it may be that the infection is spreading eastward."

Tarr looked with sympathy at the unconscious woman, thinking she looked mostly Sheelian, with her plump face and high forehead. "So we're off to this other continent?"

"Some of us are going there," answered Dr. Cross, a middle-aged woman who seldom smiled but was smiling now. "Dr. Johnson thinks it would be a good idea if you returned to Kozak with him."

"Why?"

"Pallas," said Dr. Johnson with grandfatherly patience, "Governor Opher was expecting you for dinner, and that was hours ago. It's now the middle of the night. He's been waiting a long time."

"But we've got so much to do—"

"The governor has complied with all of our requests," said Kajada. "We should comply with his. This mission has a diplomatic component, and devoting one person to that task is an acceptable use of resources. I would advise you to spend time with the governor and collect information."

"Fine," muttered Tarr, tapping her combadge. "Tarr to bridge."

"Ardelon here."

"Dr. Johnson wants me to go back to the planet with him and be diplomatic. I'm sorry, but I couldn't find any sign of Rawlings and Chance."

"OSI on Hajee is probably deserted," interjected Dr. Johnson. "People certainly went home to be with their constellations and families."

"Did you hear that?" asked Tarr.

"Yes, we'll keep looking," Ardelon assured them. "They've got to be down there somewhere. You go ahead and be charming, and try to get some sleep, too."

"Sleep? What's that?" Tarr strode onto the transporter platform and motioned to the grey-haired doctor to join her. "Dr. Johnson, let's go have dinner."

"I won't be joining you," he said with a twinkle in his eye. "I'm certain that Governor Opher won't mind."

Tarr nodded to the human on the controls. "Put us down in front of OSI."

A moment later, they materialized on the landing pad in front of the immense red pyramid and its protective walls. It was night, and a foggy chill engulfed Tarr and made her shiver. She glanced around, expecting the street to be deserted at this late hour, but several onlookers pressed forward, eager to get a look at her. A hovercraft parked on a side street suddenly rose into the air and cruised toward her.

"Good night, my dear!" called Dr. Johnson, as he bustled off to the entrance of the OSI complex.

A whooshing noise grabbed her attention, and she turned to see the hovercraft settle onto the landing pad. At the controls sat Governor Opher, beaming at her with his perfect teeth, cherry skin, and windblown red hair.

"They said I was crazy to wait out here, but I knew you would come back." He tempered his joy with a concerned frown. "How goes the battle?"

She walked over to the hovercraft and climbed inside. "The researchers seem happy—they've made a connection with Tanas as a possible origin point."

"You don't say? That's good news, is it?"

Tarr shook her head puzzledly. "I keep wondering. Why Quinntessa? Why now? It's awfully convenient."

"Convenient for whom? Certainly not us."

"For someone who didn't want much interference." Tarr shook her head. "Never mind. It will be good to eat something. Where are we going?"

"My home. The First Light Constellation." He lifted a box off the floor of the hovercraft and handed it to her, smiling awkwardly. "This is a gift, but it's actually not a gift. It's practical. It's unlikely you'll shed your uniform. If you wear this, you'll pass as one of us—in case we encounter Divinians."

She lifted the top of the box and was stunned to see what appeared to be a handwoven coat made of blazing yellow, purple, and red threads, woven together in a tapestry depicting island life. It was at once the most artistic and showy piece of clothing she had ever seen.

"Thanks. It wasn't necessary." She couldn't hand it back—the question was whether she would put it on. Wearing the fantastic robe, she would look like a queen from some old human fairy tale.

She had to confess, it was rather chilly on this foggy night. Not a star was visible in the gray sky, and the aquatic layer hung in the air like a damp mop. Tarr shivered, stood up, and put on the coat. The biological textiles were unexpectedly warm, yet lightweight, and the wrap flowed down to her knees like a purple waterfall.

"It's gorgeous," she said, realizing that for the first time.

"No, *you* are gorgeous," Opher corrected her. "The coat is merely a coat."

Pallas sat down, at unusual loss for words. "What's for dinner?"

"Anything you wish," answered Opher, working the controls. The hovercraft lifted gracefully off the pad and headed down the street. For some reason, Tarr was glad to get away from the imposing pyramid.

"We're mostly vegetarians," Opher continued. "And of course we eat seafood, but we have replicators if you desire *Earth meats such as beef,* or whatever."

Tarr bristled. "I don't eat *beef.*"

"Really." He piloted the open-air craft down a deserted paved street lined by stylish shops and charming dwellings, topped by elaborate walls and spacious balconies. Flowers and vines blossomed from a cornucopia of pots, boxes, and small plots, and their scents mingled and hung in the fog like incense. Some of the blossoms were so vivacious that they shined right through the fog. Tarr looked down at her flashy coat and realized where the muse came from.

In due course, they turned down a street lined with more stately homes—mansions surrounded by high walls. On this street, the fog reminded her of pictures of Earth in the twentieth century—places like Sydney, Australia and Boston, United States. It seemed like ambassadors row, with houses that were too impossibly grand for one person.

They stopped in front of an intricate wrought-iron gate, and a servant rushed from an alcove to open the door for her. Even before the hovercraft had settled to the ground, he was holding the door open and bowing halfway to the ground. After Tarr stepped down, the footman remained in this toadying position until Opher has also exited from the craft. She couldn't help but notice that the servant appeared to be full-blooded Nya.

"Any orders, sir?" asked the servant, staring at the ground.

"Go ahead and charge it up, Megill. I'm not going out again tonight."

"Yes, sir."

Tarr wanted to ask Megill how he had fallen to this lowly position in life, but she remembered that she was expected to be diplomatic. This had to be the one job in the universe for which she was least suited.

Opher placed his palm against a security scanner, and the gate swung open. He smiled warmly at Tarr and motioned her to place her hand on the scanner.

"Why should I be scanned?" she asked enquiringly.

"All guests need to register," he answered mildly.

Tarr nodded. "I see it makes sure I'm of mixed blood."

"Due to the late hour, you won't see the club at its finest," said Opher, ignoring her comment. "But there should be a few night hawks up at this hour, and hopefully we can roust a cook to make us a meal."

"I don't want to disturb anybody," she protested, imagining some poor servant being dragged out of bed to tend to her culinary needs.

"Our cooks would fight for the right to serve you," Opher assured her. To Pallas, that thought was more frightening than the idea that they would be forced to serve her.

They walked along a bucolic stone pathway that wandered through a garden bursting with blossoms and flowering vines. The perfume of the flowers was almost overpowering, and it mingled with the unmistakable scent of food—real food—cooking on a real oven.

"Do you see," said Opher with a smile, "they remembered you were coming. I wouldn't be surprised if the whole house stayed up to greet you."

Looming ahead of them in the fog was the mansion, which had to be five stories tall and two hundred metres wide. The elaborate building had giant columns, broad porticos, and balconies on every floor, and it was as large as most government buildings on Earth. The house was certainly big enough to house hundreds of people, not counting servants.

They ascended a wide stone staircase and passed between two massive columns. From the open door came the sounds of laughter and strange music played on a reedy string instrument, like a zither. A doorman bowed politely to them as they entered, and Tarr noticed that he was unique, not a uniblood. She realized what Opher had said about unibloods not even being allowed into the building. They needn't apply even as servants, unless they were content to park hovercraft.

They entered a foyer that was decorated with extravagant velvet furnishings, lamps with stained glass and tassels, and numerous hologram portraits morphing continuously on the walls. From the incredible array of faces on the ever-changing portraits, Pallas assumed they were past members of the First Light Constellation, going back hundreds of years.

Word of their arrival spread quickly through the luxurious club, and members began to emerge from various dining rooms and bars that opened onto the central foyer. They approached Tarr with admiration and delight on their faces, and the music and conversation faded away. Pallas wanted to crawl into a shell, or at least a dim engineering room. Instead she was wearing a coat that glittered like the sunrise, and dozens of Quinntessanites gathered around her, awe in their eyes.

"Yes, she is as striking as we heard!" proclaimed a tall dowager as she delicately approached Tarr. The older woman held out a clawed hand, and Pallas had no idea what her ancestry could be. Still she took the offered appendage, which seemed to be the expected thing to do. At least the other Quinntessanites murmured and nodded their approval.

"The First Light Constellation is greatly privileged," said the older woman with a reverential bow. The others applauded this statement with zest.

Opher stood behind her, beaming like a proud father. Tarr could not believe all this fuss and attention was for her, and she fought the temptation to laugh it off or make a spiteful comment. She had to be diplomatic, which meant bowing and smiling while several dozen strangers gushed over her.

We're risking our lives to save you people! she wanted to yell at them. *But you're hung up on the accidental circumstances of my birth.*

Mercifully, Opher put an arm around her shoulders and shepherded her through the crowd into a plush dining room. Waiters in red uniforms formed a line that led to the best table in the house, one, which overlooked a beautiful tile fountain. Tarr couldn't get over the feeling that she had stepped into a dream—one that wasn't even hers.

A waiter held her chair for her, and she sat down quickly. At last, the other diners returned to their tables, as if it were proper to resume their social gathering now that the royalty had been seated.

Opher looked at her, amusement and pride on his handsome face. "You really didn't expect this, did you?"

"Are you kidding?" she whispered. "Most places I go, I get shot at."

Opher looked shocked. "Well, not here. Not on Kozak or anywhere on Quinntessa. Here, you will always be special—the ideal of uniqueness." He glanced at a server, who was instantly at his side.

"Blood wine?" asked the waiter.

Tarr scowled, thinking that the worst thing about being half-Reptilian was that she was expected to like Reptilian cuisine. "Just water."

"Two waters!" ordered Opher domineeringly. "And bring us the fresh fish appetizers."

"As you wish, Governor," said the waiter, stealing a glance at Pallas before he hurried away.

Opher stared at her and smiled with undisguised pleasure. "I'm certainly glad you came to Kozak first, and not some other continent. Or else we might have lost you."

Tarr scowled. "I'm not something to be won or lost."

"Of course not! I didn't mean that. I only meant that some other continent could have gotten the chance to woo you, and we might have been deprived of your presence."

She shook her head with disbelief. "Wake up and realize that there's a plague devastating half this planet! And you're worried about whether I like it here or somewhere else!"

"Death and sickness come and go," said Opher, "but a uniqueness like yours has not been seen in centuries. Since your arrival, our morale couldn't be higher—it's as if we have seen perfection."

"I'm far from perfect."

"Not in our minds," said Opher, reaching across the table and taking her hand. She didn't pull away, only because it seemed cruel to be mean to someone who worshipped her. "We trust in your people and the OSI to neutralize the disease, which means that this day will mainly be remembered for your arrival."

The waiter arrived with two glasses of ice water and a steaming dish full of fresh seafood morsels. Tarr had to acknowledge that the smell of real food caused her taste buds to water, and her resistance began to break down a little.

Following Opher's example, she speared a morsel with a silver needle and popped it into her mouth. As soon as she tasted the delicacy, expertly cooked in a rich cream sauce, she knew that she wasn't going anywhere for a while—not until her stomach was good and full.

"This could be your life," said Opher, "every single day. You would certainly be elected to the Canyon Constellation, but your duties could be light. Or full, as you wish."

Despite her good intentions, Pallas laughed out loud. "Are you telling me that, even though I just got here, you would make me a leader?"

"You already are my leader," answered Opher, his black eyes sparkling with sincerity. "I'll gladly spend the rest of my life at your feet, and I won't rest until I convince you to stay."

"Wait a minute. You just *met me*, and you're asking me to *marry* you?"

"Not exactly," answered the governor. "I'm asking you to have a child with me and join the First Light Constellation, yes. If you wished to stay with me in a matrimonial arrangement, I wouldn't resist, but I don't believe in monogamy."

Pallas chuckled as she speared another delicious tidbit. "What if I don't want to have children right now?"

"Oh, you wouldn't actually carry and bear children—that would be beneath you. For that, we would use surrogates."

"Surrogates?"

Opher nodded and looked around the graceful dining room. About a third of the tables were occupied, and all of the diners were clandestinely watching them. He only had to point to a tall, blue-skinned woman with a plume of pink hair for her to stand up and strut over to their table. Tarr didn't know exactly why, but this woman reminded her of the women of easy righteousness who followed the Reptilian fleets. Then he pointed to a less tall, red-skinned woman with a plume of green hair and she followed in a sashay after the first woman towards their table.

"Pallas, this is Alekos and Thetys who work as surrogates. The four of us could bond tonight, if you wish. My quarters are large enough."

"I would like that," Alekos assured her in a husky voice.

"I'd enjoy mating with you," said Thetys as she lightly touched Tarr's shoulder.

Tarr blinked at the three of them, realizing that she had just been propositioned for a foursome. Or had she? "Wait a minute. Your idea of a first date is for all four of us to sleep together?"

"The sex isn't really necessary, of course," answered Opher, "but I enjoy interspecies sex. The more bizarre the better! I think I would especially enjoy it with you. The surrogates extract our eggs and sperm through a bonding process that's quite harmless I assure you. Alekos and Thetys, or any other surrogates of your choosing, would carry our babies to fruition. We could raise the children together, or you could be the donor, or I the donor. It wouldn't matter to me, as long as we created healthy offspring."

He smiled warmly at her. "The physical bonding is necessary for conception inside the surrogates."

Only hunger and curiosity kept Pallas from dashing out the door. "I think I need more food. I'm flattered, but I've got to tell you...you move a little fast for me."

"As you point out, we may not have that much time." Opher shrugged and picked up his glass of water. "I could recommend the *shark fin steaks*, which I understand is a human dish."

"I recommend that, too," said Alekos, staring blankly into the crowd of people.

"So you have babies for a living?" asked Tarr informally.

"Yes, and you fight everybody."

Pallas picked up her glass of water. "Well, they're both dirty jobs, but somebody has to do them."

"Pardon me," said Alekos, bowing her head. "I'm not myself tonight. Yes, I'm a surrogate. I've been taking a year off, but I might cut that short for Opher and yourself. Excuse me, I...have to be somewhere." The statuesque Quinntessanite dashed from the table and out of the room, into an adjoining café. Thetys followed after her but at a slower walk.

Opher looked embarrassed, then regretful. "It hasn't been easy to maintain a standard of courtesy under these circumstances. I suppose you could say we're not coping all that well."

Tarr looked around at the sociable dining hall, with its holograms, potted plants, antique lamps, handwoven tablecloths, velvet booths, and plush chairs. Several happy diners smiled back at her, and she had to remind herself that it was the equivalent of three o'clock in the morning. "I think you're coping quite well."

"Do you feel at home?" he asked hopefully.

"No," said Pallas with a smile. "But I'm a drifter—I don't feel at home anywhere. One of the ways to my hearts is through my stomach, though. So impress me."

In the beach house, James stepped back and surveyed the large mirror on the wall of the second bedroom. He had given Cordette the master bedroom, because it was cheerier, with its big windows and deck. She was sleeping, because they both wanted her to conserve her strength for their escape attempt, whenever it came. James tried to tell himself that the inoculations were supposed to delay the worst symptoms, too, but he had seen too much suffering on Hajee. Once the disease took hold, the onslaught was swift and sure.

At least Cordette was resting and eating. She seemed to enjoy the fish broth, and they had plenty of that in their reserves.

He sighed and looked back at the mirror, which he planned to demolish in order to reach the circuits contained inside. If it was transmitting *out*, maybe there was a way to use the transmitter to signal Ardelon. James knew enough not to touch the mirror again, and he didn't want to attack it at close range. That last jolt had almost killed him—but not quite. There was a chance that its defenses were programmed to become even more lethal with repeat attacks.

So James stood in a corner of the room with a pile of rocks of various sizes, gathered from the beach and tide pools. Near him was an open window, which was his quickest escape route. It was essential to find out what the mirror was hiding, especially if it was a panel of holodeck controls. James picked up a watermelon-sized rock and hefted it, deciding he had better aim for a corner.

He reared back and threw the rock into the full-length mirror, only his aim was a bit off. It struck more toward the upper center, and the mirror shattered a microsecond before it erupted in a gaseous explosion. James dove out the window into a thicket of sand and scraggly bushes just as a wave of heat blistered the windowpanes.

When he lifted his head from the sand, he saw choking black smoke billowing from the window, and he heard a shout. "James! What happened?"

James ran around to the back of the house, where Cordette was standing on the deck, looking frail and worried. She clutched a blanket around her trembling shoulders, as black smoke wafted over the house, contrasting sharply with the seamless blue sky.

"I was looking at the mirror again," explained James.

"By setting the house on fire?"

"Let's see what I did." James climbed the stairs to the deck and entered the master bedroom. He stalked across the tile to the bedroom door and felt it with his hand before opening it; there was a bit of heat but not much.

When he opened the door, smoke billowed in, and James spent several seconds coughing and rubbing his burning eyes. But a draft blew most of the smoke out the French doors into the crystal sky, and he was able to enter the hallway. Reaching the second bedroom, he glanced vigilantly around the edge of the door.

The room lay in ruins—blackened with chunks of glass and some kind of mucky brown residue that covered everything. Nothing was burning. Where the mirror had been fixed on the wall, there was only a rectangular hole, filled with melted residue, shattered glass, and chunks of scorched building material.

"You're not going to be able to tell much from *that*," said a voice behind him. He turned to see Cordette, keeping her distance.

"No, said James dolefully. He stepped into the room and kicked at a pile of debris on the floor. "I've never seen a mirror self-destruct. Have you?"

Cordette coughed and leaned against the wall. "Do you have a Plan B?"

"Yes," he answered with determination. "We're going to build a raft with a sail."

"From what?"

"Actually, the raft is already built—it's that small pier out front. If we need more stability, we can lash together some of these doors. I'll look for a pole to use as a mast, and you can gather sheets, blankets, curtains—anything we can use for sails."

Cordette grimaced and shook her head. "You'll be stuck with me...in the middle of an ocean. It might take days or weeks to reach a port. I can't go with you, James. You have to try to save yourself—while you're still healthy."

"Nonsense," James answered with an encouraging smile. "We got into this mess together, and we're going to get out together. If you feel weak, I'll do the work. We also have to pack food and water. I'd better get started."

As he strode down the hall, Cordette called after him, "James!"

"Yes?"

"Thank you." The young woman couldn't smile, but her dark green eyes glittered warmly.

"Thank me when I get you back to the ship." James kept a smile on his face until he had stepped outside into the warm sunshine, then he frowned bleakly. Cordette's skin looked as pale as the white beach house, and it had begun to peel on her face and arms. He had no idea what that meant, but it couldn't be good.

James' frown deepened as he strode toward the small pier. Cordette was a young woman, just starting to find her own place since her family had been assassinated and her royal title denounced, and he'd had no business involving her in this madness. True, she had volunteered—but without his personal problems, maybe he wouldn't have agreed to this foolhardy mission. If he hadn't said yes to the Dominion, Cordette wouldn't be here—it was as simple as that. All those pretentious ideas about helping people and saving lives, and now he couldn't even save himself and his wife.

He would have liked to blame Ardelon and the Dominion, but what were they but a reflection of him? Were any of them really out to save the Adirondacks Expanse—or just give some meaning to their misguided lives? James Rawlings gave a cynical laugh as he stood watching the rickety pier float on the creamy water. Somehow he always knew he would die alone, at the end of a pier to nowhere.

CHAPTER ELEVEN

PALLAS TARR WHEEZEED when she sat up in bed and saw the size and wealthy luxury of her guest room inside the First Light Constellation. She had seen it the night before in dim light as she staggered into bed in a food-induced coma. Good food was not on the list of perks for a guerrilla freedom fighter, and she had taken advantage of Opher and the First Light Constellation. If the governor had thought he was going to take advantage of her, however, he soon realized it wasn't going to happen.

Seen by the golden light of dawn, the pearl-lustre furnishings and pastel drapes and cushions were tasteful and refined. Intricate montages decorated the walls, made, from plants, shells, and found objects that must have been gathered locally. Shiny-pink flowers blossomed from there vases, giving the soft colors of the room a vibrant distinction. It was certainly the nicest room Tarr had ever slept in, which wasn't saying that much, she decided.

She staggered out of bed, still wearing the bravura coat Opher had given her. Several suits of Quinntessanite clothing lay spread on the vanity table, as if awaiting her approval. A gold tray of fruit, toast, and tea graced a flowing desk. Pallas had to ignore these offerings for the moment, as she fumbled under her coat for her combadge.

She finally found it. "Tarr to *Solaris*."

"This is Vantika on the bridge," came a friendly voice. "We wondered what had happened to you, but Opher assured us you were okay."

"I was definitely okay," mumbled Tarr, suppressing a burp that would do any Reptilian proud. "I got wined and dined last night, and you ought to see this room they put me in."

"I haven't seen Governor Opher," added Vantika with cheerfulness in her voice, "but I hear he's really something."

"Yeah, yeah, very handsome, and he treats me like a queen. Well for the most part. Where's the captain?"

"He's due to wake up in a few minutes. Is it an emergency?"

"No," said Tarr, glancing around at her luxurious surroundings and the pot of steaming tea. "I'm just checking in."

"Ardelon said you should stay on duty there, and help the governor as best you can. Kajada is going down to OSI in a few minutes, and Cross is on the continent of Tanas, tracking down that lead. The clinic in Hajee is busy, but it's tapering off."

"What about Rawlings and Chance?"

"No sign of them," replied Vantika. "We're still looking, but there's a growing fear that maybe a Divinian patrol got them."

Tarr scowled. "We know they were going to the OSI on Hajee, right?"

"But it was deserted. Even Dr. Johnson says the workers there were probably sent home. Rawlings reported some Divinians operating under the cover of this Horrell Coalition on foot around OSI in Hajee, but since they've basically left us alone, we don't want to start something on a hunch."

"Those two picked a bad place to disappear," griped Tarr. "I'll check in later. Out."

As she rifled through the pile of clothing, looking for something at least slightly subdued, Tarr heard strains of music come wafting through the open window. At first she thought it was instrumental music from some electronic device, but then she realized it was singing—a choir. A smidgen of applause and laughter told her it wasn't a recording but live music.

Tarr crossed to the window and peered into the courtyard of the First Light Constellation. Befitting the name of their lodge, forty or fifty people were gathered around the fountain in the courtyard to great the dawn. When Tarr opened the window to get a better look, several of them caught sight of her. At once, there was a flurry of activity as the chorus formed ranks and came to attention, all-staring at her.

Uncomfortable with all the attention, Pallas almost ducked out of sight. Then they began singing. Their voices floated upward like an orchestra of horns and strings, an intricate arrangement of soaring harmonies covering half-a-dozen octaves. Passers by gathered in the courtyard to listen, but the concert was directed only toward Pallas in a display of admiration and affection. These people were complete strangers to her, but they seemed to adore her.

So I'm going to wake up and be serenaded, she thought. *My duties can't get any more bizarre than this.* Despite the beauty of the music and the soft voices, Tarr wanted to blend into the crowd—she didn't want to be the object of a command performance.

She looked for Opher in the crowd and found him lurking off to the side, under a tree. He was dressed in his finest stripes and ruffles. Upon seeing her looking at him, he bowed rather like a jester and motioned toward the choir. *Yes, they are magnificent,* agreed Pallas, and she couldn't help but to flash him a smile. At this, the chorus seemed to sing all the louder and lustier.

These aren't people about to die! she thought with a pang of fear. *They can't be, not people as lively and ecstatic as these. Surely they are right—the plague must be happening someplace else, to someone else.*

Clutching a computer pad in one hand and a case of isolinear chips in the other, Kajada materialized on the street outside the OSI building in Xifo. He looked up at the red pyramid, uncertain as to why such an imposing structure was actually needed. His brief ventures into the complex had led him to believe that most of the OSI facility was housed underground, not in the pretentious pyramid.

In most of their buildings and dwellings, the Quinntessanites showed acceptable restraint and taste, but this complex was grandiose for no apparent reason. Its only functions seemed to be to impress the locals and serve as a landmark, and Kajada preferred structural design that was more practical. According to Lieutenant Rawlings report on Hajee, the pyramid probably contained a defense system with a beamed weapon, but even that seemed unworthy of the massive structure and its impressive shielding.

The loss of Rawlings and Chance was troubling, not only because every person was needed, but also because they weren't actually Dominion. In reality, Kajada decided, having only two people missing in this entire operation was an accomplishment. Still, that didn't prevent him from regretting the loss of two young officers who didn't deserve this fate.

"Sir! Mr. Kajada!" called a voice.

Kajada whirled around to see a Bolaa rushing toward him from a storefront across the street. There could be no mistaking those mammoth ears, uneven teeth, and bald skull—he was a full-blooded Bolaa. As he crossed the street, he looked in every direction, as if worried about being followed. But there were few Quinntessanites on the street at this early hour of the morning, and no one seemed to be paying any attention to them. Instead of approaching Kajada, he jumped behind a tree trunk and motioned him over. Kajada complied.

With his silver-brocaded vest, sashes, jewelry, and bright trousers, the Bolaa's apparel rivalled a Quinntessanites in showiness.

"Thank you...thank you for seeing me," he wheezed, out of breath. "Someone who works in the OSI complex told me your name. I knew you would come back here eventually. My name is Kep. This isn't a very good place to talk—why don't you come with me to the Zoran Constellation? It's not far."

"I have business inside," answered Kajada, pointing to the pyramid.

"Anything you do in there would be a waste of time. Come with me instead. You'll learn more."

When Kajada considered this request, he remembered that he had been scheduled to dine at the Zoran Constellation the night before, but hadn't kept his appointment. Information gathering was part of his mission and their efforts to stem the disease were proceeding as planned. He could spare a few minutes for this Bolaa.

"Very well," answered Kajada. "I will accompany you."

The nervous Bolaa grabbed his arm and spirited him down a side street. "My name is Kep...oh, I already said that. You're Kajada if I'm not mistaken?"

"That's right. Why are you so anxious?"

Kep gave a sour laugh. "Why am I so anxious? Oh, nothing to be anxious about—ship destroyed, profits gone, stuck on a plague-ridden pesthole, surrounded by Divinians! On top of that, I'm forced to deal with the Dominion, of all people. What's to be anxious about?"

"Others have the same situation as yours. But be thankful that you are not on Hajee." Kajada continued walking down the narrow street, and the Bolaa had to hurry to keep up with his long strides.

"I'm *grateful*, I really am! Hey, I'm risking my life to see you, and I didn't do it just to complain." Kep looked around the deserted street; the heavy dew of the sea still clung to the lampposts and wrought-iron railings. Choral singing lilted over the rooftops from somewhere in the quiet city, as dawn nudged over the buildings and stole down the streets.

"About five weeks ago, I brought some laboratory supplies here," whispered the Bolaa. "I didn't know I was going to get *stuck* here because of it."

Kajada tilted his head and replied softly, "Are you saying that you know who infected this planet?"

The Bolaa smiled, showing a row of crooked teeth; he grabbed Kajada's arm and steered him toward a row of hedges that ran along the sidewalk. "We Bolaa are businessmen—it would insult our heritage if I were to give you valuable information without getting something in return."

"What do you want?"

"I wish to get off this blasted planet!" he nearly shouted. "You've got a ship—you could take me!"

"None of us are leaving until this plague is under control."

"Yes, but it's safer up there, isn't it?" The Bolaa pointed into the gray sky. "The transporters cure you, or so I've heard."

"The best I could offer is to take you aboard our ship and let you speak with our captain. It's not a cure, but a trip through our transporter is effective during a certain stage of the disease. You could always be reinfected."

Kep's scrawny shoulders slumped. "So it's hopeless. We're all stuck here...for the long haul.

Kajada stopped abruptly and drilled the Bolaa with ebony eyes. "If you know who started this deadly disease, it is your duty to tell us. It could help save the population and the planet, and bring the doers to justice."

"I only dealt with a consortium," mumbled the Bolaa. "Knowing them, I doubt if they even knew who the customer was. The people who removed the cargo were wearing environmental suits—I didn't get a good look at them."

"Then you have no information," said Kajada snappily.

"I do so," inhaled the Bolaa. "I'll tell you something that none of the Quinntessanites will ever tell you. They're so image-conscious—they always keep up appearances no matter what horrible things are happening under the surface."

Kep took the tall human's elbow and steered him down the street, their shoes scuffing the old-fashioned cobblestones. "There's a war being waged on this planet, and I don't mean between the Dominion and the Divinian Empire, or between the doctors and the plague."

He looked around and stopped, waiting until a small bird fluttered from under a shrub and flew away. He breathed heavily and continued, "For centuries, the Organziation of Species Improvement has controlled the Quinntessanites' reproductive functions, but OSI has gotten too big and greedy. In some places, they put in holographic doctors instead of real ones—things like that. So a few years ago, some wealthy Quinntessanites formed competing companies to do the same work—making hybrids."

Walking once again, the Bolaa continued to glance over his shoulder and around corners. But they seemed to be alone. The air was empty of sounds except for the occasional creak on a balcony. "The competition has been brutal," he whispered, "sometimes resulting in industrial sabotage—if you get my drift."

Kajada raised an eyebrow. "Are you saying this plague may be the result of industrial sabotage?"

"Well, it has effectively crippled OSI—they're not the monopoly they used to be. I'd heard that a few of the smaller companies had gotten together to pull a dirty trick on them. When somebody has a monopoly on reproduction, sometimes competitors will do almost anything to get rid of them."

"If you think about it, the local companies will probably survive this outbreak, but OSI has gotten swamped by plague victims. Most of their facilities are closed, and their operations are shut down. Worse yet, they've had to open their doors to the Dominion and people from outside. Believe me, OSI is the picture of egotism, and they wouldn't be talking to *you* unless they were desperate."

Kajada nodded, recognizing an accurate observation. He quickened his pace, a feeling of urgency taking charge of him. "We believe the disease is genetically engineered."

"And who better to do that than genetic engineers?" Kep frowned and kicked a stone in the street. It skittered into the gutter. "I should've gotten off Quinntessa when I had the chance, but they've got the only good restaurants in the Adirondacks Expanse! Even though I'd heard there was a disease on Hajee, I didn't think anything of it. Then *boom!* Without warning, that big Divinian freighter blasted my ship out of orbit, killing my whole crew. We were told the freighter was a *hospital* ship, for heaven's sake! I'm so glad you shot them down. Luckily for me, I was down here, negotiating a return cargo."

"I'm sorry," said Kajada, abruptly stopping. "I could not enjoy a relaxed meal with this knowledge. I have to act on it."

"But you've got to be my guest at the Zoran Constellation!" insisted Kep. "Later tonight. Please! It would get me more credit. The lodge is right around the corner on Zoran Lane. Just come in and ask for me—Kep."

"I will try to make it," vowed Kajada with a bow. "You have been most helpful. If the captain wishes to speak with you, I presume you are staying at the Zoran Constellation."

"As long as I can afford to," mumbled the Bolaa. "Of course, in these times, who worries about pilling up credit?"

"Indeed." Kajada turned in the other direction.

"And please, bring your captain, too. He's uniblood human, right? And remember, I gave you something for free. You owe me."

As Kajada strode rapidly down the sidewalk toward OSI, it all began to appear very logical. The outbreak could have been a dirty trick gone askew, or even an accident. He had to verify Kep's information and find out who controlled these smaller genetic companies.

He tapped his combadge. "Kajada to *Solaris*."

"Bridge here," came the reply. "This is Vantika."

"Is the captain on the bridge?"

He could hear the bristle in Vantika's voice, as she responded, "No, he's not. Can I help you?"

Kajada ignored her annoyance and pressed on. "When precisely will he return?"

"I couldn't say exactly. He has rented a glider. We think that gliders may be the best way to look for Rawlings, because the Divinians don't usually fire on them."

"You're alone on the bridge?"

"Yes, and I kinda like it that way. Want to leave a message?"

"Please hail me when he returns. Kajada out." He continued walking along the street, but he was suddenly conscious of movement on a roof four stories above him. He whirled around to see something duck into the shadow of a large vent. Kajada couldn't be sure what he had seen, or if he had seen anything at all. A curtain in a balcony window moved—perhaps that was what had distracted him.

Except for a few lemurlike primates in the rural areas, Kajada hadn't seen any animals running loose on Quinntessa. He wondered whether a few of those primates sneaked into the city at night, to go through garbage and whatnot. On the other hand, there could be people observing him. The doers of this calamity were still at large, according to Kep. Kajada walked more quickly, keeping an eye on roofs, balconies, and windows, and his hand didn't stray far from the butt of his phaser pistol.

He tapped his combage. "Kajada to Tarr."

"Hello, Kajada," she said, her voice lifting, as if coming off a laugh.

"I'm sorry to bother you, but I have some important information to verify, and the captain is unavailable. I would prefer not to investigate alone."

"Give me a few minutes, and I'll be there. Where?"

"The OSI building in Xifo."

Ardelon beamed with delight as the sea-glider under his command soared over endless ocean, which looked like blue enamel rimmed in gold from the morning sun. The sun was so bright that it stung his eyes, and the sky looked as endless as space. Ardelon had flown many crafts in his varied career, but never one so responsive and natural. Gliding with the wind made him feel at one with the elements, and the brush of the wind against the fragile hull was like a gentle drumbeat. He glanced at the compass and shook his head. It was hard not to get distracted by the beauty.

Lining up his wings with the horizon to keep level, Ardelon edged the antigrav lever upward. He knew that powerful and sophisticated gravity suppressors were working in the underbelly of the glider, but to him it felt as though a sudden draft had caught his wings and lifted him upward. Since he usually worked in artificial gravity, trying to avoid the problems of weightlessness, it seemed strange to seek safety in weightlessness. The farther he rose above the ocean, the more his sense of wonderment increased.

When the sea below him began to ripple past like a cascading waterfall, Ardelon sat back and relaxed. It felt as if he were standing still, not moving at all, but he had to look at the sky to keep from becoming disoriented.

He stared into the glittering horizon. He could understand why they were so popular. Not only were they practical transportation, but also they kept adventurous, young Quinntessanites at home rather than exploring outer space.

Ardelon checked the sensors, but they were designed to search vertically for wind currents, not horizontally for lifesigns. He had navigation and weather casting tools, but he already knew the weather around Hajee was delightful, as he flew by dead calculation. And so Ardelon used his eyes to survey the coastline, picking out the carved bays, green bluffs, white cities, and copper beaches from a distance.

Harnessing the wind, Ardelon masterfully guided the glider into a low approach that took him directly over the nearest cityscape.

As he swooped over a sparkling bay, which sheltered a few sea-gliders and sailboats, Ardelon felt like a seagull coming home after a long flight. Only this was a home that was too quiet, too heavenly—the noisy flock had moved on. As he flew deeper into the city, the sight of the empty streets, silent buildings, and deserted courtyards gave him a sudden fear. He didn't know this place or its people, but he could feel their restless ghosts walking beneath him.

In a thousand years, this place would be like a ghost planet and no one would know what had happened to its people, only that they were gone forever. Ardelon could see the red pyramid in the distance, looking alien among the traditional town houses and decorative buildings.

He wished he had told Rawlings to stay away from the place, but so many operations were going on at once that it was hard to anticipate the risks. Rawlings had been certain there was information to be gathered here, so Ardelon had let him come back, even after they had scarcely escaped the first time. Now it was probably too late to do anything to help them. No matter how many ways he justified it he had lost the one member of his crew who could make a big difference in their struggle with the Divinian Empire.

His troubled trance broken, Ardelon leaned to the right to view the pyramid as he swooped past. The ruby like pyramid was impressive, but it couldn't overcome the gloomy pall of the abandoned city. It was like the biggest tombstone in a dark cemetery.

He checked his compass.

In a slow bank, the glider came around to catch an air current that took him by the south side of the oval complex. Ardelon spotted the landing pad outside the south gate, as well as the wreckage mentioned by James. A moment later, he overshot the pyramid and had to dip lower to catch a current that took him by the east wall.

On this pass, Ardelon spotted movement on the street adjacent to the complex. Looking closer, he spotted two black-garbed figures moving equipment into a decrepit building. Glancing the other way, he thought he saw a hole in the east wall of the complex, but he soared past before he could tell for certain.

Ardelon scowled. He knew he shouldn't push his luck with the Divinians. He recognized those launchers they had and they could shoot him out of the sky in a microsecond. James had pushed his luck, and now James was gone. He shoved the antigrav lever upward, and the glider soared high above the pyramid. Ardelon couldn't tell which he was more eager to put behind him: the Divinians or Hajee itself.

That's what I have to do with Rawlings, he finally told himself, *put him behind me*. As he sped away, Ardelon stole a fleeting look at the dead city and wondered whether any of them would get off this planet alive.

Only a hundred kilometres beyond the northern coast of the continent of Azzopardi, James Rawlings swayed uneasily on the deck of the raft he had strung together from doors and the strongest planks he could find on the small pier. Dusk was blanketing the glistening sea, and he feared launching and sailing into the darkness, but he was anxious to test his new craft, with its single mast and sail.

He glanced back toward the house and could see Cordette seated by the front door, wrapped in a blanket. It was hard to tell if she was even awake. The young woman had been watching his progress out of support for his plan, although she hadn't been able to help much. James still entertained the thought of taking her with him, but it seemed more unlikely with every passing minute. How long would it take them to sail this raft to land? Days? Weeks? That is, if they were wildly lucky and made it at all.

James knew, unless they did something quickly, it would be too late to save Cordette. Even if they were rescued or escaped, she would be too sick for the transporter to help her.

"I'm trying her out!" he yelled. In the murky dusk, he thought he saw Cordette wave back.

James checked his rigging, made from curtain cords then he cast off from the dock and unfolded his sail, made from the curtain. To his amazement, the wind grabbed the sturdy curtain and dragged him across a stretch of jerky surf. The planks and doors shuddered under his feet, but the raft held together for the first few metres of its maiden voyage.

Three minutes later, he was about sixty metres offshore, where the water was considerably calmer and deeper. Out here, James figured he could make decent speed, and he was filled with a scatter-brained sense of achievement. Maybe there really was hope for them to escape. They would be slaves of the wind, forced to go where it led them, but that was better than sitting ashore waiting to die.

His bliss was cut short by a sudden jolt that nearly pitched him overboard. James gazed over the side, thinking he had struck a sandbar. When he realized there were dark shapes—huge shapes—moving just under the surface of the water, he got down on his hands and knees for better balance.

Not a moment too soon, as his fragile raft was jarred again, and three planks of wood shattered. This time, he got a glimpse of an elephantine trunk and a spiny fin attached to a huge black form that slid across the water like an oil slick. Maybe these marine creatures were just being playful, he hoped, although this kind of play could have him swimming back to shore.

Suddenly one of the creatures rose out of the water and tried to board his raft, smashing it in half and nearly swamping James. He clung to the mast to keep from plunging into the cool, salty brine, and this time he got a close look at the monster before it eased back into the water. It was shaped like a lumbering manatee, but it had a mouth like a lamprey, with rows of jewel-like teeth glittering in its round, sucker-shaped mouth. The giant leech slid back into the water with a final grin, as if to say that dinner looked delicious.

Water sloshed over the sides of the raft, and the creatures began to swim in frenzy. Without thinking, James began calling for help.

He quickly realized how pointless that was, because his shouts only agitated the nightmarish shark things squirming under his raft. They were large as walruses, but sleek, with sucker mouths ringed by rows of teeth. In their agitation they no longer had the will for concentrated attack, but they smashed and jarred the raft until it was little more than a bundle of driftwood tied together.

James snapped off his mast and used it as a spear to ward off the beasts, although that had little effect. As the raft broke apart, he curled up on a last door, hoping he would drown before the giant lampreys mauled him to death.

From the shore, James heard a disharmony of sounds: high-pitched screams, piercing tongue tweets, and the frenzied slapping of water. He turned to see Cordette, about fifty metres away, standing in the lagoon hip deep in water, making a terrific racket. She ducked her head under the waves, while she continued to slap the surface, and James figured she was shrieking underwater.

Whatever she was doing, it was working, as the huge lampreys peeled off one by one to slither in her direction. James wanted to shout to her to watch out, but she had to know what she was doing. He quickly grabbed a good-sized plank and used it as an oar to row the door like a boat. He was very careful to ease his oar gently in the water, realizing that movement and sound attracted the creatures. Fortunately, he couldn't compete with the unearthly racket that Cordette was making.

He watched nervously as she flailed in the water, attracting certain death. "Get out! Get out!" he yelled at her. She managed to crawl out onto what was left of the pier just as black waves roiled under the waters of the quiet lagoon.

James lifted his oar out of the water, realizing that he had to be still. But Cordette dragged herself to a spot on the west side of the island and began to create her diversion all over again. With darkness fast approaching, he could no longer see the awful creatures, so he just kept rowing—slowly, calmly—toward the beach. Incoming waves picked up the door and propelled him the last twenty metres, until he fell off in the surf and staggered onto shore.

"Cordette! Cordette!" he called, stomping through the wet sand.

He found her, lying unconscious in the damp marshes near the lagoon. She was soaking wet, her frail body wracked with shivers and burning with fever. James picked her up and carried her into the house. He carefully undressed her, dried her, and laid her in her bed. After cleaning up the room, he stood by the French doors, alternately watching Cordette and the triple moons float on the dark sea.

"James!" came a hoarse voice.

He rushed to her side. "Are you all right? Can I get you anything?"

"Some broth, in a while," she whispered. "But first, I have a request."

"Anything."

"When I die, please feed my body to those creatures."

"What?" asked James, in shock.

"Like most Takarains, I believe in renewal. So give my body to the sea creatures...they can benefit from my death.

Don't worry, I heard the doctors say that the animal life is unaffected by the plague."

"You're not going to die," said James without much conviction.

"You're a bad liar, James," she rasped, her voice degenerating into a ragged cough. When she recovered slightly, she added, "It's my last request."

"You won't—" He stopped. "What do you want me to do?"

Her rheumy eyes looked sick but oddly peaceful. James looked down, unable to say anything for the lump in his throat. Finally he croaked, "You saved my life...I want—" He tried, but he couldn't get more words out of his mouth.

"I know." She nodded her head weakly. "There is one thing I want you to know. I love you with all my heart."

James laughed in spite of himself. "I don't care that you're a clone! I love you with all my heart too. And you've lived a life that for the most part you could have only chose. You married *me*. And married we'll be until your *end*. Now I got to tell you a story. If you think this is a mess, wait till you hear about what happened to me five years ago—"

CHAPTER TWELVE

PALLAS TARR AND TY KAJADA stood outside the gleaming metal door in the southern gate of the OSI complex on Xifo. She was literally stamping her foot, because they had been waiting here for twenty minutes—with no response to their presence. It didn't seem as if the powers within would ever recognize them and let them enter. Kajada stood calmly at attention, aggravating her impatience even more.

"Let me go get Opher," she mumbled. "Maybe *he* can get them to let us in."

"The fact that they are avoiding us is very revealing," said Kajada.

Tarr grimaced, "Well, you may want to stand here all day and find that revealing, but *I'd* like to get some work done."

He looked at her and cocked an eyebrow. "Were you getting work done when I hailed you?"

"No," she divulged. "I was enjoying real food at the First Light Constellation. These people have real food not those ragtag rations we get some of the time."

"We must verify the information I received."

Tarr grimaced. "Do you really think that the Quinntessanites are killing each other with the plague?"

"You are half-human," said Kajada. Our kind used to inflict biological warfare upon one another with unspeakable constancy."

"But these aren't humans! Quinntessanites are much more refined." Pallas shook her head.

"I'm sorry, but it sounds like this Bolaa was just trying to get something out of us—like a ride."

"Maybe," granted Kajada. He looked directly at the area just above the door and spoke vociferously. "If we cannot verify this information with Dr. Johnson, we will have to contact the smaller genetic companies. Perhaps they will be more open with us. Come on Tarr we're leaving."

Abruptly Kajada turned and walked away. Before Pallas could even take one step to follow him, the metal door whooshed open.

"Well, it's about time," she criticized as she charged into the complex. Kajada strode fast behind her.

They walked down the sloping red corridor, now more familiar than strange, and entered the sleek turbolift. Kajada surprised Tarr by immediately opening up his tricorder. She watched him study the device as she went through the usual disorientation.

"As I thought," said Kajada. "We have been transported."

"What?" asked Pallas. "Are you sure?"

The shielding makes it difficult to obtain an exact reading, but we are deep under the surface of the planet—*not* two hundred metres, as we were told. If my suspicions are correct, the OSI complexes spread throughout Quinntessa are nothing but empty monuments, with defense systems. There is only one OSI facility, and all the imitation turbo lifts feed into it through transporters."

The door whooshed open, and a glum Dr. Johnson stood before them, looking more stooped than he had before. "You are correct, Mr. Kajada—yes, you are. Except for a few scattered recovery homes, this is OSI. We have fooled and baffled our fellow Quinntessanites for almost three hundred years, and now we're paying for it. We call ourselves 'miracle workers,' but when our people come to us looking for a miracle, we're fresh out. We're phonies...with big buildings and a lot of parlor tricks."

"Somebody on this planet has created and unleashed a very sophisticated chimera," persisted Kajada.

"Well, it wasn't us!" snapped the minuscule doctor. "OSI has been ruined by this thing. We've lost the confidence of the people, and our operations have been exposed to strangers. The pyramid on Hajee is under siege by Divinians, and we've lost control in half-a-dozen other cities. In fact, our most secure wing—this one—is no longer safe."

"How many rooms are there like this?" asked Kajada.

"Nineteen. Six of them have been cut off—even I can't get in. We've had serious sabotage."

"Why didn't you tell us any of this before?" insisted Tarr.

The little man gulped. "Pride. Disbelief. We've controlled this planet for centuries, and we maintained control even when the Divinians came in. We bribed them and shared our research with them—they weren't a problem. Yes, we had a few competitors, but nothing we couldn't handle...until the plague came. Now, overnight, it's all crumbled down around us."

"So who's doing this to you?" asked Tarr.

Johnson shook his head, his spotted forehead crinkling in thought. "I would have said it was our competitors, but I don't think so. The scope of this is beyond them...somehow."

"Who are your competitors?" asked Kajada. "Do you have a list of them?"

The little man nodded and crossed to his chic desk. From a drawer, he removed a small computer pad, which he handed to Kajada. "Here they are, plus the information I have about them. I thought about confronting them, but I kept thinking it wouldn't get worse. Well, it has."

As he read the data, Kajada raised an eyebrow. "One of them is Governor Opher."

"Yes, yes," said Johnson with a dry smile. "We only tolerate each other. And starting an operation like this, even on a small scale, requires considerable funds. You'll find Quinntessa's finest families on that list."

"This is ridiculous," griped Tarr. "Governor Opher is not going to devastate his own planet for a business advantage."

"That's the conclusion I reached," said Dr. Johnson, scratching his unruly mane of grey hair. "So who's doing this to us?"

Suddenly, the floor under their feet trembled, and the lights in the waiting room flickered. Dust and paint chips floated down from a crack in the ceiling. Tarr and Johnson looked around nervously, while Kajada closed the pad and put it safely in his belt pouch.

"What's happening?" asked Kajada coolly.

"Divinians!" Dr. Johnson moved toward the turbolift. "We've already evacuated the patients, and there are just a few of the staff left. As you pointed out, transporters link our facility, so once they've breached one of our pyramids, they can attack anywhere. They must be smashing their way from one wing into another."

The little man stopped in front of the turbolift door, looking expectantly at it. When the door didn't open, he pounded on it. "Something's wrong!"

The room shuddered even more violently, and the lights went off and stayed off, plunging them into total darkness. A lantern beam finally pierced the blackness, and Tarr trained her light upon the turbolift door. It was solid like a glacier.

"Is there another way out of here?" She strode across the room to the revolving bookcase. "Where does this go?"

Johnson hurried after her. "Yes, yes! Come on!"

Leading the way, the little man in the lab coat ducked into a passage behind the bookshelf. Tarr and Kajada followed, and they found themselves in a featureless corridor that ended in a junction with six similar corridors. At the end of one of the hallways, sparks glittered on the wall. When Tarr pointed the light in that direction, it became clear that someone was cutting through the panel with a beamed weapon.

Dr. Johnson whirled around, looking stricken with fear. "They're here!"

"Which way?" she commanded.

"It doesn't matter...we're damned!"

Tarr grabbed him by the collar and pushed him down a third corridor, heading in the opposite direction of the sparks. Her light caught colored stripes on the corridor walls, which probably would have told her where to go if she only knew the code. She just moved forward, pushing the minuscule doctor ahead of her. Kajada drew his phaser and brought up the rear, protecting their escape.

They reached a door, which probably should have opened automatically but didn't. Kajada and Tarr applied all the strength they could muster and pushed it open. All three of them slipped inside. She expected to end up in another waiting room, but a quick flash of her light showed they were in some kind of operating room, with huge metal bins on the walls.

Dr. Johnson juddered. "The morgue."

"Are those bins empty?" she asked.

"Probably."

From behind them came a clattering sound, as a chunk of metal fell into the corridor. Loud voices sounded, followed by thudding footsteps. Kajada immediately shoved the door shut, as Tarr shined her light around the room, trying to find anything that could help them. Her beam caught the doctor opening a bin on the bottom row. It was empty.

Tarr moved her light to the right to reveal a large sign on a pedestal—universal symbols for "Biohazard! Danger!" superimposed over an impressive skull logo. She grabbed the sign and placed it directly in front of the door, so it would be the first thing anyone saw when they opened the door even a crack.

A metallic thud sounded, and she turned to see Dr. Johnson climbing into the body locker. He waved just before he shut it and went into hiding. Kajada walked quickly around the large room, stopping at a metal door that looked like one of the fake turbolifts. He began fiddling with his phaser; Pallas couldn't tell what else he was going to do, because at that moment she heard voices on the other side of her door. She padded across the floor as quietly as she could, turning out her light as soon as she reached Kajada. In absolute darkness, they flattened themselves on the floor and waited.

These Divinians have come from Hajee, she told herself. *The plague is bad there, and they may not even know where they are in this labyrinth.*

Grunting, groaning, and scraping sounds issued from the darkness, followed by a clang as the Divinians slammed the door open. A strong light struck the sign, and from a distance she could see it reflected on their shiny black heads, which were covered with gas masks. They shined their lights around the room, bouncing off the glossy lockers, but they didn't advance into the morgue. Despite the crisscrossing light beams, the room remained as still as the death promised on the sign.

Nearby an explosion sounded, and the ground trembled. When an officer barked orders, the lights retreated into the corridor. Amid grunting and groaning, the door was pushed shut, and the room was returned to merciful blackness.

Tarr rolled over and turned on her light, shining it at Kajada. He squinted at his phaser, making an adjustment to the weapon. "I've got an idea. Hand me your phaser now."

"But they may come back any minute," she protested.

"I need our phasers to supply power to this transporter," he replied. "Our weapons will be exhausted, but we'll make it to the surface."

Tarr couldn't argue with that, and she turned over her weapon. "Do you need some light?"

"No, I have my own. But you can help me get the door open. I have to find the override controls."

Putting her hip into it, Tarr was able to help Kajada get the turbolift door open. The enclosure was similar to the others, only larger, in order to accommodate gurneys. Kajada used his tricorder to locate the access panel then he set up his light. He removed a compact tool kit from his pouch and set to work.

Mumbling under her breath about Divinians, Tarr went back into the morgue to find Dr. Johnson from his body locker. When she pulled out the drawer, he blinked at her. "Are we safe?"

She whispered, "No. But Kajada has an idea to get us out of here. Are the turbolifts the only way up?"

"There are some vents, but being this far down, I'd extreme dislike to guess how long that would take." He sobbed pitifully.

Tarr grimaced at him. "Anything else you want to tell us about?"

"Not really," garbled Johnson. "We've reached the end—there's nothing left to hide or protect. It's up to you to save us."

"That's great. You've got a mass murderer, the plague, and the Divinians running amok—and only the Dominion to save you." Pallas Tarr offered a hand to pull him out of the body locker. "Let's hope you're lucky enough not to need one of these for real."

Aboard the *Phoenix* in the middle of a night, Tetzlaff felt a tap on her shoulder. Tetzlaff turned angrily to see her young female servant Leedora. "What?" she cracked.

"Sorry to interrupt you, General," answered the young human woman, shaky in her boots. "We have a hail for you on one of the public channels."

"That's ludicrous!" sneered Tetzlaff. "I'll have your head for annoying me."

The young human woman gulped and took a step back. "I'm sorry, General, but he was quite insistent. And he said that if you refused to speak with him, I should mention a word."

"What's that?"

"Quinntessa."

Tetzlaff stared at the young woman, and it would be hard to say which of the two women looked more frightened. Tetzlaff manufactured a smile. Then she turned away and strode toward her private study. "You're dismissed."

"Thank you."

As soon as she entered her private study and closed the door, soothing lights came on.

Tetzlaff?" asked a scratchy voice that had been electronically altered.

"Here?" The general swallowed hard and balled her hands into fists.

"Guess who this is?"

"I know. Why should you be bothering me now? I've sent you all the relevant—"

"Quiet!" hollered the altered voice. "Don't presume to think you can fool *me*. This is a warning that I know where you are every minute of the day, and I know everything you do—and *don't* do. Against my unequivocal instructions, you've sent a fleet to Quinntessa—to annihilate it!"

Tetzlaff lowered her voice, hardly believing they were discussing these matters aloud. "I am not the entire government of the Divinian Empire," she insisted. I delayed for as long as I could, but the Melosha Council is up in arms. All they can think about is the plague and the Dominion—"

"Enough excuses!" boomed the voice. "I could find a million failures who make excuses, but you were chosen for your autonomy and heartlessness. Sending a fleet to Quinntessa endangers the entire experiment and my best operative. Now thanks to you I will be forced to rescue my operative and end the experiment early—before your ships stumble in and annihilate the planet. You had better pray to your god that our records are recovered as well."

"Or what?" cracked Tetzlaff rebelliously. "I don't like to be threatened—even by *you*."

"I don't make threats," said the voice with steely calm. "I only make promises. In fact, I promise you this. Cross me again and *you'll be* dead! Do I make myself clear?"

Tetzlaff felt like protesting to him. Then she remembered with whom she was dealing. "Yes, it's clear," she mumbled through gritted teeth.

"Good. You have to delay the annihilation of Quinntessa as long as possible. Overstate the amount of Dominion vessels, if you have to. I'll notify you when it's safe to continue. And call off your garrison—they're wrecking mayhem with my operation."

"Yes, sir," answered Tetzlaff in a hoarse whisper. She wasn't going to mention that she might not be able to hold off the fearful cowards on the council or in Central Command. They could always replace her with someone more agreeable. But her benefactor knew that and was counting on Tetzlaff's substantial opinionated skills.

"Don't keep anything hidden from me again," warned the raspy voice. "Good-bye."

When the general stepped out of her private study, she finally unclenched her fists and found that her palms were dank and perspiring. Few beings had such an effect on her. Still in a daze, she returned to her bed.

A light flickered on inside of the transporter/turbolift in the bowels of the darkened OSI complex. Kajada motioned to Tarr and Johnson to come inside. "Move it," he urged. "There's only a few seconds of power."

They did as they were told, although Tarr kept her light shining on the empty morgue and the door that they had forced open to get in. Although she hadn't seen the Divinians since their brief visit, she had heard them ransacking nearby rooms. They couldn't be far away, and this sudden burst of power might alert them.

"Get in the center," ordered Kajada, reaching into the access panel. Tarr could see their two phasers, jury-rigged to the circuits, with Kajada about to connect two couplers.

"Is this really going to work?" asked Dr. Johnson uncertainly.

"I'm not sure," answered Kajada as he continued to work.

"Then maybe we should—"

Suddenly there was a smash and the sound of enraged voices. Tarr gazed out the door of the turbolift and could see three beefy Divinians pushing open the door to the morgue. She quickly killed her light after one of them pointed at her.

"Now would be a good time!" she warned Kajada.

"I'm trying."

The Divinians stormed the morgue in force, and their lantern beams crisscrossed the room like a laser show. A phaser beam streaked over Kajada'a head and blasted a hole in the wall, but that didn't stop his nimble fingers from connecting more circuits and wires. Finally finished, Kajada took a step to join them in the center of the turbolift just as the lead Divinian charged into view.

"Raise your hands," ordered Tarr, hoping a show of having no weapons would buy them a few seconds.

It did, as the lead Divinian levelled his weapon but didn't fire immediately. The odd feeling of disorientation engrossed Pallas not a moment too soon, and the Divinians were caught by surprise when the inactive transporter suddenly initiated. They shouted and fired their weapons, but Tarr, Kajada, and Johnson disappeared in a curtain of flashing molecules.

A moment later, they found themselves in the same place—the turbolift—only Divinians were not threatening them with phaser rifles. The door was closed, and the lift was dark, forcing Tarr to turn on her light. Kajada and Tarr immediately threw all the strength they could muster against the door. "Help us, please," said Tarr.

Johnson also pushed, but the other two did the majority of the work as they heaved the door open half a metre. Tarr squeezed through first and dropped into a crouch, guardedly shinning her light into the darkness. With relief, she saw that they were in a ruby-red corridor that sloped upward, and she motioned to the others to follow her.

When they reached the next door, Dr. Johnson was able to open it with a pass card. "The outer wall is on a separate circuit," he explained.

Tarr pointed her light back down the corridor, but she could see no sign that gangs of Divinians were chasing them. After Johnson and Kajada exited into the street, so did Tarr, and she decided that warm sunshine had never felt so good.

She glanced around, but the streets appeared absolutely uninhabited. "Where are we?"

"Hajee, it looks like," answered Johnson, grimacing at that conclusion.

"Let's get under cover," said Kajada, pacing toward a desolate storefront just across the street. Tarr and Johnson hurried after him.

Once they were off the street, she tapped her combadge. "Tarr to *Solaris*."

"Vantika here," came the reply. "Where have you been? I'm reading your communication signal from the continent of Hajee!"

"It's a *long* story," she answered. "Three to transport."

"It will take us two minutes to get into position. Please wait."

Tarr tried the door to the shop but found it locked. She picked up a rock and threw it though the front display window. The glass shattered with a cracking sound and crashed to the floor.

"Let's move to higher ground," she ordered.

She led the way, not pausing until they had reached a stairwell, which led to the roof. With a sign, she halted their mad dash and slumped against the door. Johnson, who was panting deeply, sat on the top step, while Kajada coolly took out his tricorder.

"There's no lifesigns in the immediate area," he reported. "We're safe for the moment."

"Thanks for helping me," inhaled Johnson.

"This isn't over yet," defied Tarr. "How do we find out whether Opher—or any of your competitors—started this disease?"

The little doctor scratched his grey whiskers. "I know what Governor Opher fears the most—that the plague will strike Kozak. When that happens, his reaction might tell us something."

"Interesting," said Pallas, wiping a gleam of perspiration off her forehead ridges. Before she could say anything else, her combadge chimed. "Tarr here."

"Stand by to beam up."

"Finally," she exhaled.

All nightlong and all the next morning, James Rawlings had been digging a hole on the south side of the island, using pots and pans as shovels. Fortunately, the sandy earth was reasonably soft, and his improvised tools were good enough for the job, if slow. James paused every few minutes to catch his breath and listen for sounds from the house. He had found an old dinner bell and had hung it by Cordette's bed, hoping she would use it to call him, if she needed him.

He felt shamefaced, thinking he should stay by her bedside until the end. But Cordette had insisted that he pursue his latest escape plan, although it was the craziest one yet. They both knew that the clock was ticking for him, too, and he was beginning to feel tired. Hours of digging and no sleep were making him feel that way, James told himself, because he refused to acknowledge that the disease infected him. On the other hand, a sense of urgency propelled him to crouch on his knees for hours on end, digging this monstrous hole.

The long hours paid off when he reached a metal box containing machinery—the valves, gears, and circuits that controlled the flow of fresh water from the pipeline into the house. While getting Cordette a glass of water, he had realized that life on the island wasn't static—fresh water came and went everyday. The pipeline came from somewhere, carrying water then kept going...somewhere else. From observing the pipeline in the ocean, he estimated that the pipe itself had to be about three metres in diameter, large enough to accommodate him if it wasn't totally filled with water. He wouldn't find that out until he broke into the pipe.

When he looked up to wipe the perspiration from his temple, James spotted something in the crystal blue sky. Shading his eyes, he gazed at what appeared to be a large white bird, soaring high above him. When he stared closer, he realized it was a sea-glider, similar to those he had seen floating in the bay at Hajee.

He bounded to his feet and waved frantically, yelling at the top of his lungs. The plane, in spite of this, never deviated from its course or altitude. Even if the pilot were looking directly at the little island, James told himself, it was doubtful he could see him from that distance. Yet, spotting the glider gave him hope, just knowing that not everyone on Quinntessa was dead or dying.

As soon as he began digging again, he heard the peal of the bell inside the house. James tossed down his tools, jumped to his feet, and rushed inside. Even before he reached the master bedroom, he heard atrocious gasping, and he rushed inside to find Cordette thrashing on the bed, puffing for breath. He hastened to her side and hugged her trembling body.

Somehow his presence reassured her, although her frail chest continued to heave with the struggle to breathe. He felt her hands grip his back, as if trying to hang on.

"I won't let you go alone!" he assured her. "I'm here."

"Thank you," she rasped. Cordette gave him a final squeeze then her fingers loosened and slipped from his back. Her entire body went limp, and he gently laid the young Takarain woman on the bed. Despite the ravaged state of her body, she wore a peaceful look on her face.

James stood up, wiping the tears from his eyes. Enraged, he yelled at the top of his lungs. "Are you happy—you bastards? What did you achieve by killing her?"

He whirled around, half expecting to see the little grey-haired hologram, gloating at them. But no one was there—he was alone in the chic beach house. A breeze ruffled the curtains and blew through the bedroom; despite the hot sunshine outside, the air was bizarrely freezing.

It was time to go.

James wrapped Cordette in her bedcovers and carried her to the lagoon. He unwrapped her body in the waist-high water then tossed the sopping blankets into the water. As Cordette had done for him, he slapped the water, calling the creatures. Gawking closely at the waves, James finally saw black shapes moving beneath the velvety indigo, edging closer to the sounds. He climbed out of the water a few seconds before the sea creatures reached Cordette's body. The water began to churn, and he turned away.

Fighting back tears, James Rawlings strode toward the pit he was digging. Before he returned to work, he stopped to look at the endless horizon of three-tone blue. He said a silent prayer for Cordette. Then he turned his mind onto more pressing issues. He didn't know who the doers of this terrible disease were, or why they were doing this to Quinntessa, but he knew one thing: he was going to stay alive long enough to stop them.

After hearing a report from Tarr and Kajada, Captain Ardelon stroked his chin thoughtfully and looked at Dr. Johnson. "So it's possible that your own people—former colleagues of yours—planted this terrible disease on Quinntessa?"

The little man sunk into a chair in the mess hall of the *Solaris*. He looked extremely embarrassed. "Yeah, it's possible. All of our research would suggest that *somebody* planted this disease on Quinntessa, and I've wracked my brain trying to figure out whom. And why. The Divinians could have done it, but why? If they wanted to annihilate the planet, there are more effective means that are less hazardous to them. Alternatively, if somebody wanted to destroy OSI, they've accomplished that."

Ardelon nodded and looked at Kajada. "What do you say?"

"Just that we cannot hope to be successful if unidentified groups continue to introduce this disease. Even those who have been treated can contract it again."

"We're fighting a deep-rooted crusade against this mania," said Ardelon, "trying to find a place to draw the line in the sand and contain it. Hajee is under control, but the number of people left there is relatively minor. If the disease spreads across Kozak, Tanas, Azzopardi, and the other continents, we'll be overrun. And now you're saying we don't have OSI to help us?"

"I'm sorry," mumbled Dr. Johnson. "None of us were prepared for a disease like this...and the ramifications. Most of the people on our staff are already helping you, but the Divinians have rummaged through our facilities. I'm at a loss at what to do."

Tarr grimaced, as if reaching a very unpleasant decision. "I've got an idea for testing Governor Opher's honesty, but it's risky. It could cause a rampage."

"The whole planet is already an armed war zone," said Ardelon. "Dr. Cross and her staff were fired upon when they landed on Tanas and killed instantly. The Divinians are liable to pop up anywhere. When all's said and done, I'd say it's too late to worry about a rampage. While the medical teams do their work, we've got to do anything it takes to track down this mass murderer."

"Agreed," said Kajada.

Dr. Johnson nodded seriously. "Pallas and I go down to the First Light Constellation tonight and try her plan on Governor Opher. If it's not him, we'll keep looking."

"Captain," said Kajada, "you and I have been invited for dinner at the Zoran Constellation, a lodge for unibloods. Since the Bolaa already gave us valuable information, we might learn more by going there."

"Okay, but let's all be careful and keep in contact," said the captain. "Rawlings and Chance are still missing, and I don't want to lose anybody else."

He looked at Pallas' clothing and managed a smile. "Where do I get something like that?"

CHAPTER THIRTEEN

STANDING IN THE MIDDLE of a large, mucky hole in the ground, James looked with satisfaction at an access panel he had uncovered atop the main pipe. It was large enough for him to fit inside, just barely. More important, the panel would mean he wouldn't have to punch his way into the pipeline, an action he didn't think he had the strength to perform. Using a spoon handle as a screwdriver, he opened the access panel to reveal a rapid flow of dark water surging past on its way to some unknown destination.

Although there appeared to be some clearance between the top of the pipe and the water level, James wanted as much clearance as possible. So he went back to the control box, where he had already removed the cover. Putting his back into it, he cranked the outlet valve all the way open siphoning as much water as possible into the beach house.

Then he jogged inside the house and turned on every faucet full blast. Water was soon gushing into the tub, shower, and various sinks at an enormous rate, and James laughed, thinking that the exquisite house would be ruined in a few minutes. He felt scatter-brained, slightly feverish, and he tried to tell himself it was mere exhaustion.

Now he needed a float. There was a small wooden table in the living room that he had not used building the doomed raft. With his spoon, he unscrewed the legs from the table and hefted the tabletop glad it was a fairly considerable hunk of wood. It would have to carry him a long way—how far he didn't know.

James gathered some food from the reserves and wrapped them in the waterproof shower curtain. He thought about changing from his mud-covered clothes into clean clothes, but what was the point? Anything he wore would get soaked. It would also be dark soon, but there was no reason to wait, as day or night would look the same inside that pipe.

With a last glance at the beach house—and final thoughts about his fallen wife, Cordette—he walked out the front door of the house and didn't bother closing it.

A minute later, James stood straddling the pipeline staring into the rushing water and thinking he was about to take the ride of his life. There was a good chance he would drown, or get chewed up in a hydroelectric plant, or meet some other such fate, but he couldn't worry about that. It would be a faster death than the alternative. At least in the pipe he wouldn't die of thirst, he thought ruefully.

Taking a deep breath and a firm grip on his small raft, James plunged into the pipe full of rushing water. The raft was nearly ripped from his hands by the first surge, but he managed to hold on and right himself. Soon he was speeding along in absolute blackness, and the sensation reminded him of two pursuits from his youth. One was bodysurfing at the beach, and the other was riding the hydrotubes at an aquapark.

James was pleasingly flabbergasted to discover that the water in the pipe wasn't that cold. Heated by ocean currents, it was about the same temperature as the lagoon. He had no idea how much clearance there was above his head, which he kept securely planted on the tabletop. Besides, there was nothing to see but blackness and water—and nothing to do but hang on, stay awake, and ride it out.

As blackness embraced the city of Xifo, Ardelon and Kajada materialized on Zoran Lane, just outside a grandiose mansion that bore a golden sign proclaiming "Zoran Constellation." A uniformed doorman, who appeared to be Zantalus, looked curiously at them, then he broke into a smirk.

"Ah, you are the Dominion unibloods," he said with honour at his own powers of examination. "Member Kep has been waiting for you." With a grand flourish, he opened the door and escorted them inside.

For some time, Ardelon had been accustomed to frugal living conditions, and he was freely taken aback by the luxurious splendor of the Zoran Constellation. Crystal chandeliers, rich brocaded furnishings, and centuries-old tapestries graced the lavish foyer. Several grand rooms opened off the foyer, and Ardelon raked with curiosity into the open doorways. Laughter and the clinking of glasses came from what appeared to be a restaurant filled with people. In a enigmatically paneled library, patrons coddled in the quieter pastimes of reading and card playing. A ballroom with a high arched ceiling appeared to be empty.

"So this is how the underprivileged live," he whispered to Kajada.

"It appears so," answered Kajada. "Imagine what the First Light Constellation is like."

"These people are trying to prove something, so it may not be as ostentatious as this."

"Mr. Kajada!" called a voice.

They both turned to see a stocky Bolaa rushing toward them, a snaggletooth smile on his face. "Captain Ardelon I presume. It's a honor!"

The captain smiled back. "Meeting a Dominion captain isn't usually considered a enormous honor."

"You're the heroes around here. Everyone says so. Without you, Quinntessa would be alone in this time of catastrophe." He lowered his voice to add, "Thank you for coming. This should get me another two months credit here."

"Glad to help you," said Ardelon.

"Let me introduce you around." Slipping between them, Kep keenly grabbed their arms and steered them into the dining room. What followed was a fast-inferno round of introductions with vendors and uniblood VIPs. Ardelon tried to determine whether any of these people could furnish them with helpful information, but most of them asked whether there was any room on the *Solaris* for passengers.

"Lay off," grumbled Kep to a persistent Shavadai named Salli. "These are *my* friends—if anyone gets off this planet, it's *me*."

"We're not taking on any passengers," said Ardelon. "Quite frankly, the life expectancy on a Dominion ship is shorter than it is on Quinntessa."

The Shavadai laughed vigorously, and his antenne twitched. "Maybe it is. But don't worry because I'd say the Divinians like you."

"Why do you say that?" asked Kajada.

"Because they're letting you operate unencumbered here, even after you destroyed their ship," answered the Shavadai. "I sell supplies to the Divinian garrison on Azzopardi, and they're under orders to leave you alone."

"What?" asked Ardelon, taking a seat at the Shavadai's table. "Are you sure of that?"

"Yes. I just flew there myself by sea-glider two days ago, and they don't know what to make of it. General Tetzlaff, the military commander of the Adirondacks Expanse, gave the orders herself."

"But they just recently attacked the OSI complex," said Kajada.

"Well, you aren't the OSI, are you? They don't trust the OSI, and I can't say I blame them."

Ardelon asked, "Did you see two prisoners in the Divinian camp? Two of our people?"

"Are you even listening to me?" mumbled Salli. "Although they really don't like it, they're under orders to leave you alone. If you've lost two people, somebody else must have them."

The Shavadai sipped a tall glass of ale and grinned self-righteously. "However, they told me something else which you would pay greatly to find out."

"What is that?" asked Kajada.

He chuckled. "When I'm safely aboard your ship on my way out of here, I'll tell you."

"That won't happen for a while," replied Ardelon.

"Better not wait too long," warned the Shavadai. "For the time being, I'll keep looking for some other way off Quinntessa. If you want to do business, you know where I am."

"Come on, let's eat," said Kep, guiding Ardelon and Kajada to an empty table. He rubbed his hands together. "Did you bring any money with you?"

"No," answered Ardelon. "Being in the Dominion doesn't pay very well."

The Bolaa sighed. "Well, let's see how good my credit still is."

Ardelon lowered his voice to ask, "Is that Shavadai trustworthy?"

"Yes, and well connected...for a uniblood."

"Can you guess what his information is?"

Kep tugged considerately on a gigantic earlobe. "Let's see...he speaks privately to Divinians, and he wants desperately to get off the planet. Maybe he knows that a big fleet is coming to blow us to kingdom come."

"A reasonable conclusion," decided Kajada.

The Bolaa sat down at an empty table and rubbed his hands together. "Are you hungry?"

"All of a sudden, I'm not," said Ardelon.

"Please, sit down," insisted Kep. "To die on an empty stomach is so wrong."

Pallas Tarr smirked graciously at the well-wishers who greeted her when she entered the First Light Constellation with Dr. Johnson in tow. The two of them were afforded the royal treatment and escorted to Governor Opher's private booth at the rear of the dining hall.

"The governor has been notified and will join you in a moment," said the servant, smiling and bowing courteously.

"Thank you," answered Pallas.

"Can I get you something to drink and show you a menu?"

"No, thank you, we won't be staying for dinner."

The Quinntessanite looked dejected. "That's unfortunate."

"We're only here to see Governor Opher," said Dr. Johnson, looking and sounding very grave.

"I see," answered the confused waiter. "Perhaps I will have the honor of serving you next time."

When he was gone, Johnson whispered to Tarr, "I hope you know what you're doing. Opher is a very powerful man."

"I know we can't sit around and wait—we've got to find out who's behind this. There's an old human proverb: You don't know who your friends are until you start a fight."

The conversation in the dinning hall raised several decibels, and Tarr turned to see Opher cutting a swath through the room, shaking hands and greeting people at every table. With his cherry skin, red hair, and impressive build, he was a magnificent male specimen, the finest being that genetic engineering could produce.

"Did you have anything to do with Opher's birth?" she asked Johnson.

"Yes," he answered, glowing with superiority. "Gorgeous, isn't he. But I could combine the same species a hundred more times and not get another one like him. I just wish he didn't know how special he is."

The little elf's eyes twinkled. "And *you* are his equal. It would be wonderful the children you two could have, even naturally—"

"Perhaps some other time," she mumbled, cutting him off. May-be there would be another time when she could return to Quinntessa to stay—to live in grand style with a perfect man like Opher. Much of that depende d on what happened in the next few minutes.

The governor approached their table, flashing his incredible smile. "Pallas, you're looking totally beautiful tonight. And, Doc, this is a pleasant surprise."

Johnson grimaced. "I'm afraid it won't be pleasant in a minute. Take a seat please."

"What's going on?" asked Opher, slipping into the booth beside Tarr. He gaped with trepidation at the Dominion officer, as if fearing the news concerned her. This made her feel guilty about the lie she was about to tell, but she was committed to her plan.

With her voice a barely audible murmur, she alleged, "We've found cases of the plague here on Kozak. I'm afraid an outbreak is in progress."

"What?" he wheezed.

"Please," cautioned Dr. Johnson, "we've got to keep this news secret for now. We don't want to start a panic, and there's a chance that we can contain the disease where we found it."

Opher looked like a man who had been struck by a Bolaa stun whip. "Are you sure they're native Kozakians? Perhaps they came from Hajee or Azzopardi—"

"No, they're from right here," insisted Tarr. "Actually from several outlying villages."

"Several!" Opher buried his face in his hands.

Johnson patted the big man's shoulder. "It was rather unrealistic to think that Kozak would be spared this problem, but perhaps we've caught it early enough."

"What can I do to help you?" asked Opher anxiously.

"For the moment, nothing public," said Pallas. "You might want to prepare whatever emergency procedures you had planned to use, but I warn you—the OSI complex is shut down."

"What?"

"It's been turn upside down by Divinians," said Pallas. "Kajada, Dr. Johnson and I barely escaped with our lives." At least that much was true, she thought sorrowfully.

Dr. Johnson had been right—Opher looked like a man who had just seen his worst fear become a reality. If it turned out they were wrong about him, and he had nothing to do with this, then her lie would probably come back to irk her. She could probably forget about any more spectacular meals at the First Light Constellation.

"What about your genetic company?" asked Dr. Johnson. "With OSI out of commission, we'll need your facilities."

"But we have only twenty or so beds," mumbled Opher. He rubbed his handsome face, still juddered with doubt. Tarr assumed that he would be upset with this information, but she found his surprise to be somewhat odd.

"I'm sorry, Opher, but we're really busy now." She rose to her feet, and he quickly followed suit.

"When…when will I see you again?"

"Hard to say, but maybe this will hold you over." Pallas reached up, wrapped her arms around his broad shoulders, and gave him the kiss he had been yearning for days. His mouth met hers in a bittersweet mixture of zeal, lovability, and extreme anxiety. She knew that even if she had lied to him about the disease, there was no lie in her kiss.

He was so distracted that he didn't notice when her hand curled under his floppy collar and affixed a tiny tracking device to his shirt.

Tarr pulled away from Opher half-heartedly, unsure whether she had made a horrible mistake or had just rescued millions of lives. There were muted whispers in the dining room as the patrons voiced their approval of this fairy-tale romance. Little did they know that the romance had just ended.

She hurried out of the room before her emotions betrayed her, leaving Opher to stare after her in disbelief. Dr. Johnson rushed after Tarr, but he didn't catch her until she was in the street, pacing down the sidewalk.

"That must have been hard," he said tenderly.

"It was." She stepped around the corner into a side street and took out her tricorder. Even in the blackness, she could see the blip that was adjusted to the tracking device, and it was moving. "He's going somewhere. He just left the First Light Constellation."

Johnson stared around the side of a building. "I can see him—he's in a hurry, heading the other way."

She tapped her combadge. "Tarr to Ardelon."

"Ardelon here."

"Target is on the move."

"Got him," said the captain. "We'll meet you en route. Excellent job, Pallas."

"Yeah, real excellent job," she mumbled cynically.

"You promised me this wouldn't happen!" barked Governor Opher, pounding his fist into his palm as he paced the back office of a grocery store in the old section of Xifo. "You *guaranteed* it."

"Get, real," came the malicious response. "There are no guarantees in an experiment like this. More to the point, you got what you wanted—OSI is history."

"We'll *all* be history if this keeps up! Hajee was bad enough, but did it have to happen here? When are you going to deliver the antidote?"

"Soon. We need a few more days." The speaker knew this was a lie, as there was no magic antidote—never would be. "Those idiot Divinians upset several experiments when they attacked OSI—I wish I knew who caused that. But if the disease is spreading this fast, we'll be done soon."

"Now! I demand you put an end to it now!"

"Or what?"

"Or I'll tell the Dominion everything! I'll tell the Divinians. I'll *expose* you."

The other party's eyes narrowed. "That would not be a good idea. For one thing, you would be ruined."

"I don't care anymore!" snapped Opher with anger. "This has got to come to an end, do you hear me?"

"I hear you...all too well."

Out of the blue a loud beep sounded in the unkempt back office, followed by a pounding on a distant door. A voice broke in over the communication channel: Intruders at the public entrance!"

"Delay them!" Furious, the speaker turned to Governor Opher. "You *fool!* You were followed!"

"I don't see how that's possible. I took side streets and watched out for—" Opher's dark eyes widened in horror. "What are you going to do with that phaser?"

"What I should have done long ago."

The phaser spit a red beam, which gnawed a burning hole in Opher's stomach. With a moan, he staggered to the door but collapsed halfway there. His assassin pressed a button, opening a secret panel, and hurried out the exit into the alley.

"Use your phasers!" ordered Ardelon when the door to the grocery store wouldn't budge.

As several Quinntessanites observed with dismay and interest, Tarr and Kajada stepped back and blasted the metal security door with full phasers. It began to crackle and liquefy.

"What are you doing?" demanded one of the onlookers, a robust Drey'auc/Chunak.

"It's all right," said a small man in a white lab coat. "I'm Dr. Johnson from OSI, and this is official business."

His words pacified the crowd for the moment, although it was unlikely the quiet row of shops ever saw this much excitement. As the door disintegrated into molten gobs, a phaser beam streaked from the store, barely missing Kajada. The onlookers wheezed and ran for cover, but Kajada stood his ground and coolly returned fire. A moan issued from within.

Kajada kicked what was left of the door off its hinges and leaped over the melted metal on the ground. Ardelon, Tarr and Dr. Johnson charged into the store after him, and they found a strapping Quinntessanite sprawled across a dozen packages of baked goods, a gaping wound in his chest.

Kajada knelt down and felt for a pulse, then shook his head. "He is dead. I regret that my phaser was on full."

"You had no choice," said Ardelon. He turned to Tarr, who was studying her tricorder. "Where's Opher?"

"Not far." She led the way through the grocery store to the rear, where she found a door marked with symbols meaning "Private. No Entry." Levelling her phaser, Tarr pushed the door open and charged into the room.

A moment later, Ardelon wished he had been the one to go initially. Lying in the middle of the small, unkempt office was Governor Opher, crumpled on the floor like a pile of rags.

Distressed, Tarr bent over the body and put her head to his chest, listening for any sign of life. From the brutality of his wound and the pool of blood, Ardelon doubted he was alive.

Still he tapped his combadge. "Ardelon to *Solaris*. Stand by to beam one to sickbay."

"That won't be necessary," said Dr. Johnson, feeling for a pulse. "He's quite dead now."

"Belay that order," said Ardelon unhappily.

Pallas jumped to her feet, fierce rage and tears in her eyes. "I killed him...as surely as if I had pulled the trigger."

"No, you didn't," said the captain, putting his arm around her trembling shoulders. "We'll find out who did."

"How could his murderer have escaped?" enquired Kajada, scanning the small room with a tricorder.

"For heaven's sake!" gasped a voice. Ardelon turned to see a female Quinntessnite standing in the doorway, her hand covering her mouth and an appearance of terror on her face.

"What's on the other side of this wall?" he questioned, pointing to the wall opposite the door.

"An alley," she exhaled.

"Kajada, you're with me," ordered the captain. "Pallas, you'll probably want to stay here and—"

"No!" she said through clasped teeth. "I want to come with you."

"I can handle this mess," mumbled Dr. Johnson. "I'll take a look around, too. The three of you go ahead."

There was no time to argue, as Ardelon led the way out the door, through the shop, and into the street. Since they were in the middle of a block of stores, he motioned Kajada to go one way, while he and Tarr ran the other.

An onlooker yelled at him, "What are you people doing?"

"Have you seen anyone suspicious, running?"

"Just you."

Figuring no one at the front of the store had see anything, Ardelon dashed to the corner with Tarr on his heels. They took a left onto a side street and ran to the alley behind the grocery shop. There was no one in the area—not the murderer, not a witness, not anyone they could question.

Ardelon had seen dark alleys before, but none more sinister than this. He drew his phaser and a handheld lantern, but Pallas charged ahead of him, anger in her eyes. The captain almost called after her to wait, but he knew she wouldn't when she was in a state like this.

He tapped his combadge. "Kajada, where are you?"

"Making my way west down the alley," answered Kajada.

"Keep an eye out for Tarr—she's headed right for you."

"Understood."

Since the alley was covered from both ends, Ardelon looked around the vicinity, trying to figure out where they were in the strange city. While in pursuit of Opher's tracking signal, they hadn't paid any attention to where they were going. He had to admit that they were lost.

A nippy puff of air brushed his face, bringing with it the earthy scents of salt, fish, and rotting seaweed. Ardelon followed the breeze to the end of the block and saw that the street stopped at the dockside. Lights flickered on the black water of the bay, where quite a few boats and sea-gliders floated in serene repose. Some of the docking slips were empty.

Our prey escaped via sea-glider, he thought to himself. *That's why they chose this place as their headquarters—to be close to the sea-gliders.*

His combadge chimed, jarring him out of his trance. "Tarr to Ardelon."

"Here."

"We've finished searching the alley—there's no one here."

"I think they escaped via sea-glider," said the captain. "Let's go back to the ship and run some scans—"

"There's a problem," Tarr cut in. Kajada's been arrested."

CHAPTER FOURTEEN

WHEN ARDELON GOT BACK to the front of the store, he found Tarr and Dr. Johnson arguing with two Quinntessanites wearing square like hats and blue uniforms with ornate piping and epaulets. A large hovercraft was also parked in front of the store. Kajada was nowhere in sight, although numerous onlookers had remained to watch the continuing drama.

"What happened?" questioned Ardelon.

"I tried to explain to them," said Johnson with frustration. "I told them that we were fired on initially, and that your man returned fire in self-defense."

"Excuse me," said a tubby officer, "are you the Dominion captain?"

"That's right."

"We have to arrest you, too."

"Hold on," replied Ardelon, trying to stay cool, "are you going to give us a chance to explain?"

"We have accounts from some witnesses. They all tell us that you were trying to break into this shop, and the shopkeeper was trying to protect his place of business. No one denies that you fired first at his locked door, and that the other human killed the shopkeeper. Not only that, but we found our governor dead inside. In my forty years of service, this is the worst case of violence we've ever had on Kozak."

"Do you understand who these people are?" questioned Johnson. "And what we're trying to do? We were chasing the people who are responsible for unleashing the plague on Quinntessa!"

The officer scowled sceptically at him. "Are you saying that Governor Opher was responsible for the plague?"

"It appears so," said Johnson.

"Any proof to back up this libellous statement?"

"If you'll allow us to search his genetic company, perhaps we can find proof."

"There will be a full hearing," the other officer assured him, "and plenty of search warrants. Which one of you killed Governor Opher?"

"None of us!" shouted Tarr. "This is pointless. People are dying by the tens of thousands, and you're worried about two people."

"He was our *governor*," persisted the officer. "That's the highest office in the land."

"I *know* who he was," said Tarr, looking fiercely at him.

Her anguish and reddened eyes had some effect on the officers, who evidently knew who she was, too.

"You're not a suspect," said the officer with compassion. "But until we find out what happened here, we have to hold the other human and your captain."

Ardelon momentarily believed making a run of it and ordering Vantika to beam him back to the *Solaris*, but they needed cooperation, not more discord. As unibloods, he and Kajada were obviously at a disadvantage.

"I'll go with you," he told the officers, "as long as you realize that these arrests could further the spread of the plague."

The officers scratched their chins and looked at one another with indecision. Ardelon had the impression that their jobs were predominantly ceremonial on the usually peaceful planet.

"Take note of him," beseeched Dr. Johnson. "Captain Ardelon's ship and the medical teams he brought with him are the only things standing between us and catastrophe."

"But he ordered them to fire their phasers!" yelled an onlooker. "I saw it!"

The tubby officer, who was the elder of the two, took an unfathomable breath and came to a decision. "Dr. Johnson, if you will vouch for the captain, we'll allow him to remain on his own cognizance until the hearing. But we have to hold the other human, because he admits to killing the shopkeeper."

"I'll vouch for all of them," said Johnson. "They only want to help us."

"Where is Kajada being held?" questioned Ardelon.

"In the Collective of Municipal Rule," answered the officer. "You can visit him in the morning."

Dr. Johnson strode up to the officers and said, "Right now, we've got to get to Genetic Development—Opher's company—and search it."

"We can't get a search warrant until morning," said the tubby officer adamantly.

Tarr snarled with rage. In a few days you'll be lying in bed and dying a miserable death. I hope you'll remember these delays you caused us. Better yet, I hope you come to us to save your life—or the lives of your children—and we say, 'Sorry, it will have to wait till the morning.'"

The officer's dark complexion paled some shades. He eventually motioned to the hovercraft and muttered, "Come on."

They could see the fire burning in the night sky from blocks away, the flames rising above the profile of the city like rocket thrusters. Quinntessanites were running to and fro, pointing helplessly at the inferno, and their driver stopped the hovercraft and watched in bewilderment. The air smelled like burning tar, and sparks floated in the blackness like unpredictable meteorites.

"That can't be!" he cried out. "The automatic sprinklers and transporters...the suppression foams...we haven't had a fire in Xifo in a hundred and ten years!"

He tapped a button on the instrument panel of the hovercraft and yelled over the mayhem, "This is Officer Nem calling headquarters. There's a fire in section thirteen, near the corner of Starlight and Moon—"

"In the Genetic Development building," said Dr. Johnson, drawing the apparent deduction.

"Yes," agreed the officer, staring at his passengers and understanding that they might have been telling him the truth about Governor Opher. "Call out the Nation Guarders and rush them to—"

"I wouldn't do that," advised Dr. Johnson. "Don't get anywhere near that building, unless you're wearing an environmental suit. You don't know what might be in there. The safest option is to keep people away, and let it burn to the ground."

The officer stared in surprise at the doctor and licked his green lips hastily. "Belay that order. Let's cordon off the block and keep people away. Just let it burn."

"Let it burn?" asked a flabbergasted voice on the communication channel.

"That's right. Don't let anyone get near it, unless they're wearing an environmental suit. Possible biohazards."

Ardelon sighed despairingly and leaped out of the hovercraft. "I don't think we're going to find any information in that building. Looks like this was deliberate sabotage. Pallas, contact the ship and head back as soon as you can. I'm sure Vantika could use some relief on the bridge." He began walking away.

"Where are you going?" she questioned.

"Back to the Zoran Constellation. There's a man I've got to see. This feeling inside of me says we're running out of time."

General Tetzlaff exhaled a remarkable sigh of relief as she read the coded message on the hidden screen in her study. At last, she was free to do what had to be done. She had also survived the most dangerous partnership she had ever undertaken. If this message hadn't come, she was probably only days, perhaps hours, away from losing her post as military commander of the Adirondacks Expanse. She would make the Melosha Council and Central Command very happy with her next order.

"Experiment cut short," read the message. "Move in and clear out the Dominion. Await my order for final resolution."

Tetzlaff knew what that final resolution was—the end of the thorn in her side known as Quinntessa. Now her place in history and the next great reign of the Divinian Empire was assured.

She swiftly sent another message: "Await my arrival, and begin Phase Three. Prepare for Phase Four.

All during the night, James Rawlings hurtled through the blackness, clinging to a chunk of wood and shivering in his wet clothes. Inside the pipe, he didn't know if it was night or day, sea or land, hell or heaven—whether he was ill or merely exhausted and half-crazed. All he knew was that the instincts for survival and revenge were stronger than the temptation to let go and end it, although that thought was never far from his mind.

Did you survive all those years, put up with all the ridicule and unfairness, give up everything you worked for, and come all the way to Quinntessa...just to die?

No! James answered the voice within him. *I have to make my life—and my death—mean something. I'm alive for a reason, and there's something I have to do.*

James wasn't sure he was destined for success in the Divinian Empire anymore, as he had once been convinced. He thought about the love of his life, Cordette Chance, and how he should never have let her come along on this crazy assed mission. What was this situation but a bunch of disconnected, often incomprehensible events from which a person tried frantically to make some sense? The only thing in his life that had ever made any sense was Cordette, and he had lost her forever.

His fingers and legs were painfully cramped as he clung to his board, and he had lost his meager supply of food in the rushing water. But none of that seemed as important as the understanding he had just reached. When he got out of this, he would redeem himself. He would no longer let life drag him along like this current—he would bend it to his will.

Without warning, the artificial river dropped away beneath him, and James plunged headfirst into blackness. Reluctantly, he yelled and thrashed his arms, losing his small life raft. At the last second, he ducked his head, put his arms out, and dove into a cold, dark pool of water. He protected his head, certain he would smash into a shallow bottom, but he came out of his unexpected dive in water that was plenty deep enough to swim in. James stroked and kicked with all his might, and he broke the surface, stammering for air.

Treading water, he looked up and saw a million stars, twinkling like the brightest lights of Sidney, Australia or Los Angeles, USA. "Yeah," he breathed appreciatively, smacking his hand on top of the water. As his eyes adjusted to the night sky and its tiny but vibrant bits of light, he could see that he was swimming in a small basin, with a dam looming on one side and a lower embankment on the other.

I made it! Where he was hardly made any difference, as long as it wasn't that damn island.

Knowing he was too weak to tread water for very long, James swam toward the low side of the basin. He finally found a rock edge and dragged himself out of the chilly water. Collapsing on the rock embankment, he lay there for several minutes, letting the water drip off his shivering body. He was only half-alive, but he was alive.

James staggered to his feet and looked around, unable to make out much in the blackness. If anyone was around, he couldn't see him or her. In the distance was a wavering light—it looked like no more than a campfire, but that was enough to give him a new destination. Now he wished he hadn't lost his food.

Picking his way carefully through the dark, James walked away from the basin and found himself on a dirt path. The closer he got to the wavering light in the distance, the more it in fact looked like a campfire, and hope spurred him to walk faster. Soon he heard voices, talking rather loudly, as if they expected no one to be nearby. He couldn't tell if it was friend or foe, but he doubted if his tormenters from the island would amuse themselves with anything as low-tech as a campfire. He was hoping these were Quinntessanites—either rural workers or people who had fled the cities.

As he staggered through the brush, he could see their seated shadows huddled around the campfire. With their backs to him, he had no idea who they were, but from their voices, he assumed they were mostly males. James figured he had better not charge into their midst without announcing himself, so when he got close enough he cleared his throat noisily.

"I'm Lieutenant Rawlings," he said, his voice sounding hoarse and hollow in his own ears.

The men jolted up as if a bomb had gone off, and he could see them grabbing what looked like weapons. In the dim firelight, he still couldn't see their faces, but he wanted to appear harmless. So he held up his hands and said, "I'm with the Dominion. I got separated from my—"

One of the men charged toward him, rifle levelled at his chest. In seconds, he got close enough for James to make out his bony face, black hair, and black uniform.

Real Divinians! James thought briefly about trying to escape, but how far could he run in his condition? In fact, he felt so weak that he didn't think he could stand on his feet for much longer. But he kept his hands raised high and a smile glued to his bearded face.

Unfortunately, Divinians were not known for responding well to human charm. This one raised his phaser rifle and fired a searing beam that hit James in the chest. That was the last thing he remembered before he pitched forward into the dirt.

"I told you, Captain Ardelon, I won't give you any information until you take me away from Quinntessa. That is my firm price."

The speaker, a Shavadai named Salli, sat stone-faced at his table in the Zoran Constellation dining room. Ardelon sat across from him, his hands folded before him and his face just as relentless as the green-skinned alien's. The Bolaa, Kep, sat between them, and he was the only one who looked animated, except for the servers who bustled around them decisively.

"Don't agree to anything," Kep cautioned Ardelon. "*Let me* negotiate for both of us."

The Shavadai hooted. "What have you got to bargain with, Bolaa? You don't know anything, and you don't have anything. All your goods are floating in orbit around the planet."

"I have my *mind*," answered Kep, tapping his large frontal lobes. "And a strong desire to get out of here myself. Besides, I was right about Governor Opher, wasn't I?"

"Yes, you were," agreed Ardelon, his voice barely audible over the clink of glasses and ricochet of silverware. "That's why I came back here—to see what else I could find out."

Salli arched an eyebrow and waited until an older Chunak couple shuffled past. "Horrible thing about the governor. Who ever thought *he* could be involved with this tragic disease? Everyone is talking about it. As I told you, Captain, I have a very valuable piece of information, but I won't part with it for free."

"Salli doesn't know anything," jeered Kep. "So he talked to a few Divinians who are also stranded here—big deal. Those boneheads don't know any more than the rest of us! Captain Ardelon is the only one with a starship—he's the only one in a strong bargaining position."

The captain nodded. "Actually I have *three* ships under my command, all of them in orbit: the *Solaris*, the *Scorpion*, and a hyper-drive shuttlecraft."

Now the Shavadai leaned forward with avid interest. "A shuttlecraft, you say? Now *that* is something worth negotiating for, especially on Quinntessa. How much gold do you want? Name your price."

Ardelon grinned and leaned back in his chair. "Gold doesn't do me a bit of good—no place to spend it. Your information isn't all that valuable either, because any fool could guess at it. The Divinians must be planning to come back here with more ships—maybe a whole fleet. And when they do, we'll run for it, and you'll still be here. If the plague doesn't get you, they will."

The Shavadai frowned. "Make your point, Captain. What do you want?"

"Don't hurry him," said the Bolaa, smiling. "A good negotiation must be savored, like good wine."

Ardelon leaned forward and whispered, "I need four things. It would be good to know exactly when the Divinian ships are returning, and in what strength. I also need to know what happened to my two missing crewmen. Just because you didn't see them doesn't mean the Divinians don't have them. We need to ask them straight on if they know anything about Lieutenant Rawlings and Ensign Chance."

"What else?" muttered the Shavadai, not enjoying this tough negotiation as much as the Bolaa.

"Kajada, one of the humans on my crew, has been arrested for killing a man who was working with the people who brought this plague to Quinntessa. If there is any sort of influence you could bring to bear on the officials, it would be appreciated."

Salli sneered, and his antennae twitched wildly. "Anything else, while we're at it?"

"That's all I can think of right now. If I think of anything else I'll let you know."

The Shavadai moaned and slumped back in his chair, while the Bolaa nodded with satisfaction. "What will you say to that, Salli?"

"I'll say that this human wants an awful lot for his shuttlecraft."

"That's all I want from *you*," said Ardelon. "From you, Kep, I want someone to gather information about Opher's company, Genetic Development. He's still got co-conspirators here on Quinntessa, and we've got to run them down."

"I'm going on the shuttlecraft, too?" questioned Kep excitedly.

"Yes, because I reward those who help me." Ardelon rose to his feet and looked at the Shavadai, sensing other diners glancing at him. "Salli, you still have your sea-glider, don't you?"

"Yeah."

"Good. I'll meet you at the bay in an hour, and we can take a little flight to look for my missing crew."

"But I haven't agreed to any of this yet!"

Ardelon smiled. "You haven't said no, so I'm taking that as a yes. You might want to load up some supplies to make it look good. See you in an hour."

The Dominion captain strode away from the table, with many of the members of the Zoran Constellation watching him go. Kep nodded his head in admiration. "For a hum-man, he's an awfully good negotiator. Wouldn't you say so, Salli?"

"A month ago, we would have laughed him out of the constellation." The tall Shavadai rose to his feet. "Now I had better put some supplies on my glider."

CHAPTER FIFTEEN

KAJADA SAT IN a cell with a force-field grid protecting the open door. There were four other cells linked with his, all of them opening onto a central corridor, but the other cells were empty. His jailers had left him reading material, food, and water, but he ignored these niceties to sit in calm and mull over the actions that had landed him in this tight spot.

He had killed a man. The killing had clearly been in self-defense, but that knowledge didn't tone down his conscience at all. For Kajada, it was a cause to wonder what he was doing on the Dominion crew—a group of people who lived a life so dangerous that it might be called suicidal.

After recent events, he had no doubt that Quinntessa had been chosen by unknown parties as a breeding ground for this disease for the very reason that it was isolated and vulnerable. A civilized society derived from the Union of the

Dominion, it was a perfect microcosm of the Dominion as a whole. If anything, the mixed-species Quinntessanites were more disease-resistant than a typical populace, which made them the perfect proving ground for a biological weapon. If the disease could succeed here, then no Dominion planet was safe.

But who would endanger millions of people for an experiment? Not even the Divinians were so evil.

That question brought him back to the life he had taken. Had the shopkeeper lived, he might have furnished valuable information. Dead, he was nothing but a mystery, and a reason for the Quinntessanites to distrust the Dominion. He was also the cause of Kajada's imprisonment and pending trail.

Try as he might to justify his actions, Kajada now saw that he had acted recklessly. Was he prone to acts of passion and poor judgement?

Kajada laid back on his narrow bunk, realizing that he couldn't answer these questions himself. Perhaps he wouldn't survive his stay on Quinntessa, which made his introspection moot. One thing was certain—there was nothing like being incarcerated in a cell, awaiting trail for murder, to make a person think.

Suddenly there was a group of Quinntessanites outside the cell and trying desperately to turn off the forcefield to Kajada's cell.

James Rawlings squinted into the blistering sun and licked his scorched lips, wishing it was still night. He croaked something, some plea, which only the circling seabirds heard *(and how happy they would be to gobble my eyes from my head, he thought, how happy to have such a tasty bit!)*, and he rested for a few moments before looking around. He was lying in hot sand on the beach, imprisoned in a crude cage about a meter high and four metres long, made of sticks and wire. Had he any strength, he could probably smash his way out of this handmade cage in a few seconds, but he was tremendously weak. His throat felt raw and his glands swollen; he couldn't see himself, but he imagined from his peeling skin that he looked somewhat awful.

James knew he was dying of the plague.

On his hands and knees he raised his head like a groggy fighter…and some distance ahead, perhaps ten metres, perhaps twenty (it was difficult to judge distances along the strand with the fever working inside him, making his eyeballs pulse in and out), he saw something new. Something which caught his attention on the beach.

What was it?

He kept his eyes on whatever it was that stood on the strand ahead. When sand fell in his eyes he brushed it aside. The sun reached the roof of the sky, where it seemed to remain far too long. James imagined he was in a desert, somewhere desolate.

When the sand fell in his eyes once more he did not bother to push it off; did not have the strength to push it off. He cried the sand out of his eyes. He looked at the object, which finally came into focus for him.

He could make it out now, fever or no fever.

About twenty metres away, under a canopy that gave them ample shade, a group of eleven Divinians sat in a circle playing a card game. Every now and then, one of them would look in his direction with jaded eye, noting that he was still there, and still alive. Behind them on the bluff loomed a small fortress, which he assumed was the actual garrison, but it appeared eerily silent, perhaps deserted.

James turned to look at the vast ocean, gleaming in the sunshine, out of place in its beauty in the middle of his personal hell. He had always thought of oceans as a symbol of life and freedom, but this one seemed like a hallucination, summoning him to a freedom he could never attain. It mocked him with its eternal splendor, telling him that it would go on for eons and eons after he was gone. If this was to be the last thing he saw before he died, he almost wished it could be something not so painfully beautiful.

He licked his lips again and rubbed his thumping head. James felt as though he had been unconscious for days, but it had probably only been a few hours since the Divinians had stunned him and tossed him into this cage. Looking around his enclosure, he figured it was some dead fisherman's lobster trap, or whatever the Quinntessanite equivalent of lobster was. Would they make him die like this, staked out in the heat? Or would they at least give him some food and water? Maybe he could provoke them into killing him outright.

"Hey!" James shouted, his voice sounding as rough as his shaggy beard. "Give me some water!"

When the Divinian did nothing but look at him, he shouted, "Come on, you cowards! Afraid of an unarmed man?"

The guards looked at him and chuckled, but one of them stood and shuffled toward him. His phaser rifle was slung casually over his shoulder, as if he knew he needn't fear this prisoner.

He stopped about eight metres away from the cage and snorted. "We're betting on how long it takes you to die. I've got you down for twenty-seven hours. Think you can hold out that long?"

"Maybe if I have a drink of water," rasped James.

The Divinian shook his head. "Sorry, but we're not allowed to aid you either one way or another. We can't give you any food, drink, or medicine; and we can't beat you senseless either. This has got to be a fair contest."

"What makes you such experts?" mumbled James. "Maybe I'll live for a week."

"I don't think so. I've watched seventy percent of our own garrison die, so I have some experience. I'd say twenty-seven hours is just about right, although you look pretty strong. Maybe I should've taken thirty-one."

The guard laughed, sounding oddly jovial and half insane. "I might not even be here in thirty-one hours to see you die. It's just as well that I took twenty-seven."

"Where are you going to be?" questioned James hoarsely.

"Far away from this pothole." He turned and shuffled back to his comrades.

James laid his head on the hot sand and wondered if he could burrow into it for some protection from the sun. But the wooden bars extended underneath the cage, and he didn't have the strength to break them. He supposed he could untwist the wires that held the structure together, but his captors were sure to notice him working on it.

Bored, he turned back to look at the endless sky, stretching across the blue sheen of the ocean. Yes, he was going to die—and the way he felt now, he didn't think it would even take twenty-seven hours. It was best to sleep, he decided, and conserve his strength, while waiting for a miracle to happen.

Who am I kidding? thought James. *Miracles happen to other people, not to me. What did the old country song say? "Just a roll of the dice. Lady luck left my side."*

Just before he closed his eyes, he caught sight of something in the clear blue sky. James rubbed his eyes and stared into the glare, wondering if it was real or only his fevered imagination. After several seconds, the apparition was still there—it looked like another one of those sea-gliders, headed their way.

A sudden babble of voices made him turn to look at the Divinians under the canopy. They had seen the glider, too, and a few of them rose to their feet and took up arms in apparent defense of this lonely stretch of beach. Others remained seated in the sand, lacklustre and listless; they looked every bit as resigned to death as he was.

He struggled to listen to their conversation against the gentle flow of the waves to the shore. "It must be Salli," said one. "Did we order more supplies?" asked another.

Supplies? James turned to watch the white glider make its graceful approach. Hope sprang into his heart, although he knew such hope was futile. Anyone who dealt with the Divinians wasn't likely to save him, or even care if he lived or died.

The approach and landing of the seaplane was quite impressive as it glided across the creamy water and set down on its sleek pontoons with hardly a splash. Six of the eleven Divinians formed a line in the sand, although they kept a safe distance away from him. There appeared to be two people in the craft, and one of them opened the hatch.

The visitor threw something into the water—it was a compressed-air raft, which instantly expanded to its full size. James watched with interest as a lanky Shavadai stepped carefully into the raft, oar in hand, and began rowing leisurely toward the shore. The Divinians on the beach began to relax, apparently not viewing this new arrival as a threat. Some of them went back to their card game.

The raft scraped into the sand, and the Shavadai climbed out, trying to maintain his dignity as best he could in the small boat. As he ambled past James, he looked at him with mild interest, although he didn't stop to talk. His destination was clearly the Divinians and the fortress on the hill.

"Salli!" shouted one of them with disapproval. "What are you doing here?"

The Shavadai nodded. "Just making my rounds. I thought I'd see if you needed anything. I've got some nice salted fish and a case of Hanka ale."

"Go away, you scavenger!" yelled another Divinian, although he didn't sound very angry. "We don't need anything, except to get off this lousy rock."

"I can't help you there," said the Shavadai with a resigned smile. He pointed to James in the cage. "I see you've found some entertainment."

"Yes, one of those meddling Dominion. But he's not going to last long—he's got the plague."

"I see," mumbled the visitor. "Are you sure you don't need anything? Your great fleet hasn't shown up yet."

"They will. They're on their way. Now get out of here, before we put you in a cage, too!" At that remark, there was a round of laughter among the Divinians.

"Okay," said the Shavadai, holding his hands up. "I'm not looking for trouble, just customers."

"Who's that in your glider?" asked another guard, peering suspiciously at the sleek craft floating in the surf.

"Just my new pilot. I'm showing him the route."

"Well, there's no sense coming back here again. We'll be gone before we need any more supplies."

"Lucky you," grumbled the Shavadai, sounding as if he meant it. "I'll cross you off my list. So you're sure?"

"We're sure," growled a large Divinian, hefting his phaser rifle. "Now if you don't get out of here in twenty seconds, I'm going to use your glider for target practice."

"I'm going!" To another round of laughter, the Shavadai hurried toward his raft. As he passed James, he gave him a wink, which was an odd thing for him to do. *He probably caught a grain of sand in his eye,* thought the prisoner.

"Help me!" moaned James, but the Shavadai was already pushing his raft into the surf to make his escape.

The lieutenant watched forlornly as the merchant rowed back to his craft and climbed aboard. He hauled his raft in after him, letting out the air as he did. Without further ado, the sea-glider floated majestically into the air; like a giant bird, it caught a wind drift and soared away.

James watched the glider sail into the sky, a feeling of despair gripping his chest.

"It's definitely your man down there in the cage," Salli told Captain Ardelon as the glider cruised away from the Divinian garrison. "But he's sick."

"How bad?"

"Not that bad—he's still talking."

Ardelon took a deep breath, grateful that they had at least found James. "There was no sign of a female Takarain in their camp?"

"None. And there's no more time to look for her. They sounded like their fleet could show up any minute."

Ardelon punched some numbers into his computer pad. "Are we out of their range of fire yet?"

"Yes—just barely."

The captain tapped his combadge. "Ardelon to Solaris."

"Tarr here," answered a familiar voice.

"I'm sending you some coordinates—it's Rawlings, and I want you to beam him up immediately. Tell Dr. Russ that he's got the plague, and she's got to drop everything to save him. Stand by." Ardelon took off his combadge and plugged it into the pad. He watched intently as a stream of lights showed the data transfer.

"We've got the coordinates," said Tarr. "Activating transport." After seconds that stretched forever, she reported, "We've got him!"

The captain let out a long sigh of relief. "Okay, that's two items crossed off our list. Salli, are you ready to take command of that shuttlecraft?"

"Right now?" asked the Shavadai, horror-struck. "We're flying over an ocean. Who's going to fly my glider?"

"We're going to abandon it."

Salli gulped, and his antennae twitched. "Abandon it? Right here...in the middle of the ocean!"

"If you're leaving Quinntessa, you won't need it anymore."

"All right," mumbled the Shavadai. "You're a very decisive man, Captain."

"I have to be." He pulled his combadge off the computer pad and fastened it to his chest. "Pallas, do you still read me?"

"Yes, sir."

"Lock onto the two of us and beam us up. And alert Conner on the shuttlecraft to stand by for a shift in personnel."

"Yes, sir."

The hard-faced Shavadai looked extremely displeased to be losing his fine sea-glider. Ardelon reached forward from his co-pilot seat and patted him on the shoulder. "Think of it as a trade-in for an even better shuttlecraft."

"Right."

A moment later, they disappeared from the cockpit of the sea-glider, while it continued its graceful flight, sailing unmanned into the blue horizon, like a great white albatross.

When they materialized on the transporter pad in the cargo hold of the *Solaris*, now converted into a sickbay, Ardelon rushed immediately to the bed where Lieutenant James Rawlings lay. Dr. Russ and her assistants were working on him with their medical equipment, plying him with hyposprays.

James lifted his head and stared at Ardelon in utter astonishment. "Am I dreaming this? Or have I died and gone to heaven?"

"Neither one," answered Ardelon with a smile. He looked at the doctor. "Is he going to be all right?"

"We got him not a moment too soon," answered Russ. "The biofilter took care of the multiprions, but he has some tissue damage and secondary infections. He's going to be laid up for a while."

"Not too long, I hope. We need him badly." The captain gazed down at James. "Where's Ensign Chance?"

"Dead," said James roughly, tears welling in his rheumy eyes. "We broke into OSI...and then—"

"Tell me later. Right now, you have to get well." Ardelon patted his newfound comrade on the shoulder.

"I got a miracle," rasped James. "I never thought I would get a miracle."

"Let's hope for a few more." Ardelon returned to the transporter platform, where the Shavadai stood in stunned silence, staring around at all the equipment and bustle of activity. "I'm a man of my word. You'll have your shuttlecraft in just a moment. Then I suggest you take it and get as far away from here as possible."

"What about Kep?"

"There's no time to wait for him. I'll give him passage on my ship." A metal pan clattered to the deck behind them, as if underscoring the urgency. A weary doctor picked up the pan, then teetered unsteadily on her feet until a colleague helped her to a chair."

The tall Shavadai nodded gracefully. He stepped upon the transporter platform and squared his shoulders.

Ardelon turned to the transporter operator. "Beam him to the shuttlecraft, then beam Connor back here. Activate when ready."

"Yes, sir," answered the human on duty.

The Shavadai gave him a noble wave as he vanished in a column of sparkling, swirling lights. The captain immediately left the cargo hold and hurried the length of the scout ship to the bridge, where Pallas Tarr was on duty at the conn. The peaceful blue curve of Quinntessa filled the viewscreen, giving the false impression that all was well on the watery world beneath them.

"Any emergencies?" he asked, slipping into the seat beside her and turning on the sensors.

"The struggle goes on," she answered. "Three members of the medical team on Hajee came down with the plague, and they're being treated along with everyone else.

"I've learned that a Divinian fleet is headed this way." He started scanning the landmasses on the planet beneath them, looking for kelbonite deposits, or anything that could mask the presence of a small starship. "We've got to find someplace down there to hide this vessel."

"Wouldn't it be easier to run for it?"

"Yes, but we're not going leave without Kajada and our doctors. We'll hide this ship and leave the *Scorpion* in orbit. When the Divinians show up, the *Scorpion* can run for it, so they'll think all the Dominion have left."

"That's risky," mumbled Pallas. She snorted a laugh and gave him an ironic smile. "Maybe this will be our first step to getting out of this crazy life."

"What do you mean?"

"Governor Opher offered to let us stay here, remember? Even Kajada said it was a good idea for us to start planning how to get out of the Dominion. He's right, you know. We can't keep up this crazy life forever. If the Quinntessanites protected our identities, this would be a good place to hide from both the Divinians and the Dominion higher ups."

Ardelon shook his head. "There too much left to do. Besides, they'll all keep hunting us to our graves. Do you think we could go from being Dominion to being law-abiding citizens just like that?" He snapped his fingers.

Tarr shrugged. "Maybe. Given the right circumstances."

"It's only a pipe dream," said Ardelon. "But I'll it in mind."

"How's Rawlings?"

"Worse for wear, but he's going to liv Ensign Chance is dead. We need to contact D see when Kajada's hearing is."

"Johnson checked in, and he said that the hearing is tomorrow. On a lighter note he told me why he has a human name. The family that adopted him when he was four was the Johnsons. They were in fact uniblood humans who lived on Quinntessa for decades. Then Tarr lowered her head, and her voice sounded far away. "Opher's funeral was less than an hour ago. That's one bastard I won't miss."

"Maybe you can hide it from others but you can't hide it from me. You were really starting to care for him, weren't you?" asked Ardelon, knowing that if Pallas didn't feel like answering, she wouldn't.

Her shoulders sagged, and her tough smokescreen faded just a little. "It's hard not to like a man who worships you and wants to give you the world. Like most of the men I like, he turned out to be rotten. Why am I always attracted to the rotten ones?"

"Because you're a rebel at heart. Despite that, someday d a man who deserves you." Ardelon continued console, and he smiled when all his scans turned is locations. "I think I found a place. Let's take surface right now."

about the Divinians down there?"

"The ones who are left are sitting around, waiting to be picked up. They're no threat anymore."

The captain opened a channel and contacted the Scorpion telling Captain Raine all that had happened, and all that was about to happen. She was not adverse to the idea of running for it when the Divinians showed up in force. He also contacted their mobile clinics and filled them in.

That accomplished, Ardelon took over the conn and eased them onto a reentry course. "Is Kep aboard?"

"Yes."

"Have him come to the bridge."

Throughout this entire mission, Ardelon had the urgent feeling that time was running out for them. He didn't know what to do about, except to plunge ahead with the task at hand. Maybe he needed to slow down and withdraw from the conflict.

A few moments later Kep entered the bridge. "Captain," he whispered. "You called for me."

"Have you found out anything else?"

"Only that Opher recently got a large inf[...] into his company and was poised to compete wit[...] would seem that he did all of this for profit, w[...] sick."

"Me too."

Suddenly a blip on Tarr's console station chirped. "Captain Ardelon!"

"Go ahead, Tarr."

"Captain! A huge starship had just entered orbit, and the Scorpion is under attack!"

In orbit over the shimmering blue planet, a mammoth starship bore down on the tiny Rambler assault vessel, peppering it with a withering barrage of phaser beams. The *Scorpion* tried valiantly to return fire while swerving back and forth, but the highly advanced starship had taken her by surprise. The Dominion ship trembled from one blast after another, and her aft sections were aflame, spitting vibrant blue and gold plumes.

"All power to rear shields!" shouted Tessa Raine on ⬛⬛⬛idge. Her scarred skinny face was worried with fear. ⬛⬛⬛ evasive maneuvers!"

⬛⬛⬛ ship shuddered violently, and the conn officer ⬛⬛⬛ console to stay in his seat. "We've lost all power ⬛⬛⬛ields down to seven percent!"

⬛⬛⬛them!"

"They're not answering!" shouted tactical. "We're dropping into the atmosphere—"

Another blast jolted them, and sparks and acrid smoke discharged into the cabin, causing Raine to gag. The captain dropped to her knees to avoid the worst of the smoke, but she felt herself floating as the ship lost artificial gravity. The deadly barrage never stopped for an instant, and the tiny ship absorbed blast after blast. The scorched, bloodied face of her helmsman floated past her stinging eyes.

"Long live the Dominion!" yelled Captain Raine with her last breath.

Upon entering the atmosphere, the assault vessel turned into a flaming torch, and a moment later it exploded into a riot of silvery confetti and burning embers. What was left of the *Scorpion* fluttered through the upper atmosphere of Quinntessa like a gentle snowstorm.

CHAPTER SIXTEEN

ARDELON STARTED TO STEER the *Solaris* back towards the upper atmosphere. "Tarr! Ready shields and weapons—now!"

"There's no rush," came Tarr's subdued response. "The Scorpion is gone."

Ardelon's jaw dropped, and Pallas grimaced and ground her boot into the deck plate floor.

"How many Divinian ships are there?" asked Ardelon, certain that the enemy fleet had arrived.

"Only one ship," answered Tarr. "But she isn't Divinian. At least she isn't like any Divinian ship we've ever seen before."

"What is she?"

"Unknown. Her hyperdrive signature doesn't match our computer."

"…doesn't mean much," mumbled Ardelon, "…out-of-date their ship's data was. What's she

"She just beamed one person up from the planet." A tense pause ensued as they waited for more information. "The ship is leaving orbit...they're powering up to go into hyperdrive. Whoever they are, they're gone. They have scrambled their hyperdrive signature so we can't track them I'm afraid."

Ardelon frowned, wishing now that he had kept the *Solaris* in orbit. "If we had been up there, could we have made a difference?"

"I doubt it. Maybe a Dominion Seeker ship could have handled them, but not us."

"Well, that's it," said a voice behind Ardelon. He turned to see Kep, the Bolaa, shaking his round head. "It sounds like Opher's murderer has just made his escape."

Things seemed to keep getting worse for Ardelon and his crew. His best friend Kajada lay dead in a puddle of his own blood. The shopkeeper's relatives who Kajada had killed broke into his cell and dragged him out onto the middle of the street and murdered him in cold blood. Ardelon looked at friend and yelled, "What have you done to him?"

Ardelon couldn't take it anymore. He a rage like never before. *That's it I've had it u* thought Ardelon.

First Dr. Cross and her staff had been fired upon when they landed on Tanas and killed instantly! Secondly Captain Raine and her crew aboard the Scorpion had been destroyed defending Quinntessa for an ungrateful populace. Even young Cordette Chance had died trying to uncover the mystery of the plague. But no the last straw was here said the voice inside Ardelon. Seeing his very best friend murdered in this fashion for essentially defending himself against one of the co-conspirators of this plague was the absolute last straw.

Anger and frustration surged through Ardelon's veins, and he looked around for the gaudily uniformed officers who had arrested Kajada. When he spotted the portly one, Ardelon strode toward him and glared at the Quinntessanite. "Opher's murderer—the one most responsible for the plague—has just gotten away in an unknown starship. And they destroyed our sister ship. In the meantime you let Kajada be murdered by the family of one of the co-conspirators who he had to kill in "

Quinntessanite looked flustered, but he held The persons responsible for his murder will justice. They will be arrested and brought to

"I find that unlikely to believe. You people have a sorry excuse for law enforcement. It's unreasonable," said Ardelon. "After all the effort we've put in, and all the risks we've taken you don't give a damn about us."

The officer looked at him with hatred in his eyes. "What are you people but a bunch of two bit space pirates?"

"This planet is at a crossroads. It's a former Dominion planet that's no longer acknowledged as that. And the Divinians want to destroy it. Maybe we should let them. You don't give a damn about us and now we don't give a damn about you. In fact let's help the Divinians out a little." Ardelon tapped his combadge. "Vantika, do you read me?"

"Yes, sir."

"We're absolutely done with these genetic freaks. They've caused nothing but trouble for our sincere efforts. I want you to take off and fly over Xifo, destroying buildings at random. In fact, go ahead and level the entire city. You can start with the First Light Constellation."

"Yes, sir. Preparing to launch."

The Quinntessanite officer blanched, paling several shades. "You can't do that! It's...it's against the laws of decency!"

"What do I know? I'm a two-bit space pirate! "I make my own laws," snapped Ardelon. "I'm Dominion."

The stout Quinntessanite gulped then he looked around at his fellow citizens, whose expressions made it clear that they didn't want their city destroyed in order to make a certain point. They slowly backed away, except for Dr. Johnson, who pushed through the crowd.

"Everybody stop it right now!" pleaded the doctor. "These people are *dying* for us. They've risked their lives and their freedom for us. Our own National Patrollers are shooting down gliders that try to land here. Our own Governor Opher was partly responsible for this horrible disease. These are *not* normal times."

After a moment, the officer heaved a sigh. "I'm sorry, sir. Please extend my apologizes to you and your crew for this situation. What's going to happen next?"

Ardelon tapped his combadge. "Belay that last order, Vantika."

"Yes, sir," she answered, sounding relieved. "What's the real plan?"

"Right now, we're going to leave Quinntessa and get some reinforcements. We'll take all our medical staffs from the clinics but leave the equipment and supplies for the Quinntessanites to use. Stay prepped for launch, because we'll be taking the ship at maximum hyperdrive speed and we'll need every second to gather the reinforcements. Ardelon out."

Dr. Johnson stepped up to the captain and warmly shook his hand. "Captain, I don't think we can ever express our gratitude for what you've tried to do for us. No matter how it turns out, we know you've done all you can. We may not be able to erect any statues to you, but the Dominion will always be heroes to us."

"Hear! Hear!" yelled someone in the crowd. Spontaneous applause erupted, and some Quinntessanites patted Ardelon on the back. He could still see fear and uncertainty in their eyes, but there was also genuine affection."

"I'll keep the clinics open," vowed Johnson. "You leave it to me."

Ardelon nodded, unable to find words to express his own feelings. Moments like this were few and far between for the Dominion, although they were the only reason the Dominion still existed at all. When he turned to follow Tarr to pick up Kajada's lifeless body, he felt a familiar tug on his shirtsleeve. It was Kep.

"What about the shuttlecraft?" asked the Bolaa. "When do we leave?"

The captain looked down at his small ally and shook his head. "I'm afraid I let Salli leave already, but you can come with us."

"You'll be the first Bolaa member of the Dominion," added Tarr.

Kep thought for a moment, then replied, "No, thank you. I think I'd rather take my chances here. These people aren't so bad after all. Good luck to you, Captain Ardelon."

"You, too," replied the captain.

A moment later, as they prepared Kajada's body for transport back to the ship, he turned to Tarr and said, "So he would rather stay on a plague-ridden planet that's about to be destroyed by a Divinian fleet than join the Dominion. What does that say about us?"

"After what just happened to the *Scorpion*, I can't say I blame him."

"I'm sorry you didn't get to see Opher's funeral."

"I've got a feeling I'll see more funerals before this is all over," she answered solemnly. She whispered to him, "Why did you promise reinforcements? That's something you can't guarantee. Why bother to leave the clinics operating?"

He lowered his voice to a low whisper. "We saved them from the plague for the most part but we can't save them from the Divinian fleet. The least we can do for these people is give them a glimmer of hope. Let them take their minds off their problems before their apparent demise."

General Tetzlaff rubbed her hands together and smiled, thinking how good it would feel to finally be rid of the obstacle known as Quinntessa. Destroying the planet would not only please her superiors and exterminate the plague, but it would destroy any trace of her involvement with her secret benefactor. It would also rid the Divinian Empire of a worthless planet that was more trouble to govern than it was worth.

And she would do the deed herself, to achieve the maximum recognition and credit.

"Coming out of hyperdrive in forty seconds," the bridge captain of the *Phoenix* reported to her.

"Excellent," Tetzlaff said with a satisfied smile. She had only been able to scrounge nine ships on the spur of the moment, but she still figured that would be enough to scorch the planet. If they didn't kill everyone and everything with their weapons, the nuclear winter they caused would annihilate everything in a few days. From what she knew of the planet, the inhabitants were relatively peaceful and had no working starships, so they wouldn't be prepared for an all-out conflagration. They would have no place to hide.

"Coming out of hyperdrive," reported the bridge captain of her flagship.

General Tetzlaff rose from her seat and stood before the viewscreen. *What an ugly little planet,* she thought when it came into view—*all blue and watery, like weak eyes.* "Any sign of the Dominion?" she asked.

"None," answered the officer on ops. "There are no ships in orbit."

The general nodded, thinking that the cowardly Dominion had run for it. Or perhaps they had all succumbed to the plague. It was just as well, because her crew needed all of its firepower for the task at hand.

"What about the garrison?" asked the bridge captain.

Tetzlaff frowned, her neat brow knit with concern. "According to their last report, most of them have already died from the plague, and the rest are getting sick. We have no facilities to care for them, and we don't want to stay here any longer than absolutely necessary."

The bridge captain nodded. He knew they had the facilities but nobody wanted to risk getting the plague, and the whole purpose of this operation was to make sure that the plague died on Quinntessa.

"I'll make sure that they are all decorated for bravery," said Tetzlaff. "Posthumously."

She looked at another viewscreen and could see the other eight ships in her fleet spread out behind her, ready to execute her commands. "Have the fleet take positions and power up weapons," she ordered.

"Yes, sir."

"Fire!"

Their weapons raked the planet in an inferno that blazed across all the little continents on Quinntessa. Everything and everyone who wasn't dead yet soon would be. The nuclear winter had begun.

EPILOGUE

NINE HOURS LATER, Ardelon sat alone in the *Solaris'* mess hall, eating his ration pack and watching the telemetry from the subspace sensor relay they had left in orbit around Quinntessa. Quinntessa was a remarkable planet—worldly yet unspoiled. But now it had been destroyed. There was nothing or nobody left alive on Quinntessa. He had that bittersweet feeling of defeat. It had never been their intention that a civilization hundreds of years old should be annihilated into nothing. Ardelon could only imagine the end of the people, their homes, businesses, and unique lifestyles. In a way, they had lost the battle that led to the losing of the war.

Also, they were troubled by the knowledge that the real masterminds of this biological weapon had gotten away. Where they would strike again, no one knew; but Ardelon was certain that they *would* strike again.

Hearing footsteps behind him, he whirled around to see one person entering the mess hall. The man was walking stiffly with a cane, and he slowly approached Ardelon. When the man reached Ardelon's table, Ardelon realized it was James who was using the cane, and he looked a little better than the last time he had seen him.

"What are you doing up?" he asked James, with a mild scold in his voice.

"I couldn't lie in that bed a moment longer," said James with a smile. "Mind if I join you? I heard what happened to Quinntessa."

Ardelon smiled listlessly. "Not at all. Have a seat. Quinntessa would have been a beautiful place to live. Now it's gone. All that remains is a barren rock with no life whatsoever."

"I don't blame you," said James, easing himself to the chair opposite Ardelon with some difficulty. "You did everything you possibly could to help those people. I grew up in fairly beautiful and wild country on Earth, and I miss those outdoor adventures."

"Where are you from?" asked Ardelon.

"Yukon. It's in northern Canada. It's beautiful—forests, lakes, rivers, glaciers, lots of wildlife. Most of the year, it's cold, but I like it. I miss it."

"Why don't you go back?"

The big man shrugged. "I'm not sure. Besides, there are some memories I'm not so fond of. But maybe I will go back someday."

He watched James Rawlings, who seemed to be the most troubled of all of them. The Dominion were used to the Divinian Empire messing things up, but James had never gotten such a vivid demonstration of its heavy-handed interference before. It had come as something of a shock.

Aboard the *Solaris* there were doctors from the Divinian Empire that had come initially with James. Fortunately none of them were actually Divinians just subjects of the Divinian Empire. They blended in nicely with the Dominion crew. All of the Divinian Empire doctors who had come with James were preparing to leave, but James didn't look like it. He found himself wanting to stay on the *Solaris*. That night, Ardelon found himself alone with James. They sat in silence for several minutes. Ardelon knew he had an opportunity here and he knew he should at least try it. He hadn't broached the subject yet, but it was time.

"Rawlings," he said, "we're dropping off the Divinian doctors at a neutral trading outpost. If you're going back to the Divinian Empire, you've got to go with them too. We'll part ways and hope we never have to fight against each other."

James gritted his teeth. "I can't stand the Divinian Empire anymore. If we were all school children the Divinians would be the bullies with big whips and monster trucks. They didn't give a damn what happened to the Quinntessanites."

"Why do you think it's so different in the Dominion? The aggressive Divinian Empire has destroyed more lives than you can ever imagine. What's five million Quinntessanites down the drain, as long as it keeps the Divinians happy. If you're not going back to the Empire, are you going to stay with us? Are you ready to rejoin the Dominion?"

The big man nodded slowly. "I can't believe it, but I think I am. I know you know that I was James Anderson a Dominion Battleship Destroyer Captain at one time. And you know basically my life story from your database. I don't want to be James Rawlings anymore. I want to be called Jonas Hanson from here on in. It will be a new start for me in the Dominion with a completely fresh identity that nobody knows."

Ardelon smiled at him. "No problem I can arrange it."

"Also what would it be worth if I can convince the Divinian Empire's doctors on board to join us? Could you say get me my own ship if I can convince all sixteen of them?"

"I'd say we have a deal!"

"Is there anything else I could do for you?"

"You can do a lot for us, like help us with missions that are in the planning stage. There's a mission we've talked about, but we've never had the right person until now."

"What is it?"

He looked around just to make sure they were alone. "I think I can trust everybody in my crew, but I'm not entirely sure. So I want you to keep this between you and me for now."

"That's no problem."

Ardelon smiled. "It involves raiding a Divinian shipyard. How would you like pick out your very own ship? Not just get a beat up old something."

"I'd like that very much." James Rawlings now called Jonas Hanson smiled back at him. Hanson knew this was the start of a beautiful partnership. And a new beginning for him that had already been more promising than his previous two starts.

"THE END"

Made in the USA